REMEMBER ME

Remember Me

DAVID STACTON

faber and faber

This edition first published in 2012
by Faber and Faber Ltd
Bloomsbury House, 74–77 Great Russell Street
London WC1B 3DA

Printed and bound by CPI Group (UK) Ltd, Croydon, CR0 4YY

A CIP record for this book is available from the British Library

ISBN 978–0–571–29506–7

Introduction

The Case of David Stacton

Might David Stacton (1923–68) be the most unjustly neglected American novelist of the post-World War II era? There is a case to be made – beginning, perhaps, with a simple inductive process.

In its issue dated 1 February 1963 *Time* magazine offered an article that placed Stacton amid ten writers whom the magazine rated as the best to have emerged in American fiction during the previous decade: the others being Richard Condon, Ralph Ellison, Joseph Heller, H. L. Humes, John Knowles, Bernard Malamud, Walker Percy, Philip Roth, and John Updike. It would be fair to say that, over the intervening fifty years, seven of those ten authors have remained solidly in print and in high-level critical regard. As for the other three: the case of H. L. Humes is complex, since after 1963 he never added to the pair of novels he had already published; while John Knowles, though he continued to publish steadily, was always best known for *A Separate Peace* (1959), which was twice adapted for the screen.

By this accounting, then, I believe we can survey the *Time* list today and conclude that the stand-out figure is David Stacton – a hugely productive, prodigiously gifted, still regrettably little-known talent and, yes, arguably more deserving of revived attention than any US novelist since 1945.

Across a published career of fifteen years or so Stacton

put out fourteen novels (under his name, that is – plus a further raft of pseudonymous genre fiction); many short stories; several collections of poetry; and three compendious works of non-fiction. He was first 'discovered' in England, and had to wait several years before making it into print in his homeland. Assessing Stacton's career at the time of what proved to be his last published novel *People of the Book* (1965), Dennis Powers of the *Oakland Tribune* ruefully concluded that Stacton's was very much 'the old story of literary virtue unrewarded'. Three years later Stacton was dead.

The rest has been a prolonged silence punctuated by occasional tributes and testaments in learned journals, by fellow writers, and around the literary blogosphere. But in 2011 New York Review Books reissued Stacton's *The Judges of the Secret Court*, his eleventh novel and the second in what he saw as a trilogy on American themes. (History, and sequences of titles, were Stacton's abiding passions.) Now in 2012 Faber Finds is reissuing a selection of seven of Stacton's novels.

Readers new to the Stacton *oeuvre* will encounter a novelist of quite phenomenal ambition. The landscapes and epochs into which he transplanted his creative imagination spanned vast distances, and yet the finely wrought Stacton prose style remained fairly distinctive throughout. His deft and delicate gifts of physical description were those of a rare aesthete, but the cumulative effect is both vivid and foursquare. He was, perhaps, less committed to strong narrative through-lines than to erecting a sense of a spiritual universe around his characters; yet he undoubtedly had the power to carry the reader with him from page to page. His protagonists are quite often haunted – if not fixated – figures, temperamentally estranged from their societies. But whether or not we may find elements of Stacton himself within said protagonists, for sure his own presence is in the books – not least by dint of his incorrigible fondness for apercus, epigrams, pontifications of all kinds.

*

He was born Lionel Kingsley Evans on 27 May 1923, in San Francisco. (His parents had met and married in Dublin then emigrated after the war.) Undoubtedly Northern California shaped his aesthetic sense, though in later years he would disdain the place as an 'overbuilt sump', lamenting what he felt had been lost in tones of wistful conservatism. ('We had founding families, and a few traditions and habits of our own ... Above all we had our sensuous and then unspoilt landscape, whose loss has made my generation and sort of westerner a race of restless wanderers.') Stacton was certainly an exile, but arguably he made himself so, even before California, in his estimation, went to the dogs. In any case his fiction would range far away from his place of birth, for all that his early novels were much informed by it.

Precociously bright, the young Lionel Evans was composing poetry and short stories by his mid-teens, and entered Stanford University in 1941, his studies interrupted by the war (during which he was a conscientious objector). Tall and good-looking, elegant in person as in prose, Evans had by 1942 begun to call himself David Stacton. Stanford was also the place where, as far as we know, he acknowledged his homosexuality – to himself and, to the degree possible in that time, to his peers. He would complete his tertiary education at UC Berkeley, where he met and moved in with a man who became his long-time companion, John Mann Rucker. By 1950 his stories had begun to appear in print, and he toured Europe (what he

3

called 'the standard year's travel after college').

London (which Stacton considered 'such a touching city') was one of the favoured stops on his itinerary and there he made the acquaintance of Basil 'Sholto' Mackenzie, the second Baron Amulree, a Liberal peer and distinguished physician. In 1953 Amulree introduced Stacton to Charles Monteith, the brilliant Northern Irish-born editor and director at Faber and Faber. The impression made was clearly favourable, for in 1954 Faber published *Dolores*, Stacton's first novel, which *Time and Tide* would describe as 'a charming idyll, set in Hollywood, Paris and Rome'.

A Fox Inside followed in 1955, *The Self-Enchanted* in 1956: *noir*-inflected Californian tales about money, power and influence; and neurotic men and women locked into marriages made for many complex reasons other than love. In retrospect either novel could conceivably have been a Hollywood film in its day, directed by Nicholas Ray, say, or Douglas Sirk. Though neither book sold spectacularly, together they proved Stacton had a voice worth hearing. In their correspondence Charles Monteith urged Stacton to consider himself 'a novelist of contemporary society', and suggested he turn his hand to outright 'thriller writing'. But Stacton had set upon a different course. 'These are the last contemporary books I intend to write for several years', he wrote to Monteith. 'After them I shall dive into the historical . . .'

In 1956 Stacton made good on his intimation by delivering to Monteith a long-promised novel about Ludwig II of Bavaria, entitled *Remember Me*. Monteith had been excited by the prospect of the work, and he admired the ambition of the first draft, but considered it unpublishable at its initial extent. With considerable application Stacton winnowed *Remember Me* down to a polished form that Faber could work with. Monteith duly renewed his campaign to persuade Stacton toward present-day subject matter. There would be much talk of re-jigging and substituting one proposed book for another already-delivered manuscript, of strategies for 'building a career'. Stacton was amenable (to a degree) at first, but in the end he made his position clear to Monteith:

> I just flatly don't intend to write any more contemporary books, for several reasons ... [M]y talents are melodramatic and a mite grandiose, and this goes down better with historical sauce ... I just can't write about the present any more, that's all. I haven't the heart ... [F]or those of conservative stamp, this age is the end of everything we have loved ... There is nothing to do but hang up more lights. And for me the lights are all in the past.

Monteith, for all his efforts to direct Stacton's *oeuvre*, could see he was dealing with an intractable talent; and in April 1957 he wrote to Stacton affirming Faber's 'deep and unshaken confidence in your own gift and in your future as a novelist'.

The two novels that followed hard upon *Remember Me* were highly impressive proofs of Stacton's intent and accomplishment, which enhanced his reputation both inside Faber and in wider literary-critical circles. *On a Balcony* told of Akhenaten and Nefertiti in the Egypt of the Eighteenth Dynasty, and *Segaki* concerned a monk in fourteenth-century Japan. Stacton took the view that these two and the Ludwig novel were in fact a trilogy ('concerned with various aspects of the religious experience') which by 1958 he was calling 'The Invincible Questions'.

And this was but the dawning of a theme: in the following years, as his body of work expanded, Stacton came to characterise it as 'a series of novels in which history is used to explain the way we live now' – a series with an 'order' and 'pattern', for all that each entry was 'designed to stand independent of the others if need be'. (In 1964 he went so far as to tell Charles Monteith that his entire *oeuvre* was 'really one book'.)

Readers discovering this work today might be less persuaded that the interrelation of the novels is as obviously coherent as Stacton contended. There's an argument that Stacton's claims say more for the way in which his brilliant mind was just temperamentally inclined toward bold patterns and designs. (A small but telling example of same: in 1954 at the very outset of his relationship with Faber Stacton sent the firm a logotype he had drawn, an artful entwining of his initials, and asked that it be included as standard in the prelims of his novels ('Can I be humoured about my colophon as a regular practice?'). Faber did indeed oblige him.)

But perhaps Stacton's most convincing explanation for a connective tissue in his work – given in respect of those first three historical novels but, I think, more broadly applicable – was his admission that the three lives fascinated him on account of his identification with 'their plight':

> Fellow-feeling would be the proper phrase. Such people are comforting, simply because they have gone before us down the same endless road ... [T]hough these people have an answer for us, it is an answer we can discover only by leading parallel lives. Anyone

with a taste for history has found himself doing this from time to time . . .

Perhaps we might say that – just as the celebrated and contemporaneous American acting teacher Lee Strasberg taught students a 'Method' to immerse themselves in the imagined emotional and physical lives of scripted characters – Stacton was engaged in a kind of 'Method writing' that immersed him by turn in the lives of some of recorded history's rarest figures.

*

Stacton was nurtured as a writer by Faber and Faber, and he was glad of the firm's and Charles Monteith's efforts on his behalf, though his concerns were many, perhaps even more so than the usual novelist. Stacton understood he was a special case: not the model of a 'smart popular writer' for as long as he lacked prominent critical support and/or decent sales. He posed Faber other challenges, too – being such a peripatetic but extraordinarily productive writer, the business of submission, acquisition and scheduling of his work was a complicated, near-perpetual issue for Monteith. Stacton had the very common writer's self-delusion that his next project would be relatively 'short' and delivered to schedule, but his ambitions simply didn't tend that way. In January 1956 Monteith mentioned to Stacton's agent Michael Horniman about his author's 'tendency to over-produce'. Faber did not declare an interest in the Western novels Stacton wrote as 'Carse Boyd' or in the somewhat lurid stories of aggressive youth (*The Power Gods, D For Delinquent, Muscle Boy*) for which his *nom de plume* was 'Bud Clifton'. But amazingly, even in the midst of these purely commercial undertakings, Stacton always kept one or more grand and enthralling projects on his horizon simultaneously. (In 1963 he mentioned almost off-handedly to Monteith, 'I thought recently it would be fun to take the Popes on whole, and do a big book about their personal eccentricities . . .')

In 1960 Stacton was awarded a Guggenheim fellowship, which he used to travel to Europe before resettling in the US. In 1963 the Time magazine article mentioned above much improved the attention paid to him in his homeland. The books kept coming, each dazzlingly different to what came before, whatever inter-connection Stacton claimed: *A Signal Victory, A Dancer in Darkness, The Judges of the Secret Court, Tom Fool, Old Acquaintance, The World on the Last Day, Kali-Yuga, People of the Book.*

By the mid-1960s Stacton had begun what he may well have considered his potential *magnum opus*: *Restless Sleep*, a manuscript that grew to a million words, concerned in part with Samuel Pepys but above all with the life of Charles II from restoration to death. On paper the 'Merrie Monarch' did seem an even better subject for Stacton than the celebrated diarist: as a shrewd and lonely man of complicated emotions holding a seat of contested authority. But this work was never to be truly completed.

In 1966 Stacton's life was beset by crisis. He was in Copenhagen, Denmark, when he discovered that he had colon cancer, and was hospitalised for several months, undergoing a number of gruelling procedures. (He wrote feelingly to Charles Monteith, '[A]fter 48 hours of it (and six weeks of it) I am tired of watching my own intestines on closed circuit TV.') Recuperating, he returned to the US and moved in once more with John Mann Rucker, their relations having broken down in previous years. But he and Rucker were to break again, and in 1968 Stacton returned to Denmark – to Fredensborg, a town beloved of the Danish royal family – there renting a cottage from Helle Bruhn, a magistrate's wife whom he had befriended in 1966. It was Mrs Bruhn who, on 20 January 1968, called at Stacton's cottage after she could get no answer from him by telephone, and there found him dead in his bed. The local medical examiner signed off the opinion that Stacton died of a heart attack – unquestionably young, at forty-four, though he had been a heavy smoker, was on medication to assist sleeping, and had been much debilitated by the treatment for his cancer. His body was cremated in Denmark, and the ashes sent to his mother in California, who had them interred in Woodlawn Cemetery, Colma.

From our vantage in 2012, just as many years have passed since Stacton's untimely death as he enjoyed of life. It is a moment, surely, for a reappraisal that is worthy of the size, scope and attainment of his work. I asked the American novelist, poet and translator David Slavitt – an avowed admirer of Stacton's – how he would evaluate the legacy, and he wrote to me with the following:

David Stacton is a prime candidate for prominent space in the Tomb of the Unknown Writers. His witty and accomplished novels failed to find an audience even in England, where readers are not put off by dazzle. Had he been British and had he been part of the London literary scene, he might have won some attention for himself and his work in an environment that is more centralised and more coherent than that of the US where it is even easier to fall through the cracks and where success is much more haphazard. I am delighted by these flickers of attention to the wonderful flora of his hothouse talents.

As mentioned above, it was in 1957 that Stacton set himself on the path of taking historical personages and themes as his near-exclusive focus. *Remember Me*, about Ludwig II of Bavaria, he first floated to Charles Monteith as:

> a study in madness, of the regal temperament and its reflexes, pushed to that point when it has nothing but the past to govern. It will be a short, grandiose, and thoroughly insane book. Though I don't intend to linger lubriciously [*sic*] over improper details, I don't intend to pull my punches either, and the treatment will be from the inside, and hence matter of fact. The idea of grandeur brought low fascinates me.

After the delivery of the first draft Monteith certainly pressed Stacton on the cutting, re-shaping and shifts of emphasis that he felt would be essential to the novel's creative success. '[Y]ou have set yourself here one of those supremely difficult literary undertakings', Monteith wrote to Stacton in 1956, 'where complete success is the only kind of success worth having.' Stacton, though declaring himself 'fussy as a hen about this book', was good enough to take Monteith's major points (even the unglamorous counsel that the ideal length for a novel to be priced at 15/- was approximately 80,000 words).

Remember Me is by no means 'lubricious', but through Stacton's refined, rich and evocative prose it certainly does conjure a sense of Ludwig's inner world, including his famously suppressed sexuality. The mental universe of 'The Mad King', with its complex sensitivities and creative passions, emerges as one exquisitely ill-suited to the cut and thrust of politics; and Stacton traces the path toward

Ludwig's downfall with considerable sympathy. 'Reliving another man's life is not always so agreeable', he wrote of his long labours over *Remember Me*. 'But this, too, is part of the magic of Bavaria . . . a landscape slightly mad, but altogether loveable. I hope I have been able to catch a little of its feeling here.' This would be to make the most modest estimation of his achievement, for *Remember Me* is a stunning work, the first of Stacton's novels to suggest that truly great things might lie ahead.

Richard T. Kelly
Editor, Faber Finds
April 2012

Sources and Acknowledgements

This introduction was prepared with kind assistance from Robert Brown, archivist at Faber and Faber, from Robert Nedelkoff, who has done more than anyone to encourage a renewed appreciation of Stacton, and from David R. Slavitt. It was much aided by reference to a biographical article written about Stacton by Joy Martin, his first cousin.

For three Spiegelbergs
and in particular for
Enrico d'Assia;
from time to time they, too,
have walked away

When suddenly there is heard at midnight
A company passing invisible
With wonderful music, with voices——
Your fortune giving way now, your works
Which have failed, the plans of a lifetime
All turned illusions, do not mourn uselessly.
*   As one prepared long since, courageously,*
Say farewell to her, to Alexandria, who is leaving.

.   .   .   .   .   .

And listen with emotion, but not
With the complainings and entreaties of cowards,
Listen, your last enjoyment, to the sounds,
The wonderful instruments of the mystic company,
And say farewell, farewell to Alexandria you are losing.

CAVAFY

(Copyright 1951 by John Mavrogordato.
The Hogarth Press: *The Poems of C. P. Cavafy*)

PROLOGUE

———— ⊳⊳⊐●⊏≪ ————

It sometimes happens that when we can find no comfort among the living, we turn for advice to the dead. Most of us have friends in history. But the dead are eager for life. As soon as they sense our sympathy, they invade us and take us over utterly, until we can no longer tell whose life we are living, ours or theirs. Yet the tyranny of history is not without certain benefits. It can teach us wisdom. It can soothe us tenderly. It can console us for the burden of ourselves.

Thus it was that three years ago I found myself entering into the mind and soul of someone else, an experience both peculiar and strange.

I had come to Munich, that city that so loved its rulers and so hated everything they did. I was alone. I leaned over the parapet of a bridge across the Iser and watched the progress of a dirty swan through a thin mist of rain. It had escaped from the pond built for it, and had ventured on the river. Usually swans are graceful: the posture of this swan was not. He was searching for something, though I could not see for what. For some reason I did not want to see for what. I furled my umbrella and yet remained there, not caring about the rain. I was in Bavaria at last, although I did not quite know why I had always felt impelled to go there.

It was Oktoberfest, and I was deeply moved and a little shaken. It seemed that there was something in Munich that was asking to be spoken. It was like black magic, turning white.

So in Munich I did not notice the fashionable shops; the inner courtyards, or the stout ladies in pastry shops imitating the chatter of some Vienna of the mind; but only saw the desolate bombed squares, the massive ruins of that Northern Florence invented by Ludwig I, a parochial yet imperial wilderness where, in the great state square, at dusk, with the gutted shells of splendour all around them, now only leather motor-cyclists spun in the dim light of some moth-like game. Here the grass grew wild where it had once been disciplined. Munich has the unmistakable air of a place accustomed to rule. It has it most near the Theatinerkirche, in these bomb-shattered ruins made permanent by an overgrowth of weeds.

I did not want to linger long, but no matter what I did, I should go to Nymphenberg. Actually by Nymphenberg I meant two other buildings there.

When I did go it was alone, in the rain, the soft, gentle, melancholy rain that turned the landscape purple pewter. I got off the trolley at some distance from its ultimate ter-minus, and walked along the motionless canal into which the rain dissolved, scuffing the brown and yellow autumn leaves which damp had moulded into patterns of its own. I was sad, yet content, for all my life I had known that one day I would walk down this canal, towards this palace.

Here, I knew, was an answer waiting to a question framed when people of my temperament were first born, a special, shy, negative answer as important as an affirma-tion. That question has no words. As I walked beside the canal, a desiccated leaf solemnly detached itself and eddied down to the water, where huddled also swans.

Then, in the great circular parterre, there was Nymphenberg, behind its flowers, filling one with the shock of the expected. How Dutch it looked, a Teutonic Regent's Park, but parochial once more, and curiously childish, with its horseshoe of similar villas for the attendant nobility of yesterday, surrounding the vast but somehow maternal country house.

I did the usual things. I went to see the Museum of Carriages in what was once the riding ring. The day was grey and overcast. There was not much light, and because of the rain one approached the past through slowly separating veils. In that low shed lies all of Ludwig II Wittelsbach, his carriage when he rode, his carriages. That was what I had come to see.

Here and there in the gloom was the glint of gold: the noisy but comfortable state coach surmounted by the crown he did not want and was afraid of; the carefully glassed-in and crimson cushioned prison of a state occasion. But there were other carriages, too: the small sleighs whose figureheads hold always aloft a dusty lantern, long unlit, articles for laughter and pleasure, for affection in the snow; the marriage coach that was never used; the cutters, the light dashing barouches, all there, horseless, immobile, but crisp as yesterday.

For some reason these carriages were deeply moving. The German tourists felt that and they wept, for they weep easily. Ludwig was not loved, and the unloved have an inexorable power. I could not stay with those carriages driving relentlessly nowhere. I could not stay with those Germans. I fled outside, around the palace, to the Amalienberg.

In that little placid palace garden it was still raining.

19

This seemed appropriate, for in the heart it often rains, and the Amalienberg is a palace of the heart. Deep in its heart the world must sleep alone. The Amalienberg knows that secret. I fled for good.

So that, having gone from there, I stood on the bridge over the Iser, while behind me toy bands in children's uniforms went wanly tootling through the streets; and watched the swan, that curious, bedraggled, yet determined swan, battling against the upstream current.

It seemed to me that Ludwig was all around me, and that he stretched out his hand. I took that hand, for that was what I had come to Munich to do; and I asked the question that he always asked, and to which he seemed to have found the answer.

What is love?

So insistent was that question, that for a while I seemed to inhabit him and to relive his experience.

That experience began one day long ago, in a country that can no longer be found on any map, on a late winter's morning sometime in the 1860's. But in one way or another it has happened at one time or another to almost everyone, and happens still.

PART ONE

I

———— ➤➤➤●◄◄◄ ————

Life burns us away with a fine omnivorous rush, even though subjectively the years seem banked. But when does the fire catch? In his case it caught in 1864.

11th March 1864 was an important day to the citizens of Munich. Their old king Max was dead, and their new king Ludwig would that morning take the oath to the constitution which in Bavaria was equivalent to a coronation.

Of Ludwig they knew only that he was young and handsome, and so they were prepared to feel young and handsome themselves. There would be street dancing and heavy dinners. After that they would go home. For the moment they had no worries. They slept.

Clouds lay over the city like a folded napkin. The napkin opened and the light poured down. It was the dawn of what must surely be a favourable day. They stirred. They stretched out an arm. They had no terrors, for there was no unrest in the city, and no danger of assassination whatsoever.

Nonetheless there were more troops in barracks than usual. In part this reflected the German love of order; in part it showed the German love of uniforms. In any event it explains why the citizens remained unaware of the body in the Iser.

It was discovered by two bored young policemen on early duty, who conveyed it to the morgue. The youth was not yet twenty; the river was extremely cold; he had not been dead for long; the swans had not yet discovered him; and he was extremely handsome. Clearly it was a case of suicide. The matter was hushed up only because the authorities could see no point in causing any public annoyance on the morning of the constitution oath.

There are, however, several ways of committing suicide, and among these the destruction of one's own body is merely the simplest, the least important, and the soonest over with. To destroy the self takes much longer, and is totally beyond the provenance of our guardians.

Such at any rate were the thoughts of the coroner, who finding himself up so early, was in the garden of his house watching the progress of the two puppies of his terrier, Triebschen.

The first puppy was a melancholic. The second was the good doctor's favourite. It was like a child and his one desire was to keep it from harm. He picked it up and let it slide yelping happily through his fingers. He held it in his hand, reverent for a moment to feel the quick confident life there, and then set it back on the gravel path and let it gallop with a drunken toddle towards its mother's dugs. It was white with two black spots.

The process of weaning had begun. The mother growled. The puppy stopped and cocked its head. The other puppy heard, shuddered, and squinched down under a geranium. It had already learned better. The white puppy shrugged, cocked its head once more, sniffed, yawned, and bounded forward. The mother swatted it with her left front paw. The white puppy scittered across the path and came up against the geranium.

Usually it bounded up again. Now it lay there silently,

24

watching. The process of weaning was not pretty. The good doctor stooped and picked the white puppy up. He felt for it bitterly. He held it in his hand, soothing it, stroking its tiny ears, and making faces at it. But he was too late. Even in his hand the puppy did not feel quite as it had felt only a minute before. Something had changed. Forgetting the runt under the geranium, the doctor took the white puppy indoors and gave it warm milk with a little melted butter, but even that did not seem to cheer it up very much. He was sorry. Taking the puppy he went upstairs to wake his wife.

He was a Swedenborgian, and it seemed to him that the sadness of the puppy in some way tied up with the body he had been wakened to receive, for he believed it quite possible that all events are symbolic, if only we could find the person to whom they had meaning, for they often occur in lives to which they are not pertinent, as though they had been mislaid. But events can happen to anyone, and search his memory though he did, he could not see how these applied in any way to him. And he was quite right. They did not. With a sigh of relief he continued up the stairs. Idly it occurred to him that he was probably the only person awake in Munich who was worrying about the nature of love. In this, however, he was not quite so right. He paused on the landing and went into his wife's room. It was becoming day.

But the light in Bavaria is sudden, bright, and treacherous. From definition it shifts rapidly to a high, shadowy gloom. The corners of the Residenz Palace were full of shadows, which leapt from chair to chair. The palace seemed to be waiting. The walls listened. The court was alone. And in that peculiar ancestral light it was cold and damp.

In a small bedroom that was little more than a dress-

25

ing-room an agile boy lay in bed, too active to sleep, but too frightened to get up. Pomps had come upon him very suddenly. For years he had been stuffed with knowledge, as though he were a Strasbourg goose tethered in a cage, but of wisdom he had learned none, except for the sad wisdom of the watchful young. He did not feel like a king. He felt like a boy. He did not know what would happen to him next.

All he had to do was to walk down a corridor, mount a dais, take an oath, and listen to a speech he had not even written. Yet his bed was clammy with too much tossing, and he knew the reason. It was because once he was King, he would be more alone than he had ever been, for a king cannot expect love. Everything else he may have, but not that, for love can exist only between equals, and he has none. He would not be Ludwig any more to anyone. He would only be Ludwig II von Bayern.

He had a sudden vision of his father, an impersonal beard in a court uniform, and of his mother, an alien in her own kingdom, whose most personal act it was to be allowed to wash teacups with her own fingers, at her summer chalet, as Marie Antoinette had played dairymaid at Versailles. Neither could help him now. The one was dead, and the other was dead to him. Nor was there anyone else for him to love. He thought of his governess and of his friends. He had no friends, and Fräulein Meilhaus was married now. He could only write her letters. If a prince is too sensitive to put up with the love of sycophants, where can he find love?

He had a secret. He thought he knew. He had a name he would soon be able to utter, for he could only love greatness, and for years now greatness to him had had but one name.

But as he lay in bed, that name did not help him, even

26

though he repeated it in silence to himself. For the self has many secrets, the greatest of which is the secret of its own nature, and that it would take him many years to learn. As the years went by in single file he would ask them each a question, and it would always be the same question. He could not know that now.

Against a side wall of his bedroom stood a dusky Venetian mirror in a frame of tasseled swags. It was an old mirror, of lead glass from which the mercury had fallen away in strips, leaving a mottled, distorted image of the past. From where he lay he could see it now, but it was not himself he saw reflected there. It was his brother Otto, peering out at him from the silent mirror world. It was the face of an abandoned faithful dog. The eyeballs rose too high against their upper lids. If even Otto could not be with him, then he would indeed be alone.

He waited for his servants to come to dress him, and he had ugly thoughts. He had always thought that to become King would be to force understanding from the stones around him, and to move in a celestial company. But it was not like that. There was no company at all.

It is, of course, socially considerate and convenient that we should be unable to share our sorrows; but that we should be unable to share our joys is a crime against the human spirit. He was permitted so few human acts, that even childhood seemed snug behind him now, like a shore he was leaving. As King, he foresaw, he would be permitted even fewer. Once on that sea, and it might be dangerous to seek a port.

He threw back the covers and leapt to his feet. The parquet was icy. As he stood up a knocking began at the door, at first deferential, and then peremptory, as servants always are. They had come to dress him, and he was not ready for them yet. Perhaps he would never be ready. He looked angrily round the room and then told them to come in. It was too soon. His father's body was scarcely cold.

II

⸻ ➤➤➤❖◆❖◄◄◄ ⸻

Between himself and his father there had been little
sympathy. To Ludwig his father had always been a stern
and unapproachable bureaucrat. When he heard he was
dying he felt the wild jubilance an animal feels when its
keeper disappears. But once inside the sickroom and he
felt differently about the matter. He had never seen death
before, and once the door closed behind him, he was
alone with it and saw it plain.

King Max had been recuperating from an illness in
Italy. That their monarch should take his sniffles abroad
had so incensed the public press, and of all those who fear
the public press, those who own it fear it most, that the
cabinet had clamoured for his return. He came unwillingly. Once in the capital, and death had methodically
prepared to gather him in, with the others of that day,
as an unforeseen but valuable catch.

The sickroom was too high, too dusky, and too closed
up. The state bed was very tall. And on the bed lay what
was left of his father. It was curious how important that
body had become, now that it had no importance whatsoever. A sound came from the bed. It wasn't a pretty
sound. It was the sound of an actor who has reached
those lines he never had the time to rehearse. Ludwig
moved towards the bed reluctantly.

It was the first time he had seen that expression which, like the features of the sleeping, seems to show the naked soul within. His father now looked vulnerable and human and curiously tired, for the face of the judicious public servant he had forced himself to become had dropped away, revealing the innocent face of a conscientious stoic underneath.

Ludwig was moved, and because he was moved, he was frightened. He did not want to see any more, and desperately waited for his father to die. It did not take long, but the process was far from comforting. In the hours just before death we look in the face and see for the first time how little age has been able to alter the ultimate self within. The dying in this are beyond mortality.

The King's bedroom was shadowy. His father lay under the sheets of the state bed like an abandoned bundle. Not only his country, but his priest had finished with him, and he knew it. It did not make his death any easier.

Death for Ludwig had never been and never could be the hobbled old man of the Christians, rattling his scythe. Death for him would always be a cool, aloof, and dangerous young man, Hermes Psychopompos come for a stroll down into the sulphur shades.

Yet the young men of the gymnasia, summoned to their fathers' couches in the atrium, must also have glimpsed the truth that smiling beauty is not a matter of the body, but of the spirit, so that Hermes is a youth to all ages, who comes laughing and friendly to the suicide, but it is grave and consoling to the state councillor. Age is mortal, for it is ugly, but youth is a fragment of eternity. To kings age is an occupational disease, and so is death. It is inherited. Each succeeding king is a little less alive, for the weight of the dead monarchs of his line, and ancestors are vampires. They suck out our substance. They leave nothing but a shell. That is the way dynasties die. They silt up with themselves, until they grow useless, like abandoned ports which time leaves far inland.

Even as he watched, his father disappeared, leaving behind him no heritage but his mortality. Ludwig turned and fled the room, as one would flee contagion.

Outside the corridor he bumped into that silly old man, the Archbishop. The Archbishop cleared his throat.

"The Lord has taken a good King from us. Let us now pray that he may give us such another," he said.

Ludwig merely stared at him. Did he really believe a good king was that empty, rattling shell in the bedroom? The Archbishop bowed down before him. It was certainly gracefully done. Your headsman on the block could have done it no better. For the first time he heard himself called "Your Majesty".

He did not like the sound of it at all. It was as though the Archbishop had wielded a snuffer instead of a crozier. He did not want to be King. He wanted to be alive. He did not want to be extinguished by the leaden weight of a crown. He wanted to burn. He needed privacy to think, and now he was King there would be none.

That had been three days ago. And now, deferential and contemptuous as trained nurses, the servants had finished preparing him for immolation downstairs. He went out into the ante-rooms, to his suite, a collection of uniforms without faces. The little company moved towards the stairs and then went down. Ludwig felt locked up in himself. It was difficult to walk with the proper gravity. He went down the steps with the peculiar gait of a painted steel duck at a shooting gallery. The duck

31

has no volition. It can only hope the marksmanship is bad.

A king has no identity. As a man sitting for his portrait loses for an hour or so his identity, to become merely what the painter sees in him, so, too, a king, and in particular a constitutional king, is no more than the living model of the state portraits in his own halls. He is merely a number after a royal name. His only importance is to be a link in a chain. Ludwig shrank from that.

The party reached the state apartments, the Reich Zimmer, high-ceilinged and rococo. He felt slim and naked in his uniform. The throne room lay unavoidably ahead, with courtiers ranked on either side in order of precedence. He could not turn back, but neither would he look back. He walked instead into a maelstrom of swirling tulle, amongst which stood red trouser legs like the inimical legs of wading birds. He had entered upon that long corridor which has no doors, and the emptiness was vast.

And what did the courtiers see? No doubt they thought him more pliable than he was, for he was too beautiful to have a mind. People of that beauty appear but seldom and bloom only for a little while. The young king was a work of art, and people will worship a work of art the first time they see it, for it momentarily shocks them into awe. That might seem to give him a margin of time. He saw a sea of faces. They saw a beautiful boy who had a reputation for reading too much. They could not see his future or his mind. He was seventeen, very tall and very slim. His face was the face of a kitten who knows too much. The eyes had a tarsier brilliance, which concealed the fact that they opened on vast echoing caves. The lips were as perfect as any Cupid by Canova, and his teeth were small, pointed, and white. Angels must look like this, when completely preoccupied by the necessities of their calling. But it was not so much the features, as the radiance that made him so unusual to see. It was a disembodied face. It did not belong to anybody. It was a silver death mask of someone a god had ruinously loved. And silver tarnishes.

He reached the dais and ascended the steps to stand before the throne. He glanced at the assembly, hedged in as he was by the Cabinet and officers of state, creaking around him like dead trees. From the walls of the room twelve statues of dead Wittelsbachs looked down at him. Thus would a captive animal look round the confines of his first decent cage. Thus Charles I must have gone to the scaffold, and Schiller's Maria Stuart to the block. Thus the victim was made King.

He did not listen. As everyone knew, he read too much, and he had early developed the habit of consoling himself with legends. Lohengrin, Parsifal, and Tristan ruled his mind, and he was eager for their creator. Meanwhile he retold himself a story. The prime minister stepped forward, clutching the speech from the throne.

Ludwig changed the scene. Instead of himself, Elsa of Brabant looked into the distance. She was waiting for a champion to save her from those around her court. She had prayed and her prayer was about to be answered. Her eyes were tightly closed. For a moment Ludwig also closed his eyes. From the far end of the estuary a swan appeared, sailing calmly towards Antwerp, rising and falling over the flaccid water, drawing the small boat of Lohengrin. The swan reached the jetty of that town, the saddest of the Northern ports. Elsa of Brabant and her stomachered ladies moved slowly towards the foreshore, through a landscape by Tiepolo. Ludwig II Wittelsbach opened his eyes and took the oath to the constitution. It was noticed by the assembly that his voice, though firm,

33

was thin, and had in it some abstracted quality. It was almost as though he were calling on someone.

He was.

The prime minister read the speech from the throne, a speech Ludwig had not written and had not seen. To the prime minister, however, it was clearly a moment of great importance. He was neither a sensitive nor an agreeable man, but he seemed to feel the occasion. Ludwig wanted very much to laugh. But he did not dare to laugh. Very soon now he would be able to send for Lohengrin. For the moment he concentrated on something else.

He did not precisely have hallucinations, but his mind had the tricky ability of making mental experience actual. It was sometimes an enormous help, particularly when he felt lonely, or afraid and in need of friends.

So now on the steps of the dais, beside the throne, lay the warm, palpitating bulk of a black-haired Alsatian with yellow eyes. Ludwig took comfort in his sudden presence. His name was Doppelgänger. His pink tongue flicked in and out over white fangs. He, at least, was real, and lovable, and loving. His right paw hung languidly over the dais.

Imperturbably Prime Minister von Shrenk went on reading the speech from the throne, fully aware that he would be reproduced in the newspapers as a steel engraving by the end of the week. As a matter of fact, he rather looked like a steel engraving.

Meanwhile the dog Doppel offered some comfort, except that Ludwig did not really want to remember him. He had been shot accidentally many years ago, and since then Ludwig had disliked dogs. He did not know why.

III

In former ages, when royalty attained to the throne or a dictator turned out the party previously in power, the first new acts demanded of him were preordained: he rewarded favourites; raised cronies; debased his rivals; defeated the enemy; and destroyed the memory of his predecessor. Such was the ancient prerogative of kings. Ludwig was not concerned with any of that. Suddenly, after years of anxiety, he was King and there was nothing to do. It was like arriving at a much coveted country house for tea, only to discover that it had been removed by a bomb, for the parliamentary system made the education of politicians unnecessary, and that of princes futile.

They had decided to introduce him to politics, in the same spirit in which a man who would ride breaks in a horse. They had taken the saddle and bridle off King Max, and now they were ready to slip it over him. He felt quite clear-headed and watched his ministers warily. The ministers had funnelled down into the presence of Herr von Pfistermeister. For Herr von Pfistermeister Ludwig had prepared what he was sure would be a small, but disagreeable surprise.

At the moment however Herr Pfistermeister was delivering himself of one of those lectures upon politics which seemed to be his speciality. His approach to politics was that of a chef to food. He did not actually eat it himself, but he liked to prepare it. Ludwig did not intend to eat it either. Pfistermeister was a bumbling, conscientious, narrow-minded, black-eyed, and unredeemable idiot.

They stood in the small sitting-room of Ludwig's old rooms on the top floor of the Residenz Palace, for he had refused to move into the now empty apartments of his father on the floor below. Herr Pfistermeister came to the end of a very long sentence and closed his mouth. The sunlight made what hair he had seem thin.

Ludwig cleared his throat uneasily. It was, after all, the first request he had ever made. He had never dared to ask for things before. Now he was about to command something for the first time.

"You will leave for Vienna to-morrow," he said.

Herr Pfistermeister blinked.

"I want Wagner brought here."

Herr Pfistermeister looked puzzled and then frightened. In those days Wagner was less a composer than a revolutionary. A princeling, clearly, might demand a mistress and be gratified, but a composer was another matter.

Herr Pfistermeister's face was more plastic than it looked. It now showed the exasperated anger of a man confronted with the unknown. Ludwig smiled. "Find him," he said. "This evening I will tell you what I want you to say to him."

He felt on surer ground now. The thought of this tubby, perspiring substitute for Parsifal setting off on the train in quest of someone else's Holy Grail was endlessly amusing. He could hardly wait. A great deal depended upon Wagner.

Suddenly he felt safe. He had been spied upon so long, by his tutors and his relatives, that he had forgotten that nobody can read another man's thoughts. In that lay security.

Herr Pfistermeister hesitated, and then left the room. He was almost too upset to bow.

Ludwig was very happy. He had something to look forward to now. In former ages the Wittelsbachs had patronized great men. Dürer and Orlandus Lassus had been attached to their court. Now he would patronize Wagner. Wagner, he felt, held the keys to his soul. Wagner would be his friend. Alone and friendless, one day at the house of his uncle, he had come upon one of Wagner's books. He had felt friendless no longer. He felt that in Wagner he had found a kindred soul. In the book Wagner had asked where was the prince who would foster his works, and when he read that, it was to Ludwig as though he had heard a voice in the room, a voice he had always known, that always understood him and could help him with himself. No one else was there to help. Wagner must do. He waited anxiously.

A week later Pfistermeister unwillingly announced that he had found Wagner at Zurich. To Ludwig it was the beginning of everything. Wagner was his spiritual autobiography. Wagner had written Lohengrin, and from the windows of Hohenschwangau Ludwig had long watched the white swans bringing and taking away the seasons. Wagner had the power to animate all the legends of childhood, which Ludwig had never hoped to know except as dreams. To Wagner he would have much to say. As he had thought of Elsa of Brabant on the day of his coronation oath, so he thought of her now. It made no difference that the only thing Wagner could understand about his admirers was their admiration. Ludwig could offer more than admiration: he could offer power. With Wagner he would design new rooms for his own soul to

37

move in. He had once written in a school essay that one should take as a model a real man, good and energetic in every respect, and make him a guide for one's own conduct. In order to reach the self, one had to follow someone else. Now his life would be fulfilled.

He sent Pfistermeister back to Zurich with a photograph, a verbal message to come to Munich, and a gold ring set with a ruby like a weeping eye.

To Wagner, at Zurich, Pfistermeister was no more real than he was to Ludwig. But as he listened, it was like a scene from one of his own operas, in which he preferred to live anyway. Once assured that the performance was genuine, and he knew exactly what to do. He could not sing his acceptance, but his spirit sang. It seemed impossible to him that this could at last have occurred to him, but that it should happen to somebody seemed altogether natural, for it was the plot of half his works. The hero suffers and is saved, usually by a loyal liegeman. In the cloudy metaphysics of his art, salvation was always possible, and now it was here. It was the closest he could ever come to glee. He agreed to entrain at once.

Herr Pfistermeister saw the matter differently. He had his duty to perform, but that did not mean that he liked it. To him Wagner was a dangerous radical, and a North German into the bargain. Also he used too much scent. With the exception of portrait painters, great artists lived only in the past. They had no business walking around in the world of the living, where they could be as dangerous as saints. He could scarcely get away from Wagner fast enough.

Once they reached Munich, he dropped Wagner at an hotel and scuttled off to report to the King, his forehead prickling with perspiration, as a dancer sweats most not during the performance, but immediately after it, to think what he has done wrong. The King, of course, was delighted. Pfistermeister was soon dismissed, but not before he had seen the look of ecstasy on Ludwig's face. That look disturbed him. Pleasure was not an emotion to be displayed before ministers, even by kings. It hinted at instability. Besides genius was expensive. It always demanded to be paid for what it would do next, rather than for what it had just done, and its fertility was apt to be inexhaustible. Previous Wittelsbachs had exhausted the treasury through a mania for architecture, but at least architecture served to keep out the rain and could be broken up into small livable rooms. An opera could not.

Once Pfistermeister had taken his fiscal tribulations away with him, Ludwig went back to bed. It was after midnight. The bed was badly rumpled. He went to the window and gazed across the square. Already in his life he had looked out of too many windows, for windows are mirrors which show us everything but ourselves. Seeing the square below him made him uneasy. On the opposite side of it rose the bland face of the Theatinerkirche, up whose steps had been carried the body of the king, his father, while his brother Otto and he had walked slowly behind, with the whole weight of Munich behind them.

There is a painting by Caspar David Friedrich called "The Ages of Man". He had seen it once. On a low shore projecting into the distance is the family. Walking towards them is a man in a syndic's cloak, carrying a cane and wearing a velvet beret such as Wagner wore in photographs. The father protects the family from the intruder, and is not pleased to see the man in the velvet cap. Beyond the family, far over the weak horizon, vanish a series of high-masted ships. It is impossible to tell

whether they are coming or going, but one is afraid they
are coming, just as the man in the velvet cap approaches
the family. It is a picture filled with fear, for our death
lurks in anything we love. These ships are like the great
creaking rotten barque that brought the vampire Nosferatu to Hamburg. The moment is evening, and the
light beyond the horizon only provokes profound dis-ease.

Below the Theatinerkirche, in the whitewashed crypt,
stood the lead coffins of almost half of the Wittelsbachs,
tarnished by time, each with its coronet or crown, coffins
in all sizes, to match the age of any man; and in the midst
of that shifting darkness stood the bright new sarcophagus
of his father, surmounted by a crown. In the blue shadows
the door of the church might open, the coffin might
appear in the square, and Wagner might die before
morning. The weight of his family there in their crypt
seemed to stifle him.

He closed the window, but he could not sleep. He had
a white night, haunted by the closed doors of the *kirche*,
by the thought of Wagner in his hotel, and by the "Ages
of Man", whose artist, like Wagner, was also a blond
child of the sea with great searching eyes the colour of
transparent nakedness. At last he slept a little while.

At his hotel Wagner was no more easy. Within himself
he was already a great man, but not yet to the world. Thus
must a statue wait anxiously to be unveiled, as though
it could have no reality until others saw it. The sculptor
knows better. So should the artist, too. The statue is not
the maker. The statue is the thing made. Only that
deserves our fame.

He wished that he were better dressed. It was difficult
to carry matters off from time to time, and he had had
fifty years to learn what the staff says in the pantry.

Alone in his bedroom, he tried to face the matter out.

It was a typical bedroom of the period, large, airy, high-ceilinged, but with wallpaper as maniacally fluctuant as an eye test for the colour-blind. He wondered about the sincerity of the King. The sincerity of princes can be as transient and as narrow as their intelligence. Still, the King was not yet twenty. It should not be difficult to dazzle him. He was still young enough to listen to the conjuror without watching his hands. If that were true, all would be well.

There were three operas unperformed in his drawer and six unwritten in his head. It would be pleasant not to worry about money any more. He would have to be indulgent. He had much to be indulgent for. After all, it would only be a stop-gap measure. Genius takes the easiest way out, and the easiest way out is to be dishonest about trifles. He would do whatever was expected of him. The interest of royalty, like the attention of birds, could not be held for long. It dissipated at the first cracking of an incautious twig. He would need patience only for a while.

He slept until wakened for his interview. At the Residenz he waited in the ante-room. The door was open, and he entered. In the room he saw two young men, for the King was with an aide-de-camp, Paul of Thurn and Taxis. In him, too, Ludwig had once hoped to find a true friend, but Wagner could not know that. Yet even so there was a togetherness about the two young men that did not belong to men, in Wagner's opinion, but only to men accompanied by women. It was a peep into a world he was not meant to see, as a man leaning over a staircase in a country house he has visited before, sees far below him the mistress talking to the maid he had previously forgotten to tip. It worried him. So much depended on their meeting. To Wagner, Ludwig and Paul resembled those marvellous portraits by Philip Otto

Rünge in which the people are like dandified fruit. They seemed to stare at him with the same svelte, velvety, edible incuriosity. Ludwigmade a motion and Paul left the room.

Suddenly self-conscious, Wagner advanced. There was no denying that the King was ravishingly beautiful, with a silvery androgynous charm, but it was a disturbing beauty. It consisted of something besides beauty that he did not know the name of, but which made him feel soiled and ashamed. Then the King smiled. It was a radiant smile. Suddenly Wagner felt that everything would be all right.

Ludwig felt nothing of the sort. He had expected Siegfried and Lohengrin, or Merlin at the least. What he saw was a small man with short legs and a head that lurched on his shoulders like a burlap sack stuffed with eels. The vision lasted only a second, but it lodged in his mind, for the reality of his latest illusion might be useful later. After all, he had loved before. At least he had learned that much. But now, wanting only to see the ideal self, he rushed forward to embrace the man he regarded as the Master. Reality is thought: illusion resides in the senses and the fingertips. It was better to touch as soon as possible. Ugliness was one thing. The ugliness of a man who wanted something and was afraid he wouldn't get it was quite another. That ugliness he had instantly to abolish, for if he saw it, he would see nothing else. He had not known before that the patron must be careful not to see too much.

Wagner was not conscious of being ugly at all. They talked for almost two hours. Ludwig had never talked with a great man before, and Wagner had never talked to a rich one, so there was much to say. It was like the display of the Amherst pheasant. They were both top-heavy

42

with the gorgeous weight of dreams fulfilled, the feathers ruffled out.

To Ludwig it was the correct length of time, for he longed to rush to his rooms to savour the experience alone. To Wagner it could not be long enough. He hated solitude. He could only live in public, surrounded by much human noise. Ludwig felt sorry. Wagner was so obviously terrified that the meeting might fail. Ludwig had to prove that it had not failed. He asked the composer to come to Berg in May.

But in a way to have him gone for the time being was a relief. He was content to sit alone in darkness and to think. He would give Wagner anything. Together they would create a world better than this one. The only safety in the world is the safety of a work of art. It is the safety the inarticulate long for. They know it exists, but they cannot enter it. With Wagner he would. For the first time in his life, to be alone filled him with a delicious thrill.

But Wagner could not think without the presence of a woman. He went back to his hotel to worry; and in the absence of any of those great placid creatures on whom he begot their husbands' children and his own works, sat down to write a letter. He had at last found his prince, and would do anything to keep him, but the world must know that, for already, he understood, Ludwig had a certain moral reputation that could not but soil his own. And yet he felt excited. He was on the threshold of that greatness he had so long planned for himself, the door to it had been unlocked, and as a result he felt grateful. "You cannot conceive the magic of his eyes. If only he remains alive. It is such an incredible miracle," he wrote to his last mistress but one.

Indeed, the eyes were peculiar. They seemed to have

the ability to see around events to what lay on the other side of them. If he had not known all kings to be basically irrelevant, Wagner would have been disturbed, for those eyes remained in his mind even when the face was no longer clear, like the staring eyes of a forest, that look out at the passing traveller, see everything, and say nothing. To see everything is to see too much. There were things which Wagner did not wish to have seen. To his letter he added a prudent footnote: "He is unfortunately so beautiful and intelligent, so full of feeling and so marvellous, that I am afraid his life might vanish like a dream of the gods in this vulgar world." If the letter were to be intercepted, that would read nicely, for though compliments are all very well, a private letter is usually taken to be more sincere, particularly if read surreptitiously. After writing the words, he stared at them with surprise, perceiving them to be true.

What was the King? Who was his friend in the anteroom? Would his friend be amiable or an adversary? How much power did he have over the King? Would he have to be supplanted? As for Ludwig himself, Wagner was equally uncertain. Beautiful? Yes, but beauty fades. Intelligent? Undoubtedly, but he knew nothing of music. Full of feeling? He certainly seemed to understand the libretti very well. The whole exciting business, though no doubt it would soon grow tiresome, was certainly marvellous. Adolescence was a dangerous country, but if it produced another opera, after all, why not? He would reap the King's favour like a profitable crop. He smiled and blew out the candle. All was well. He had already been granted an allowance from the Treasury. It would pay his debts. Later he could ask for more.

In some ways Wagner was an enviable man: there wasn't an ounce of pity or compassion in his soul. But he saw certain difficulties all the same. Rarely is greatness recognized, except by accident, or for the wrong reasons, for greatness is unique, and we can recognize only what we have already seen.

The King was a beautiful boy. He might have been Parsifal. But clearly he wanted to live always on the heights, into which he as clearly planned to buy his way. But genius, having no market value, cannot be sold or bought. Nor could Wagner sit all day long at Starnberg, writing incessantly and visited only by a disembodied idealist. Wagner was a man, as well as a genius. He could already tell that as a man he had desires for which the young king would have neither approval nor understanding. He would have to be careful. For the king also had desires, and they were probably ambiguous. Also those eyes saw too much. Very well, Wagner would go to Berg on the Starnbergersee for a while, if that would please the King, but he would not live there without company of his own choosing. There were some things which the King need never know.

IV

―――――▶▶▷◖◀◀――――――

So it was not so difficult to get Wagner to Berg, after all.

Royal families have always tucked away somewhere a small modest house where they go to earth to become human, only to discover they have forgotten how. Since everyone becomes an imitation of himself in time, this lends to the behaviour of royalty a curious facelessness, for from earliest childhood they have had no one to imitate but the idea of royalty itself, which has no face.

Of such somewhat pathetic domestic retreats, Berg had always been Ludwig's favourite, even as a child. It was a toy. He always felt better there, and he felt better now. It was May of 1864, and he was ecstatically happy. Wagner was established across the lake. Ludwig was alone, but to think of Wagner was even more satisfactory than to be with him, and besides, the Master must work, and as long as he knew where the ideal companion was and what he was doing, Ludwig did not care whether he was present or not. He had him in imagination, everywhere.

For instance he and Wagner might have taken a walk into the crags, and communed with the moon in the hovering insect stillness of the night, under the shade of some dead tree. Or they might have climbed the Watzmann together, that mountain which seemed the genius of the lake. Such things were better to imagine than to cause to be. It was a great pleasure to be able to walk alone in the cool night, thinking of someone else, and he savoured the experience accordingly. The night was what he would have had people be, impersonal yet tender.

The moonlight glittered supernaturally on the lake, so that through the trees the water became something more than water. The woods surged towards him, like bounding dogs, yet through the slender tree trunks the pulsating blue-white light of the lake offered him salvation. Salvation was what he wanted. He approached the shore as Parsifal approached Monsalvasch, the magic, unattainable castle of the grail. The light within the edges of the nightwood touched him profoundly. Wagner had given him a soul. If it was transformation he desired, it could be found here, where the branches interwove and grew in every direction, like the leitmotifs of the Master's operas.

In the distance rose the Alps. Across the water glimmered little lights. It was a moving moment, and he was glad he was alone. As a captive child he had looked across this water to Possenhofen. It was in the library there that he had first come across the works of the Master. Now, in another villa across the lake, the Master was near him. Somewhere across the lake he was thinking, creating, indestructible and pure. Ludwig was his inspiration.

Suddenly the lights of Wagner's villa twinkled and guttered out. The sky seemed to lighten by contrast. The night was cold. Ludwig shivered. Something seemed to have happened to his happiness. Release he must have of some kind, or else explode. By now he knew what form that release would take, and though he hated it, have it he must. It was too hard to wait for Lohengrin.

He turned and strode swiftly towards the stables, for

47

by accident he had climbed on the wave of his own lower sensations, and felt himself driving in towards shore, helpless to avert the shattering of the crest. It was at such moments that he went mad and loathed himself profoundly. Each time he did this sort of thing he vitiated the bottled-up energy that he needed to drive him higher and higher, until at last he might burst out into the milky-white meadows of the mind where the Master was, and freedom from the self as well. Each time he tried to control himself; the tension became too great and he dropped back. Each time the sense of defeat afterwards was more terrible. Servants have more uses than one, but it made him hate the sight of them.

An hour later, shuffling back to Berg, his big body furtive in the trees, he avoided the look of the lake. He dared not look at it until sleep had renewed him again, otherwise he would spoil everything. The lower desires were abominable. At the time they meant everything. Afterwards they meant the loss of everything. They worked against the Self. And sex is not love. One will never find love down there.

He entered Berg and slept until afternoon.

When he woke, it was fearfully, as though he expected to be caught out and punished. But the world had other punishments in store for him. It could wait for a while, so that for once he awoke to a world exactly as he would have wished to see it. While he slept the landscape had come alive, with that dazzling transcendence which overwhelms people when they are exacerbated, or deeply moved.

He went for a walk. Seedlings swayed between the roots of whole dynasties of trees. He loved the natural world. He could understand the pathos of snow melting drop by drop from the tip of a fir bough, in a way that

48

he could understand nothing else. Now for a moment the world seemed to return his love. It was a consolation, in a way, for he had begun to realize certain things about the Great Friend.

Wagner had never seen a tree in his life. Such was the speed of his imagination, such was its haste to arrive at its destination, that whole forests swept by him in a green blur, like a sheet of flames; and when he did reach his destination, which was the last note of the last act of the next work but one, sure enough, there was the green blur, immortal forever as a background to some of the least convincing and most ignoble gods and goddesses who ever peopled a mythology. It was a shame. He missed so much. Ludwig was aware of the dryness of each single constituent leaf in the comity of a tree.

Where could he ever find love? He had summoned Wagner to find out. But far from giving it, Wagner did not even seem capable of accepting it when it was offered. To Ludwig love was a necessity. To Wagner it was only a convenience. To realize that was very sad.

Love for the world's small things is furtive and hides out of sight, peering at infinity through the grasses with nictitating eyes. Of such was Dürer's world. Of such was his. But Wagner was not like that.

Ludwig had hoped to find refuge in a work of art. Yet all the things he loved, the fragile, the precious, the transparent, the infinitely rare, the cherished individuality of life, had no place in Wagner's world at all. Ludwig could not take them there with him, for in that world the particular did not exist. That dates the operas badly; for only those things which usually escape the attention of others survive contact with the ineffable, only those grasses too tiny to be trampled underfoot, those moments too swift to be shared.

49

And yet it was May. Ludwig was bewildered. The world was so kind, that it seemed impossible that the men and women in it could be cruel. The little inexperienced white buds of apple trees popped into day and found it wet. The most transparent of invisible snails, street cleaners of the lake, were scavenging the water. Bushes, shrubs, grass, and anything that had roots, had grown one sixty-fourth of an inch. A stream, running too rapidly, jumped its banks and obliterated a meadow with flowers, which settled in clouds like dusting powder after a cold bath. The woods turned themselves to a loving statement of that detail which Wagner could not cherish. It was their reparation to a king too young to grieve.

It seemed to Ludwig that there were angels in the wood, and that they spoke to him. When the natural world was kind or understanding, he always felt an immense joy. But he could not give that joy a name, and it did not occur to him that joy could be a form of consolation. He hurried on to meet Wagner, suppressing an emotion which, from passion, had almost turned to dread. And that dread had swept over him so suddenly, that he scarcely realized its nature.

He looked around him at the wood. But angels are invisible. Only in art can we draw the likeness of what cannot be seen. He was alone. He had realized something.

Wagner's metaphysics was built on flesh and would not survive its foundations. Wagner could never understand the cool, sand-swept cities of the androgynous, where the sexless hold their silver rites like grave children or infant Ptolemies. That was the trouble between them. Ludwig knew that. Wagner could treat an erotic boy only as he would treat a woman. He could never cast his being into those great waves of consciousness which

50

break on no shore, where the sexless swim like charming dolphins, loyal only to the advent of an Arion. Ludwig demanded a Mozart, to whom sex was merely, and justly, a parable. Wagner knew nothing about parables. He had only a myth, and it had taken him long enough to find even that.

Not for an instant had he been willing to accept Ludwig as anything but walking surety at the local bank. Ludwig knew that as soon as he learned that the Master had sent for his whole performing circus of disciples, for Hans von Bülow, and for Hans von Bülow's wife. Wagner's lungs were too small to breathe the air even of those mountains he cast up. He had to have creature comforts adapted to the plain.

It was not pleasant and Ludwig was badly shaken. Wagner had been unwilling to stay at Starnberg, so Ludwig had bought him a house in the Briennerstrasse, in Munich. Whenever he went there he felt appalled, and he soon came to avoid it. Art was solitary and pure, and now there were all these people between him and it. The house was vulgar and ostentatious. He could not find Wagner in it anywhere. It reeked of women. The house his grandfather had built for Lola Montes, the actress, must have looked like this, but at least Lola Montes had been a woman, and a lovely one at that, with the dark face of a spider. Wagner was not a woman. Why, therefore, did he live like one? His house was like the apartment of a fashionable actress. It was kitsch.

Artists were supposed to be naked, noble, and severe. Art was a religious exercise, a preparation for enlightenment. This house was like a vestry after mass. It stank of attar of roses and rose de Bengale. Ludwig blinked and longed for the woods.

He picked up a bibelot from an end table and wondered

51

what to say. The box was supposed to be of gold and tortoise shell, but the tortoise shell was celluloid and the ormulu was pinchbeck. He opened it and it was empty. It had no use. He put it down.

Wagner sat like an actress between engagements, bloated and waiting for someone. It was not for him, of that Ludwig was sure. He knew that as soon as he came in. This was Tannhäuser before him, not Lohengrin, but Tannhäuser in the body of a dwarf. Ludwig shut his eyes.

Wagner looked perplexed. Perhaps the King felt unwell? He had clearly decided to be obliging. He asked if Ludwig would be back that evening. His eyes were watery and furtive. There would be caviar and iced champagne. He might just as well have rubbed his hands together with glee. It was the food of the upper classes. In this life some of us partake of one Host, and some of another.

Ludwig winced. The vulgarity of it was appalling. At any moment Wagner might belch. Did he really believe that the pinnacle even of worldly recognition was merely to eat Strassbourg paté every day for lunch? He wandered round the room uneasily, aware of the man sitting there, but the Great Friend was gone. Only the Master remained, and the Master was a lie. Only his works were true. Ludwig wanted to cry, but he would not be seen in tears by anyone. He rushed out of the house. It was a moment of disillusion. Even back in the security of his own apartments in the Residenz, the parquet stretched around him like an ominous desert.

He could not bear the solitude. He fled to the theatre, which connected with the palace by a short passage. In the theatre the world was real, and he must somehow banish the thought of that grubby, wet-fingered little man

52

with his lolling head, or else he would lose even Lohengrin. We can forgive the gods everything but their incarnations.

It was Lohengrin he worshipped, not Wagner. Somewhere he must find a Lohengrin. For Lohengrin was a creature of the mountains. His home was in the snows and cloistered woods of Monsalvasch. He descended to flatland only to save the innocent. But in the opera *Lohengrin* there were no mountains. There was only the estuary of a dying town. The air Ludwig breathed had to be thin air. The fustian atmosphere of the house in the Briennerstrasse was mortal to him.

Once in the theatre and he felt safer. There was a performance that night of *Wilhelm Tell* by Schiller. The audience was sparse. He crept into the empty vestibule alone, after the curtain had gone up, and let himself quietly into the darkness of the royal box. From below him came the distant echoes of superhuman voices, roaring out the pathos of great poetry. He sat down with relief.

After the sleepy pears of the Briennerstrasse, to taste the pure passion of Schiller was to bite on a sharp apple, and to feel the mouth refreshed. Nobility of character conquered the tyranny of the self high in Switzerland. Salvation was over the border, in Uri. The young hero scrambled up a cardboard alp to save his people. The actor's name was Rohde. Ludwig watched him with attention. The young man had a certain address. Some of Wagner's best works had been written in Switzerland. Perhaps love might lie there. He must go to Switzerland, perhaps with this same Rohde, and find out.

With the right companion, high on the exaltation of an alp, perhaps freedom would at last be possible. For since without love we live in chains, with love freedom

53

might be conceivable. Only on such peaks lay the holiness of mankind.

Below him the curtain rang down. He would make the trip incognito. Rohde was not only handsome, but his speeches had a cold metallic fire, like the hooves of horses waiting on cobbles on a frosty morning.

When it had seemed there was none, he felt a way opening before him once again. He left before the final curtain and went to his rooms. If the greatness of Wagner resided only in his works, then his body would not accomplish Ludwig's release, nor would his friendship. He must find someone else, it did not much matter whom or whose. He felt himself once more carried along by that inferior wave which he feared only after it had reached a coast. He did not care. Children are perfectionists. They long to destroy themselves, so that they may be reborn the next day. And in keeping his imagination alive, he had also kept something of the child he had always longed to be. He fell asleep, feeling the dawn of a blessed irresponsibility.

Next day he saw Cosima von Bülow riding across the Konigsplatz beneath his windows, in an open carriage. He knew who she was. He felt she had something to do with him. He pulled himself up abruptly, sensing something he did not quite understand, but only because he did not want to understand it, for the police brought him the town gossip every day.

He put his knowledge carefully away. And it would have stayed tucked away, had Wagner not chosen to overstep himself. Perhaps all favourites become overweaning occasionally, but Wagner chose the wrong occasion.

The occasion was a command performance of *Tristan*. Ludwig had wanted them to share the work together. He had sent over designs for the stage sets. Wagner, whose attention to detail was almost mentally unbalanced, would not have it so. He sent the designs back. It was another rebuff.

As deer come down warily to the water at evening, when the critics are away, so does royalty refresh itself uncertainly at works of art, afraid that its taste may be attacked, yet eager for nourishment. Sitting in the theatre, Ludwig did not greatly care. If he wanted his pennyworth of applause, Wagner should have it. It proved him the smaller man. But that afternoon Wagner had given him political advice, and in politics he had no right to meddle. Nor should the theatre be entirely his. After all, it was Ludwig's theatre.

The performance had been tended with loving care. Wagner had insisted upon a royal audience. Almost the whole family was there. That he should look down at the stage and see his soul naked and exposed to the indifferent gaze of his relatives filled Ludwig with fury. It seemed to him that Wagner had boned him as one would bone a fish, and flung the fillets on the stage for the world to laugh at. Fortunately his relatives were too stupid to realize what was happening. Only the *Liebestod* roused part of their bodies against their will, in a sensual way. For it was not really spiritual music: it was emotional chiropractic, designed to manipulate a limping soul.

He began to watch eagerly. Lohengrin had failed, but perhaps this new work, *Tristan*, might provide the answer. For it is not for Isolde that Tristan dies, but through her. Only in casting her off, can he cast life off, and so be free. Ludwig became intent. As once travellers rolled cannon balls down the mystical corridors of Hadrian's tomb, so would he vanish into the dark corridors of this masterpiece, to hear his destiny echo at the end of it and to forget the man who made it.

It was very stirring. Ludwig decided to be magnanimous. When the curtain fell, he allowed Wagner to take his bow from the royal box, if only because it had the added merit of annoying the audience. Let Wagner be vulgar if he would, and if little pieces of ostentation like this pleased him, very well. He could produce a masterpiece, and that was all one could demand of anyone. A masterpiece was as rare as mutual love, perhaps because a mutual love was one. But Ludwig did not want to see any more of him. It was the work he wished to see. The man merely interrupted his thoughts. He fled after the performance to Hohenschwangau.

That was the highest and the most ancient of the family *schlossen*. It was from there that the original Lohengrin had set forth on his pilgrimage. Ludwig felt healthier among those heights and snows. He would not descend again to the capital until he must.

Tristan had uplifted him. He wanted to think about it. He also wanted to try an experiment. He would always be grateful to Wagner for having written it, and the other operas also, but he no longer saw any reason to be grateful to him for anything else. Besides, if reports were true, he had the von Bülow woman now, and Ludwig did not want to think of that.

Meanwhile, having no one else to turn to, he had turned back almost regretfully to Paul.

Paul of Thurn and Taxis was a cadet princeling of that prolific and serious-minded house. He was the young man whose mere presence had given Wagner the emotional key to that first successful interview.

And he was the first friend Ludwig had ever had, the first to accept his love, and also the first to reject it. But that he had accepted it at all, gave Ludwig hope. If he must make do with substitutes, then he must make do with the substitutes he knew. He had no time to seek for others.

He had first met Paul a year ago, in 1863. That was the year the family had finally recognized him as crown prince, and had given him apartments on the top floor of the Residenz. Having done that, they left him there. Along with the apartments, he had also been given two aides-de-camp. He had waited to meet them eagerly, but without much hope. Still, if they could not be friends, at least they would be company.

He did not so much remember people as the rooms and places in which he had met them. To remember the people themselves was too painful, for he had the ugly trick of remembering them clearly as he first saw them, before he managed to pretend that they were what he wished them to be.

When the door opened and Sauer and Prince Paul came into the room, he was so nervous, that at first he saw nothing but their clothes. Yet the hermit crab, foraging under the weight of the sea and almost blind, sometimes finds by accident a fellow scavenger.

Paul had been a slim, manly youth, with a curiously arrogant and withdrawn head. His costume was court military. His features were blurred and indistinct. He had reached his apogee already, as the prototype of the athletic and agreeable young man. There was nothing left for him to do but decline. But when we see a statue or a painting walking around in the flesh, immediately we are curious. We want it. Ludwig forgot all about Sauer. To this day he could not remember the man. But on first seeing Paul he experienced that shock of recognition that is so much more dangerous than love.

And as though this were love, he immediately began

57

to try to fit him into the private corners of what life he had, to fill up the empty places and to chink the disappointments of the past. That was when the pattern of his life was set. The things he tried to do with Paul, he would after that try to do with everybody else to whom he was attracted.

There was a small hunting lodge up one of the valleys of the Watzmann. He took Paul there, for it was one of the places where he had always wanted to have a friend.

In the mountains of Bavaria the forests are like green fur. In the clear, invisible wind the nap of the tree tops wriggles affectionately. In the mountains he felt free. In the mountains the Wittelsbachs were kings as they were nowhere else. In the cities nowadays the *bourgeoisie* had a permanent lien against their betters. But in the mountains the peasants were loyal. The Wittelsbachs were men up there, the heads of their clan. In the cities they were merely constitutional monarchs, and a constitution has neither emotions nor loyalties. In the city a king is only a picture in a pie shop or on the palace balcony. In the mountain woods he gets his body back.

He had only had one perfect day with Paul. But he remembered every detail of it clearly, even when the image of Paul himself had faded. For in the days when he had first met Paul, he had felt only the emotion evoked in him, and not its social nature. His first days with Paul were part of that golden past before he had learned that the objects of our desire and of our love are not necessarily the same.

There are certain days in our life whose likeness sits in the mind forever. When we examine them outwardly, we cannot see why we remember them at all, even though they have the captive clarity and beauty of a snowstorm in a paperweight. They are those days when our senses

58

capture permanently the outward semblance of the world during some great inner spiritual event that transforms our lives. This one was a day in September of 1863.

He and Paul were alone together. It was the first time Ludwig had ever been allowed to be alone with anyone. It made him move with a curious self-conscious jerkiness of which he was agonizingly aware. He became the puppet of himself, and scarcely knew which wires to pull. He so much wanted to please Paul. And in truth Paul was easily pleased, though not by him. But there was no way in which Ludwig could know that.

They climbed one of the silent valleys of the Watzmann. The higher they rose the closer together they became. The day was intimate and warm. Rank, conventions, and reserve lay behind Ludwig on the slopes below him, like discarded clothes. He longed to touch Paul's hand. He did not dare. He did not then quite understand the nature of his necessity to touch, but drew away from it instinctively. Instead he began to run.

Paul followed. He was, after all, an aide-de-camp. He had to do what his master did. They shot out of the forest like dogs after a rabbit, and found themselves in the middle of a little meadow.

Through the meadow ran a shallow brook, very wide over smooth stones. What energy it had was caught by a low dam, where it was allowed to spill over. A few dusty and abandoned fruit trees stood about in the knee-high grass. The forest rose beyond. Beside the dam there was a mill. Behind the mill was a steep-roofed farmhouse. The Watzmann lurked beyond. At the top of the Watzmann glittered snow.

In front of the mill was a yellow wooden bench. Behind the bench stood a young peasant, stripped to the waist. He had the face of a Siegfried, not that of a Lohengrin. It was a heavy, sleepy, inert face full of shadowy laughter. His skin was slippery, but his body firm. He was sweating lustily. He was planing a plank.

Ludwig paused and was envious. He himself had the wrong body for a hero. And Paul was an idea, not a body. Paul he could have. The woodsman he could not. He transferred his emotions from one to the other. He had found an ideal figure at last and he would never be able to forget it. There remained his desires, and he was afraid of them. Paul had the slim, useless figure of a drawing-room officer.

Looking at the woodsman, Ludwig became both reverent and wary. He sat down on a stump. It was something that moved him deeply, a glimpse at the thing he and Paul should have had between them, but did not. For the aristocracy could make nothing. It was born without hands. It could only express itself through others, otherwise its message died.

The woodsman was wearing lederhosen and nothing else. The sweat clotted on his hairy chest and legs. His face was finer than he was. It was a face not to be lost. They shared their lunch with the woodsman. It was a communion of sorts, but communion with a god who could not answer.

Ludwig had found what he could never be. It made him sad. It made him suddenly see through Paul, to the amiable nonentity on the other side. Physical desires, though they should be denied, could be gratified anywhere. But what he needed was greatness. Greatness was the only thing he could love, and he despaired of finding it anywhere.

Then he had met Wagner, and there had been hope. But Wagner was not great. Only his works were so. Wagner was gone. The works remained. He had dismissed

Paul when he had found Wagner. Now, having dismissed Wagner, he called Paul back. Who else was there, whom he could call?

He called him to Hohenschwangau. He had a reason for that.

Together they went down to a jetty on the lake, below the *schloss*, towards evening. The experiment had appealed to Paul's sense of masquerade, and Ludwig had known that it would. After all, there was nothing else in Paul to appeal to. For the moment Ludwig was willing to take what he could get.

A small boat was moored there, attached to a mechanical swan. Ludwig had had it manufactured secretly. For him it was a solemn moment, the moment of the test.

The two youths stood for a moment on the dock, watching the uneasy waters of the lake. Paul was wrapped up in a heavy cloak. He took it off and handed it to Ludwig. Ludwig tried not to watch. He did not want to see Lohengrin departing, but Lohengrin coming toward him. The light caught for an instant against Paul's armour. The little boat went out into the lake, turned, and started back.

Ludwig had had his back deliberately to the water. Now he watched. The swan made a slight chugging noise, ploughing woodenly through the water. The gunwales of the boat were too low. Paul had to stand with his legs apart, in order to balance, but he was undoubtedly Lohengrin. And yet he was not. He was only Paul. He had the impertinence to grin, when he should have looked remote, stern and heroic. That grin cut through Ludwig like a knife, at the same time that he was thrilled. The music of Wagner seemed to surge around the edges of the lake, in the trembling of the fir boughs. Yet as the boat came closer to the dock, he could see more clearly the cheerful, meaningless, wheaten face of Paul.

Abruptly his vision faded. His union with the works of Wagner disappeared. It had been wrong to call back Paul. He sent him away and tried on the Lohengrin armour himself, in the privacy of his rooms. He had to know how it felt to be Lohengrin, for if he was never to be saved by a Lohengrin, then he would have to be Lohengrin himself.

Paul was slighter than he, and so the armour did not quite fit. But wearing it did give him the delicious feeling of at last living inside somebody else, as though he were safe in being able to peer out at the world through another man's eyes.

And yet in this case they were not eyes that saw very much. Perhaps the actor Rohde would see more. He hoped so, though subconsciously he did not believe it. It was only a way out of an increasingly tangled wood, the easiest one that he could take. He had been King for almost a year. The ministers were trying to remove Wagner. They were censorious about all luxuries except their own. They were agitating for his marriage, and politics were not agreeable. He decided to get away from them incognito.

He took the actor Rohde with him only because Rohde had the external face that hung like a magic mirror in his dreams, now close, now far away, and with strange skin, the texture of barley soap, which could wash away care. The person he sought seemed never to be behind the face he found.

As he boarded the train for Switzerland, he had the sensation of doing something he would do again, so that it did not matter whether the trip were a failure this time or not. It was only a reconnaisance.

But he knew, even before they reached the border, that the excursion was to fail. Rohde, like Wagner, but for different reasons, turned out to be unattainable. He was too cool, where Wagner was too warm. They followed the route of Tell. He had Rohde recite the immortal speeches as they reached each site, and forgot the man in the evocative glory of the voice. He did not look at the man. He looked at the mountains instead.

There, across waters merging into mist, not far from Geneva, lay the true mountain blue, purple only in its intensity, while he walked along the shore. Up there among the ice and the rocks Rohde was nothing but a blond voice, and that was as it should be. Still, one cannot live with a voice. When he became impatient, he left Rohde snoring at the hotel, slipped out into the transfigured night, and watched the Alpinglow. Tell had no use for the endless poppy of Tristan, nor for the chypre of the Venusberg. Tell smelled of pine boughs, cold water, and his wife was a round-faced necessity in a faded dirndl. Freedom lay the mountain way.

The night was full of little surreptitious noises, as water shifted its position to something more comfortable, and small rocks redistributed themselves along the shore. Why was it that he could find in nature that union that was denied him in any human face? He faced out over the billowing emptiness of black and grey mist, and saw above the clouds the Eiger, the Mönch, and the Jüngfrau, glittering white truths which were always there for him because they were places he could never reach. A cloud passed over the moon and broke in two.

The double cloud, touched round the edges by moonlight, was like a pair of dark eyes not so much looking down, as out into space. He stood in the skull of the world, looking out through the eyes of the cloud. He had

had experiences like that before. They were the only experiences worth having.

He could see himself standing naked on a sharp rock, above the clouds, with here and there other rocks also topping the cumulus, but those empty or abandoned. He had come out at the top, into a perpetual cold day. His eyes were closed. His lips were full. A small wind tousled his frozen hair. His tall body had the length of adolescence. His hands met just below his chest in a horizontal gesture, to show the light the way in. Nothing existed up there, yet something existed that came to nourish him. He could see himself quite clearly. It was a vision of how his life should always be. From now on he would live only at night, for it is only at night, solitary in the watching hours, that the lonely find themselves in company.

He went back to the hotel, having seen that Rohde did not matter, that none of the Rohdes would ever matter. They were only a means.

Yet no matter how high we may climb, we must always come down, and it is then we crave company. When he got back to Munich it was to discover that the ministers had succeeded in removing Wagner. For the man's own good, he must send him away. But once he had gone, there was a void that nothing could seem to fill up. He had seen through Wagner. Priests see through their gods long before the pilgrims do. But he had seen through to the works on the other side, and for their sake he would continue to make the man an allowance. Besides he never totally abolished those whom he had loved. There was always the chance that they might come back. He liked to leave a way open, just in case. But the way to Wagner was paved not with love or with understanding, but only with gold.

None the less there was the void. It had to be filled up.

V

---------->>➤➲◉⊂≤<<----------

He filled it up by sending for Paul again. Paul was the
winner only by Ludwig's losses. It was a process that
enriched neither of them.

He forgot that the face of the saviour which haunted
his nights was an ideal face, and that therefore it would
match no body. But he had not the strength to withstand
the abnegation of himself. If the spirit has no friends,
then it grows restless, and there is no number of private
worlds it needs to be alone to pace up and down in. Our
solitude cannot survive in little rooms.

It seemed so little a time since he had become King
and had made his first mistakes. But it was two years,
which meant he had two less years in which to find himself. It was 1866. The years went by in single file, always
walking more rapidly, and each one in passing took something away from him. He waited for something whose
identity he could not know, but might recognize in the
procession. Like a spider of patience, he wove his web.
He remodelled his apartments in the Residenz. Even
Philip II took some trouble with the Escurial, before he
walled himself up in it for good.

It was the bedroom that gave him most pleasure. Every
time he had to satisfy the desires of his body, he would
satisfy them in some anonymous place where nothing

could touch him. His bedroom was to be his retreat into purity. He had felt much freer to indulge himself once he had discovered that the Kings of France always slept in a state bed, guarded from the world by a railing and balustrade, taking their pleasures elsewhere. It was like sleeping behind the altar in a church. No matter what people might demand of him, they could come no closer than the balustrade which divided the public part of his bedroom from the choir.

The bedroom was high and dark, but the darkness was relieved by the heavy gold of cornices and picture frames. Safe under the baldachin, above which two angels supported the crown, as they do in certain pictures of the Nativity, he was inviolable even to himself. In those moments when he could forget the sacredness of his own person, when drowsily he woke up in bed under the canopy on a cold morning, he felt deliciously safe and cradled within himself, protected from the world by his balusters. No one could get in at him, so long as the gate was closed; and should it be opened, he would hear the click. No matter what he might do anywhere else, here there was no danger that he might defile himself. Here he would always be ready for Lohengrin.

Yet to tell the truth he found the bedroom unpleasant. The private world he walked in was in the garden on the roof.

At Hohenschwangau, he had had a fountain put in his bedroom, so that he should never be out of sound of running water, which was purity itself. A clockwork moon waned and waxed across the ceiling. There he had had the forest just outside, so there a fountain was enough. At the Residenz Palace in Munich he put the forest in the roof.

Others might nod and frown at his eccentricity. To

him it did not seem eccentric. He had that capacity for direct action which to some people seems madness. But in him it was not madness yet. It was only the logic of a fairytale.

In the fairytales remembered from his childhood, when a man was cornered, he found always a tiny door somewhere, hidden from view, through which he might suddenly escape into a big and propitious world, if he but had the key. Ludwig kept the key to the wintergarden with him always.

Pacing at night alone, by the flickering light of a candle, he had only to lift a curtain in his study, unlock the door, and step back into the only reality he knew. He had only to lock the door behind him, and he was free.

Beyond the door was an enormous garden forest, lit by paper lamps. The temperature was warm. A skiff rode rocking at its rope on the captive lagoon. Sometimes it was a gondola. Sometimes it seemed like a swan. Palm trees scraped against the ceiling. A peacock looked out from behind a bunch of dates. A parrot said good evening. He crossed a little bridge and sat under a chestnut tree in the middle of a mock Indian village. Tiny castles peeped through the humbled trees. An artificial moon was reflected in the water, which at will could be made to turn blue. That was the influence of his grandfather's love for Italy. Water lilies exploded among their leaves. A fountain played in the middle of a Moorish pavilion. When he tired of it, he could always wander down into the hermit's stalactite grotto, stooping his gigantic body to pass down the narrow paths. Water played there, too.

And it was there, late at night, almost on towards dawn, while the night sky contended with the artificial moon until he had to turn the latter off, that he sat and thought about that miserable creature, Paul.

For now Paul was important again. He had realized a truth about him. At least he hoped it was a truth. For if Wagner now had, as reports said he had, the woman Cosima von Bülow to protect him, might he, Ludwig, not have Paul to be a Cosima to him? He decided to write to Paul at once. And when the answer to his note arrived, ecstatic and sycophantic, he decided that he had done the right thing, for if we do the only thing we can do, then how can it be wrong? We have no choice.

They were to meet in the wintergarden. He awaited the meeting eagerly, for he had seen almost no one for a month. He was sitting in the grotto when a footman announced Paul's arrival. He did not stir. He wanted to hear those footsteps come eagerly over the rustic bridge. He shifted enough to have a view of the path. Paul would only come in expectation of patronage, but to be able to dispense patronage was better than to have no attractions at all.

From a distance, for Ludwig was short sighted, it was clearly Lohengrin who approached him. He rose to meet him. He had decided to take him back into favour.

Like so many dandies, Paul had always the air of having a permanent nose cold. At a distance of ten paces, obscured by rustling ferns, this did not show. At a distance of ten paces the face of Lohengrin dissolved into the wheaten face of the woodsman they had seen together, the face Ludwig had always sought and would always seek, open, affectionate, yet abstracted, the eternal face of the sleeping, who are more innocent and vulnerable and wiser than we are, and yet who have no faces of their own.

Ludwig stopped, not wanting to be disillusioned. But Paul went on advancing, smiling sycophantically. For an instant Ludwig felt a pang of disappointment. The ideal

68

face faded. The face that remained, however, was at least familiar and affectionate, even kindly, and it was good to meet someone again. He had, besides, only to remove him in order to make him ideal again. Lohengrin lived always at the misty limits of the eye.

For a moment he thrilled to the beauty of an actual face, before he pushed reality away.

Spiritually the elegant are all of the same period. Paul's was the face of 1824, that last year in the modern world when beauty in a man was not culpable, but the goal of a society. In those days to possess the face of an ephebe was in itself an act of character, in the years before the rise of the cravat divorced the head from the body utterly, in the years before morals rose up and smote ethics dead. In those days the face was not a public mask, but the highest form of self-expression of which the body was capable, so that the beauty of the head was the epitome of the beauty of the body, not something alien to it. There is something elegiac about the faces of the 1820's, something withdrawn and sad, like the best parts of the Greek Anthology. Ludwig often read the Greek Anthology, but the year had changed, 1866 was no time for dandies. The world was a little ashamed of itself by then.

Ludwig and Paul had this in common, that they were both beautiful, and beautiful people share a vocabulary of gesture no one else may know. Within this vocabulary, understanding is possible. Love is not. So long as they remain strangers, they may know each other well enough.

So for an instant there was understanding between them. Wagner was right. Paul had the head and manner of a painting by Phillip Otto Rünge, that sweet, troubled, rueful face. The mouth, too, trembled with a sensitivity

69

possible only to art, and the neck supported pride like a pedestal. About the skin of such people there is always a faintly floured quality, like that of sweet cake dough, perfumed and naked on a baker's tray, the translucent quality of a glowing lamp. Ludwig gave in to desire, and stepped on to the familiar treadmill again. Sycophants have always the power to gratify our desires, and Ludwig had the power to have them gratified. But for our emotions sycophants can do nothing. You need two mirrors before you can see your own back. A sycophant offers us but one.

Perhaps a mania for the stage can be infectious. Like Wagner, Paul had learned to act, and since the perimeter of his accomplishment was slight enough to fit a stage, he acted, on the whole, quite well. His true ambition was to marry an actress and manage a theatre. He responded to Ludwig well enough. Not even Schiller in the midst of an enthusiasm could have done so well with the material given him. Love, to Paul, was pure, altruistic gratitude for being admired. It was not his fault that he had reached that age when men of his type begin to be admired by women, or that, like most matinée idols and all cats, he must have his evening on the tiles.

Besides, he found it fun to be in favour once again. It was not Paul's fault if he wanted to please so much, that he did not care whom he pleased. Why should he not be so? He was a creature of pleasure. Pleasure was his natural element, on the surface of which he skimmed like a water-scooter in search of food, held up by the surface tension of its own environment.

Meanwhile, Ludwig did not have to know and did not yet know that Paul kept an actress up the back stairs. It was almost the magic month of May again, and they both intended to make the most of it. Like most people who

70

long to experience an ecstasy, Ludwig had convinced himself of the genuineness of the next best thing. Already he felt May breaking over him like a flood. He had never prepared for May before in quite this way. Last year the pink month had solaced him for the absence of the Great Friend. This year the works of the Great Friend solaced him for what he lacked in having Paul. It was a kindly month, but inwardly he walked alone in it, as always, against the blue sky. Beauty in a man was the eternal promise of something else. Did not Schiller say that that which appeared as beauty on earth would meet us on the other side as truth? All people were alembics. Given warmth, they could distil anything.

That was the value of Paul. It was a German friendship, coming to a boil. The only condition of their indissolvable and soon to be dissolved friendship was that they should not touch, or even meet except in the fever garden on the roof. For Schwärmerei is an emotion not known to other races. The Germans believe in immanence, and at the same time hold that the immanent is the transcendent. That which is holy is not in everything, but only to be found in particular stones, rocks, trees, and combinations of words. The everyday world, to them, is out of focus. Heighten the focus and the blurred edges of what we call reality become sharply transfigured. And this is true of German emotions, too. Find the right words, and they then contain something that they did not contain otherwise. The whole husky German language is saturated with this sudden, cooling cologne. Their words may often be meaningless, but they have the smell of heaven. That is what Paul and Ludwig did. They sharpened the focus.

They lived in a perpetual condition of belladonna, until their eyes ached. Indeed the failing of the House of

Wittelsbach was not something so genetic as the Hapsburg Jaw, the Romanov haemophilia, but that their eyes ached with too much light, as a fast film will granulate too coarsely.

Ludwig was at a fever pitch to carry this emotion safely with him into May. With Paul he felt almost safe. He could do without Wagner. For that reason he commanded a performance of one of the operas, to prove to the Master that though the work was immortal, the Master himself was no longer necessary. It was as though the congregation was at last sufficiently holy to serve the Mass itself.

And then he ruined everything. On the last day of April he was alone with Paul and failed himself. He could not help it, but it ruined everything. The body should not have the power to force upon us its necessity.

He was horrified.

Paul did not understand. His performance had been admired so much, that he had only had the desire to please still more. He was clearly terrified to lose favour, for he lived by pleasing princes. That was the vocation hereditary in his family. He did not know what he had done, but he tried to roof over the misunderstanding with words. Not being able to think of anything else to do, he rushed back to his own apartments and wrote Ludwig an impassionedly apologetic letter.

It was delivered that night. Alone in the wintergarden, Ludwig persuaded himself to believe the letter. So, too, did Elsa of Brabant believe that she had never asked the fatal question, once Lohengrin was gone forever. Dawn seeped over the city and through the glass of the roof, contending with the artificial and mechanical night inside. Ludwig, his eyelids hurting him, strained for a last look after Lohengrin, but could see no one.

All the same, like Elsa, he would pretend he had not asked the fatal question. For the world of the daytime is not the same as the world of the night, nor are the people who live in it the same people they are by dusk. Therefore from dawn until late evening he could still have Lohengrin in the person of Paul. Only in the lonely barracks of the night would he realize their relationship had become impossible. We can never forgive others for their participation in our own sins. It was something he did not dare to do.

Meanwhile, in order to retain something of the magic of May, he went to Switzerland incognito, as Count Berg, with Paul, on a visit to Triebschen, where Wagner had established himself.

Triebschen was a square house on top of a hillside, over which the trees waved like great fans of seaweed. In the garden of that villa it was possible once more to talk of important things. It was even possible, or so he hoped, to show by Paul's presence, that Wagner might keep his Cosima. He had nothing against Cosima except that she was there and had a tendency to tell him what to do politically. She was the first of the over-weening women, but she was a great one. Ludwig wanted to show that he quite understood the situation, having a full life of his own. But it did not quite work that way.

It was pleasant to talk to the Master, pleasanter still to put him in his place, and to show that the greatness of his accomplishment was dependent solely upon the greatness of his patron. While he talked, out of the corner of his eye, he could see Paul lurking in the garden. Yet all the time, somewhere in a high cool room inside, Cosima was waiting to laugh at him once he had gone. He was aware of that. The Master was not so great as his works. There was something specious even at Triebschen. Paul became more mortal and less like Lohengrin every day.

So far he had been able to hide behind the shield of his public popularity. He returned to Munich almost with relief, as a man returns to his own work, after turning his hand to something a little beyond him.

But as he drove from the station to the palace, for the first time in his life the crowds booed him.

It was an enormous shock, for public popularity was one last refuge he had taken for granted, hit directly by a bomb.

He shrank into himself, feeling as though he had been slapped. His carriage had no roof. There was nowhere to hide. He could only sit erect and smile and wave.

His grandfather, Ludwig I, had told him that all crowds were treacherous, but until now he had not believed it. He felt coldly angry. He was their King. They had no right to boo. It was disloyal. For the moment he felt confused. The world fell around his ears.

There was no Lohengrin. There was only that miserable creature Paul; the hatred of the crowds, and a memory of Wagner not as he was now, plump with success at Triebschen, but as he had first seen him, a squat, ugly man with the lolling head of a dwarf, in smelly clothes, who reeked of bad tobacco and had an evil temper. As usual, whenever he felt warm towards it, his world turned sour.

He fled to Roseninsel, near Berg. There he had fireworks let off in the sky. The sky was not dark enough for them. It was instead suffused with the unattainable Alpenglow. The rockets sizzled up into the sky, following irregular courses, and burst like immortelles, shedding their dry petals of flame downward to the lake. It was pretty. Yet even there he was not safe from those booing crowds, nor from his ministers. What did they want of

74

him? Against the pale sky, the glow of the rockets seemed timid and ineffectual. But as the night grew darker, the rockets seemed to shoot higher, and the great spluttering wheels began to burn like nebulae.

It was watching them, as some fell into the lake, but others fused with the sky to become invisible, that he had an insight. For a moment it seemed a true one. One can save one's self by self-abnegation, and therefore he would abdicate. That way he would free his spirit from the petty tyranny of men, and so become truly pure. Another rocket exploded like the taut bell of a hot mushroom, and splayed out its saffron fingers in the sunburst of Louis XIV. The fingers merged into darkness. That was what he would do. He would go up gloriously in fire and disappear. They should not boo him again in Munich. They should never have the chance to boo him anywhere else. It was the first time he threatened to abdicate: there would be others.

Paul came up to him, but Ludwig did not speak, though he knew Paul was there. The starlight, the darkness, the shadows, and the abrupt, distant glare of the rockets showed him that Paul was only a man with a heavy and inert face. His eyes gleamed in the darkness, besides, with the look, slightly crafty and slightly contemptuous, of a favourite who is about to lose favour, of a white puppy afraid to be kicked. He paid no attention to Paul. He never would again.

As he watched the sky over the lake, a great burden fell from him like a cloak. He would abdicate, and his brother Otto would be King. Otto was nothing.Otto would not interfere with him in any way. He would retreat to the mountains where the peasants were loyal, and Otto might rule in Munich if he wished. He would continue to send Wagner money, for the great work must

75

go on, but otherwise he would cast Wagner loose, to float like an abandoned swanboat on the water. Lohengrin would reach shore by himself.

And yet, even as he made that decision for the first time, he knew he would not really do it. He had remembered something about his brother Otto that should not have forced its way up from the past. He shut his eyes. He remembered it too well.

It had happened years ago. He had always loved Otto. He always would. But that did not mean he trusted him. He had learned to distrust him many years ago, when they were both children, at Berchtesgaden, in the late 1850's.

The bright, autonomous kingdom of childhood, which has but one occupant, who is ruler and subject both, is dangerous training for a king. To Ludwig, even then, Otto presumed.

Ludwig had decided that later on in the day they would act out *Maria Stuart*, by the poet Schiller. Otto could have his head chopped off, after a certain amount of suffering, and Ludwig would be an executioner in yellow boots. That Ludwig should have his head chopped off, even in a play, was unthinkable. Otto knew that. He agreed to be Maria Stuart. The tortures she had to undergo were truly terrible. They had decided to hold the execution itself in the greenhouse. The door to the greenhouse was of rotten wood, the paint hanging from it like a cluster of bluebottles. The door was very narrow.

The two brothers paused to look at it. It presented a certain problem.

"I shall go first," Otto announced nervously. "I am Maria Stuart."

Ludwig was aware of the beating of his heart. He had

76

been in a temper all day. He felt a handkerchief in his pocket.

"You aren't anybody," he said. "You're only my younger brother."

Otto was stubborn. He moved towards the greenhouse door and reached for the handle.

Ludwig leaped forward instinctively. He could not help himself. Part of him knew what he was doing and part of him did not. He held Otto by the neck and pinioned his arms. It gave him the thrill of power, that strangely sexual delight, to do so. Otto began to scream. Ludwig whipped out the handkerchief, tied it round Otto's neck, shoved a garden stake through it, and began to twist.

"You are my subject. You must obey me," he chanted, turning the stick. Otto's face was shocked and blue, but he made no sound.

Otto was finally saved by their tutors, who had heard the scuffle. Ludwig tried to shake them off.

"He is my vassal. It is none of your business."

The tutors pulled them apart. Ludwig felt his head clear, and he faced reality as though it were a firing squad. He was very sorry. He loved Otto. But he would never trust him again, nor would he ever go to Berchtesgaden willingly. After all, Henry IV went to Canossa only once.

Besides there were other things about Otto, that made the thought of abdication impossible. They were not things he liked to think about, but they were not things he could ever forget, either. If a king abdicates, then he is no longer a king. A king without a throne is merely pitiable. That was not the way. He badly needed advice.

But whom could he ask for it? Wagner would answer, but only out of self-interest. There was no one. He turned to one of the grooms for diversion, a man named Kuns-

77

berg. It was only peasants he could trust. Paul sent him a last miserable letter of farewell. He left it unanswered. It was indeed farewell.

Kunsberg lasted a week. When it was over, Ludwig was glad. At least he had had the wisdom never to allow Kunsberg into the wintergarden. No one from now on should sully that place.

Late at night, habitually, tired of pacing his rooms, he unlocked the door behind the curtain, stepped inside, locked the door behind him, and without turning on the gasoliers or lighting the candles, skirted the borders of the little lake, went to the grotto, and sat in the humid darkness, listening to the secretive movements of the ferns, as they taught each other how to grow. Only a few driblets of water fell irregularly from a faulty washer. The cascade down the rocks of the grotto had been turned off. He turned it on, and watched the water glitter in the gloom. The skiff rocked on the lake. Apart from that it was very silent. The whole hostile city was asleep below him. He did not understand it. He was scarcely twenty-two. At twenty-one nothing could be as final as this. There must be a way to go on.

He closed his eyes, but there was no face before him any longer. If he could not have love, then he would have approval. If Wagner and Paul could shut him out from the ultimate transfiguration he needed, because of a secret they had about women, then he would learn the secret, too. He would marry, and then he would be like other people, and they would have to let him in at last. It was the only thing he could do, for even Kunsberg had not been Tell.

If he married, the people would love him again, and he could always keep his single self apart. Dynastic marriages need not be intimate. It took but one night to produce an heir. The problem was solved. No one would boo him again. He called for a servant and had the lights put on. He would keep vigil here in the wintergarden all night long. If he married he would be alone no longer. In the thought of that, solitude suddenly became precious once more, so he sat and savoured it.

VI

If woman there was to be, then she must resemble the Empress Elizabeth of Austria, his cousin. Perhaps in this he was right, for the Empress Elizabeth and he were very much alike. She was a legend, too. He must have another from the same nest.

But the Empress Elizabeth was anomalous. Like Marie Antoinette, she was to die by violence, but unlike Marie Antoinette, all her life she acted as though she knew it. Had the great royal martyrs survived, we should think far differently of them than we do now. Maria Stuart was a foolish and ruthless giantess. Lady Jane Grey was a frightened child too ambitious to deserve our pity. Marie Antoinette was stubborn and resentful. It is only the minor royal houses which have given beauties to the world. The Empress Elizabeth was a Wittelsbach, and certainly a beauty. She had some of Ludwig's good looks and unreal disposition. And she, too, was a legend in her own time, particularly to herself.

Unfortunately legends have the uncomfortable ability to disbelieve in each other, which is perhaps why they understand each other so well. Yet for Sisi he had a certain reverence. In his opinion she was what women ought to be, for to him women were distant unreal legends, made out of Meissen or white bisque from Nymphenberg. Perhaps he was right. Could we live in a fragile world of porcelain women, we would all willingly be vitrified. Alas, the fragile woman is an invention of the male mind, for no man can know what a woman is when she sits alone, or what she talks about with other women. The true barrier between the sexes is sexual vanity, that must always fear what it does not understand.

There was something about Sisi he could not quite define and which made him uneasy. Women hate the ideal world and try to bring it down in tinkling mockery. Women love only the present. They hate the future and forget the past. Therefore he approached the problem of women warily. Besides the problem was not one of women. The problem, as laid before him by his ministers, his relations, and his common sense, was one of marriage. And marriage is the end of youth: to the boyish, it is as though the doors of childhood closed behind them for the last time. They can hear the bolts shoot home.

But for kings marriage is an appurtenance of the strategy of state. Indeed, the moment was propitious. He had been a bachelor king for two years, and that was long enough. He wanted to see women again. He wanted to see what they were like.

The Empress Elizabeth was the daughter of Duke Max in Bayern, his uncle. There was also a younger daughter, Sophie, in the shadow of her glamorous sister, but no doubt longing for an advantageous marriage too. To well-brought-up young ladies, no other career was possible. Sophie and her family lived at Possenhofen, across the lake from Berg. He ordered the carriage and set out.

His family did not understand him, which chiefly meant that they were baffled because his desires were not the same as theirs. He found it amusing to go to Possenhofen wanting something they wanted him to want. It might even make them like him. Now that he went to see the women, they would open out their intimacy for him, like the folding doors to a dining-room, and would allow him a peep at the feast inside. He knew perfectly well that as far as Possenhofen was concerned, he was a good catch.

He had always wished that trumpets might go before him when he rode. He could not achieve that, but he did have a state coach readied, four piebald horses attached, several footmen summoned, and an equerry was sent posting ahead. He decided to go in state, and to watch their eyes sparkle with hunger like the hard black eyes of mice. It was delightful, for it was pleasant sometimes to be smaller than one was and to do less than one could.

The carriage lumbered through the cold woods. Steam rose from the horses' nostrils. Above the rumble of the wheels he could hear the regular slap of the grooms' buttocks as they hit their saddles. He was a boy of twenty-two, and unless its power be absolute, royalty matures late, if at all.

At last the carriage jounced into the grounds of Possen-hofen. From the window he could see the small turrets of Berg on the other side of the lake. It was like looking across the water at himself, and he rather liked what he saw. There was a slight rain and the drops against the window-pane were agreeable.

A footman shot up an umbrella, opened the door, and lowered the carriage steps. Ludwig got out. Since Sophie's sister was Empress of Austria, in compliment to her he had worn Austrian uniform. It suited him well. He had just had his hair curled, and the umbrella was far from wide. He scurried for the door, carrying his plumed helmet under his arm. The rain cheered him up.

Sophie was in the drawing-room whose windows overlooked the lake. Her mother, his aunt, and Sisi were also there, drawn up as for review. He lurched nimbly into the room and smiled at them. They sat clustered as though about to be painted by Winterhalter. That would be Elizabeth's touch. It was quite clear that she nowhere enjoyed being Empress of Austria so much as at Possen-hofen, among her relatives. Her eyes had the powerful look of a woman who has made a fortunate marriage.

He stayed an hour and enjoyed himself very much. It was a little boring, but easy to do. Besides, it was fun to watch Aunt Ludovica slowly trying to puzzle things out in her head. For her, marrying her daughters off must be a little like playing going to Jerusalem, but with thrones instead of chairs. There were never enough to go round. It was Elizabeth's fault, of course: if her marriage had not had such a high glitter, Sophie might long ago have found an acceptable suitor. Ludwig was highly enter-tained and only twice eyed the clock.

Then he noticed Sophie looking at him with the stub-born look of a child peering into the window of a candy shop. It made him uneasy. He made a mental note to send her flowers.

He glanced at his hat and his gloves, which he had placed on the floor beside him when he sat down. There must be a low draught in the room, for the plumes on the helmet eddied like a sea plant. The look in Sophie's eyes had disturbed him. He made up his mind to go. He would have liked to hear her sing, which was one of her more delicate accomplishments, but if he stayed much longer, she would, and then he would have to stay too long. He got up and left Aunt Ludovica to her matri-monial cobwebs.

The footman held forward the umbrella, but he re-fused it. The drawing-room had been too warm, and his curls were already unset. He walked through the light spring rain and re-entered the coach, humming to himself, and when he thought over how they had sat there, he was happy with laughter. He looked out the window as the coach rumbled away. Two little lapdogs tumbled down the terrace stairs and stood uncertainly on the wet grass, as though trying to decide what size they were. They were fluffy, like young girls. Women would not be too difficult. He closed his eyes and opened them again only when the coach pulled in to Berg.

At Possenhofen there was a lull after he had gone. Then Sisi sat back on the sofa and sniffed the air.

"So much chypre," she said. "He must bathe in it."

Aunt Ludovica frowned and rebuked her.

"Nonsense, you would have thought it excessive half an hour ago yourself," said Sisi.

Sophie looked pale. Then she caught her sister's eye, and the two of them burst into fits of giggles.

"He's only a boy, after all," said Aunt Ludovica. She was bewildered.

"And Sophie shall be Queen of Bavaria," said Sisi. The two sisters went off into the giggles again.

Aunt Ludovica stirred uneasily. It was all very well to think such things, and even to plan them, but they should not be stated so light-heartedly.

Back at Berg Ludwig sat in the darkness of his study and watched the evening turn to velvet, so that in the light from the *schloss* the discontinuous lines of the rain were like silver embroidery being invisibly woven. After all, he was King, and women love a king. They can always be depended upon to support both the Church and the monarchy. He had forgotten that.

It had been a most revealing day. It had been a test. With the one test behind him, now he felt better about

84

undergoing the second. The ministers wished him to make a tour of the kingdom, so now he would agree. Possenhofen had shown him how easy it was to please others, so long as his emotions were not involved. He thought about that. The rain had grown thinner. The farther shore of the lake was now dimly visible, and the pale lights of Possenhofen, too. He felt restless. He would make his progress through Bavaria, as his councillors wished. He could almost see the look of disappointment on their faces, when he would tell them. It would leave them with nothing else to grumble about.

So he spent a happy night, for he had learned the secret he had not known before. The women had taught it to him, for after all, women have much to teach. It was that you may do what you will, provided you show only that part of you which your audience covets for itself, and therefore imagines that it understands. He had learnt the secret of the survival of kings. To be unchanging, one must appear to be a chameleon. To see if he was right, he had to take the tour. And the way to please women was to flatter them and to give them the thing, but never the nature of the thing, they wanted.

He went on the tour. It did not teach him as much as he thought it did, for he read too much. His favourite reading was in court memoirs, and as a result his concept of kingship was already too French. It made him out of date, before he had even caught up with the present. But he could not know that.

He liked Nuremberg best. They cheered him in Nuremberg. That completely erased the fact that he had been booed in Munich. That part of him which thirsted for attention, the Achilles heel of aristocrats, was profoundly soothed. As he drove through the streets, dimly he perceived the shadowy figure of Sophie, as chatelaine to public approval. Normalcy held the keys. Therefore normal he would be. As he passed along, it was almost as though the crowds expected to see somebody beside him, and indeed he half expected it himself. As the crowds cheered him, it was as though the person beside him slowly took form, not in features, but in the gestures of the consort whom the crowd desired. Monarchs, in their origin, like Gods in heaven, come in pairs. Rulers are parents to the state. The crowds were, of course, applauding him; but the imaginary consort they evoked, so long as she could be limited to the gestures of a gracious public appearance, would warm the glow that warmed him. If it be wise, royalty will always keep itself a mirror to the populace, protected from them by a thin coating of similarity which allows the public to cheer its own image. Given that, and behind the glass they may do as they please. Very well. He would set a real mirror up before them.

Sitting inside himself, jolting over the cobbled streets, he could very well see what these people wanted and what they were applauding. And as he felt his body and outward appearance adapt to circumstances, he began to perceive a new way to be invulnerable. Insects protect themselves by mimicry. So should he. As an actress tours the provinces before coming into London, so he toured Würzburg, Aschaffenburg, and the battlefields round Kissingen, before coming in to Munich. And he wrote to Sophie. If she was to be his ally, if she was to give that presence evoked by the crowds a shape, then she must be made into a friend. She seemed docile and agreeable, and perhaps even a little colourless. All the better: he did not think about her very much.

This was his kingdom. It was also his opera. In receiving its applause, and in playing the king it wanted,

86

he got the same selfless thrill that Wagner seemed to experience over his copying desk. He determined that if he married Sophie, their public life would be impeccable. It did not occur to him that they would have to have a private life as well. Heirs did not come out of bottles.

He was so taken up with this vision of a toy marriage, that he forgot that kings can also be the victims of their own state machinery, which once they put it in motion, rolls over them like a juggernaut. The announcement of his engagement shocked him profoundly. It was too actual. The appearance was all very well, but reality was like a dash of cold water. It brought him to his senses.

The engagement was timed for the 1st of January 1867, as though it were a good intention. Perhaps it was, but whose? As he had foreseen, the public loved it. What made him sadder was that his relatives were so easily satisfied. It made him feel like an actor triumphing in an inferior play. Contempt for the author is quite salutary: contempt for the audience makes their applause too meaningless to be really worth while.

He had only to speak his lines properly, to be free of censure forever. It showed how meaningless censure was. He had merely to simulate reality, and they took it for the real thing. It made him smile, but the smile became sad.

For people will pay anything to be taken out of themselves, so long as in the process they are not forced to the effort of understanding anybody else. It was so easy. Yet the excitement of the opening night was one thing, but how does the actor amuse himself during the 80th, 90th, or 500th performance? Surely by then he would grow a little bored. Ludwig thought that over. He looked ahead into the future, and saw it blocked off by a perpetual marriage. Everything first rate was a parody of itself, but why was that so? He decided to go to the theatre to find out.

The party given for the announcement of the engagement was dull. After the speech itself, except for the flush of triumph on Sophie's face, which amused him, there was the problem of what to do next. The problem was easily solved at first. It was necessary that they appear in public in order to make the best use of their new popularity. Goodness knows how many public monuments and civic ceremonials we owe to the need felt by royalty for some excuse to show itself in public barricaded behind the safety of an event. In the absence of such occasions, the theatre made an admirable substitute.

They went to the theatre, therefore, quite often. On this particular occasion the performance was just some such comedy of French manners as they would both be living soon. It was like dropping in for a visit at his own future household. The play was familiar. Only occasionally did he notice the lines. In a box nearby he could see Uncle Max, Aunt Ludovica, and Sophie. Sisi, fortunately, had taken her laughter back to Vienna with her. He smiled inwardly.

No doubt Aunt Ludovica expected him to be difficult, and so to surprise her he decided not to be. He made a visit to their box. He took care to stand well to the front, like an angel lowering a thermometer down into the pit to test the temperature of hell. It was altogether favourable. He turned to smile at Sophie, and saw to his displeasure that her face had a puzzled, faintly frightened look. No doubt this was reality to her.

But as men and women have different illusions, so do they have a different reality. Sophie sat primly on her chair. She did not like to be exhibited. She wanted warmth and could not seem to feel it. She shrank into herself.

88

Ludwig watched without approval. "Smile," he whispered, smiling beautifully. He thought she was very stupid, but perhaps that was just as well. She had worn a dress that did not go with his uniform, which was silly of her, since the whole meeting had so clearly been planned in advance. He stared at her until she smiled. Unexpectedly, the smile became spontaneous, and he wondered what had gone on in her mind. Perhaps she also liked applause. Aware that they were being watched, he began to talk to her, his thoughts elsewhere. It did not matter what he said, so long as they should appear affable and intimate. He saw with relief that that was the sort of thing she understood. She talked easily, from the front of her mouth, as disinterested and well-brought-up girls were taught to do.

In private no doubt she would prove a bore. But then he would seldom have to see her in private. Queen she should be. She was qualified for that. But there the matter should end. He became impatient.

When the party separated to go their separate ways, he sighed with relief. Few actors go to the greenroom after the performance. They prefer the privacy of their dressing-rooms. And that was as it should be.

He had not counted on having to see so much of her. He found the engagement extended to private as well as to public occasions. It disturbed him. He had always seen lives from the front. Married lives he had seen only in their public appearance. He had not realized they had a private dimension as well. Sophie and Aunt Ludovica began to take up more and more of his day. And though he longed for company, it was not for any particular company he longed, but for an ideal. He began to look at Sophie speculatively. For somewhere under all those clothes there was a woman. No congress of statues would

89

give them the child the family and the public alike would soon be clamouring for.

Applause was pleasant, but it had a drawback. Like a fire, it had to be fed, otherwise it guttered out. He tired of the public occasions at which they both had to appear, and when he could, he fled away from them. It was enough that Sophie had what she wanted. Now she was certain of her ambition, she could be left to herself.

But even when he was alone, he could not avoid the preparations for the wedding. It was as though they were building a scaffold around him.

He had had to approve the drawings for the state wedding coach. It was being built now. It cost more than would have ten operas by Wagner, but nobody grudged the money. There was a lesson, also, in that. A golden burst of angels held the royal crown above the roof. It was like the specimen cage in which some rare bird was carried sorrowing away from its native element into captivity. He did not like the look of it.

Below him, morning and night, he could hear the carpenters fitting up a suite of rooms for Sophie. They were carving them out of the apartments in which his father had died. Dynasties are inexorable. Now the carpenters were installing a staircase from his own rooms down to hers, a narrow corkscrew stair. The idea filled him with panic. He thought that if she ever came up those stairs, something would die in him. He heartily wished that stairs might be built to twist only one way. Twist them the other way, and she would suck the soul out of him like a cork from a bottle. Let her be Queen and nothing else. Women demanded too much. She could never share his dreams, and if she learned that, she would destroy them. Soon she would leave no part of his life untouched, and his existence would silt up with marriage as would a river, until his spirit could no longer find a passage to the sea.

He had written Wagner all about it, and Wagner seemed to approve. He took some comfort from that. She must meet Wagner. Only if they got along together, could he be sure that she would play her appointed role successfully. She was a woman and Cosima von Bülow was a woman. Perhaps the two of them, having each other, would leave Wagner to him.

From below him came the sound of the carpenters. They had finished the risers. Now they were laying the treads, standing on the finished stairs, as they worked on the unfinished ones. If he had cared to do so, he could have looked down that hole between the walls to see the stairs mounting up towards him. He did not care to do so.

He thought suddenly of Aunt Ludovica. It made him shudder. After the marriage she would ask Sophie questions about what they did together. Women always did. He could already hear what they would say.

At that point a footman brought in a package and laid it on the table before him. Hastily he opened it. Inside were three photographs, mounted on stiff grey board, heavy and gilt, with rounded corners, and a small box of *cartes-de-visite* copies. He put the top photograph on the table and stared at it, as though studying his future.

It was their engagement photograph. He looked not at Sophie, but at himself, trying to trap in the features of that stranger something he could recognize. We cannot possibly be what other people see in us. It is something we refuse, and rightly, to believe. The camera photographs something that has nothing to do with our real nature at all.

In this photograph his head seemed to float above his

body. He was detached. Sophie seemed as little interested in him as she was in the moon. She held on to his body and gazed directly into the camera. Her touch on his arm was light, and yet she seemed to drag his body down. She seemed like a well-bred vampire in a romantic story, but the story was her own, not his. Her right forefinger pointed down towards the ground. His face was free of her, but his body, she seemed to say, would never be free. They had only the protection of their clothes between them.

It was, in many ways, a successful photograph. He sent her a copy at once. It was more successful, he thought, than perhaps she would know. For like conjurers, women can successfully exert their charms only on those who do not know how the trick is done. As a trip backstage can ruin the ballet forever, so does a touch of feline insight protect a man from the stratagems of women. In the picture he and Sophie looked like members of two different species. She was the huntress, not he. Her body was more real than she was. Beneath the demure white morning dress, her body twisted like that of the Lamia of Corinth, once the latter's nature had been revealed. Rather than face her as she was, he was eager to introduce her to Wagner, for he could accept her only by turning her into a character in one of the Master's operas.

He was nervous about Wagner. Wagner had gone, but Wagner as an artistic dream remained. Wagner was an ideal. Women hate ideas. Their only defence is to engulf the creative impulse and divert it into the making of children. And if he could not keep his ideals as those were expressed in Wagner, then nothing was worth keeping.

He began to be terribly afraid. Events rushed by him too quickly. He could snatch at only one or two of them.

The family had moved Sophie in to town, into the house of Duke Max. It was too close. It meant that he had to pay her visits there, almost daily.

They were to be married in August. It was already March. He could feel himself being sucked under. He did not know what to do.

In the hall of Duke Max's town house were two busts at the foot of the main staircase. One was of Sisi, the Empress Elizabeth. The other was of himself. Sophie certainly resembled her sister, and yet she was not of that litter. She was a kitten too young to scratch. He felt great pity for her. None of this was her fault. If they had not given her claws, he would marry her yet.

Ascending the stairs, he paused on that "yet". After all, nothing in his life was inevitable. It occurred to him only with his hand on the balustrade, that if he had to do so, he could always draw away from her at the last moment. At least he thought he could. More cheerfully, he went on up the stairs, bearing in his hand the gift he had brought her.

He found her alone in a drawing-room upstairs. She turned to look at him, but did not speak. She was posed neatly against a window, and the sight pleased him. In women he liked only the artificial. If she were always to be artificial, then he might be able to go through with it. She was like a rose. She had the same fresh, guileless, new-cut quality. He moved so often in a cloud of chypre that sometimes he forgot how some people had no smell at all, as though being newly scrubbed had an aura of its own. Some smells were sounds. Chypre had the heavy, wooden odour of Wagner, but Sophie was like a powder-dusted baby fresh from the bath, in a Mozart world of popularity. She was a toy. Her jerky little movements of pleasure and delight had been contrived for her at birth, and were innocent of personal artifice, for they were the ancestral strings of rank.

He paused in the doorway. She made a little smile, and it was a gesture of hers slightly to drop her left shoulder when she did so. It was almost her only gesture. Soon it would be May, and he wondered what a May in this world of hers would be like. He could not talk to her, as he had talked to Wagner, or even to Paul. That sort of enthusiastic ease is unisexual, not bisexual. She had no conversation. It would drive him mad to invent something to do for them both, day after day. The sort of silence between them was the kind that comes at the end of a love affair, not at the beginning of one.

He had brought her a portrait of Maria Stuart on porcelain. He had thought that he should bring her something that meant something to him, but not anything that meant too much. He wanted to see if she felt about Maria Stuart as he did, for Maria Stuart was one of the martyr queens.

Sophie was not interested in martyr queens. She only said it was pretty but much too large to make into a brooch. Her voice was as irritating as the bell at Mass, always tinkling away when you were thinking of something else.

She did not understand; and that, unconsciously, must have been the moment when he began to back away.

He glanced at the miniature, longing to put it back in his pocket. Profane people should not be allowed to look at sacred things. Sophie had no more intelligence than the small dogs who surrounded her, and who were no doubt chosen to match her muffs. It was as though he had given a piece of himself away. She would never give it back. It did not matter to her what it was, but it did matter that it was a gift. In the mind of a fiancée, tribute

94

bulks as large as ever it did to the consciousness of any emperor.

He could not stay in the same room with her any longer. He left abruptly. That night, from Berg, he tried to write her a letter. He tried to explain what Maria Stuart meant. She read slowly: perhaps she would understand. He felt a dreadful sense of loss.

There was a strong gale outside that night. The wind whipped the waves of the lake. It was good to get away from the small world of Munich to the big world of the elements. Unfortunately it only made the marital world ahead of him the smaller. The world dashed around his tower. Suddenly he felt himself transported to Scotland. Maria Stuart and all his dream friends stood on the hard rock shore of that impossible country of the mind. Bavaria is higher up. Scotland is farther to the north. But the land of each is holy, for it is figured forth as the faith of its people. The vast landscapes of Scotland are one of the noblest ideas of Man. They extend into the absolute.

He had retreated to fantasy. The waters of Berg became the waters of some loch. Far off, across the water, at Possenhofen, a boat put out from a dock for the last time. It carried away Maria Stuart, from the heroine she might have been, to a French world of casuistry.

He thought he understood Scotland very well. It was an immense tilted landscape where despair was not a pejorative emotion, but a cloaked companion on an endless voyage. In the distance, as it must always sound, he heard the thin and subtle music of the Skye Boat Song. Whether a song of arrival or of departure, it was one of the great laments. The Scots are ennobled by loss. Only the cry, *Great Pan is dead*, echoing across the tideless sea, rang down the mind in the same way.

He could never take Sophie with him into the world of

the ideal. Look though he would through the shadows of the gale and the whip of the sea mist, he could not see her figure there. Nor would she ever allow him to take that voyage alone.

The wind drew chains around the tower. Maria Stuart left Scotland for the last time. And far ahead of her, as she travelled down into England, far in the distance of the future, came the wavering notes of another coronach.

It did not matter. Just for that hour, while the candle guttered beside him and the wind rattled round the tower, he was secure once more in something larger than himself. Alone, like Macbeth, he sat to consult the shadows of enormous kings.

With each page he read, for he was reading court memoirs, he saw more clearly that Sophie had taken him in, not because she wished to do so, but because she was a woman of a certain time and place. The woman he would never trust. There remained that figment of his own desires, the Queen. Actors must be chosen to match their parts. He made a note to order Baron von Lütz, chief of the Royal Cabinet, to bring him the crown.

The next day, with Merk, the court jeweller, he went with it to his uncle's house, so Sophie might try it on. It was still another way his subconscious had discovered in which to abolish her.

But outwardly he thought that if he could not have the reality, at least he might have the semblance of a queen. For his purposes that might well be enough. Reality was not so important a matter, nor experience, that he should be greedy and want all of it.

When they were ushered in, she was waiting. He was even pleased to see that she was capable of showing awe.

The box containing the crown was placed upon a table in the centre of the room. It lay in a blue leather box with rounded corners. They all stared at the lid for a moment. There before them lay all that is holy in the nature of a queen. Even he had seen the female diadem only once. Merk stepped forward and raised the lid of the box, but Ludwig waved him away. The jewels with which it was encrusted twinkled slowly in the light, as though only half awake. They were full of dragon fire.

It looked more alive than she did. He snatched it up and placed it on her head. Despite his gesture, it settled reverently. There was a full-length mirror in the room, and he caught sight of her in it, before he had the courage to look at her directly. He burst out laughing. He could not help it.

For the crown had settled down on her like a snuffer over a candle. It completely obliterated her. She had not even the appearance of a queen. Whether from relief or from the chagrined look on her face he did not know. But laugh he did.

She half turned, saying nothing, and stared at him. She only stared, but it stopped his laughter instantly. He had never seen anyone look at him like that, except once or twice her sister Sisi. Incredibly, it was almost as though she felt sorry for him. He stood there.

Then she bit her lip and burst into tears. He strode out of the room, leaving Merk to gather up the crown. It was absurd to say he did not love her. It was not quite that. But she would not do as Queen. What would she do as? Something must still be salvageable.

There was only the visit to Wagner. Wagner was in Munich for a day or two. And Wagner had almost promised to come to Berg this May of the marriage.

The visit to Wagner was not a success.

The marriage came closer and closer. He began to feel that if his life was empty, then he might as well immolate himself with Sophie as with anyone else. Whether he really believed that to be true is another matter. But he had some comfort. Since the fitting of the crown, she had drawn a little away from him. Since the meeting with Wagner, she had drawn farther away yet. He had a reprieve.

But it was a reprieve with certain intimations of his coming execution. One day he held the ceremonial of the wedding before him, on an engraved card fresh from the printers'. It left him alone not one moment of the day, but on the other hand it did not leave him alone with Sophie, either. The ceremonies ran from ten-thirty in the morning until ten at night, but he and Sophie were to be allowed to rest between three and six. It would be a rest in the same room, and he did not wish that they should ever be alone together in the same room. If their life together were to be a performance, then it must exist only in public. It is the knowledge that even an uncut *King Lear* can last only three hours which makes that play endurable. The greater the tragedy, the shorter the play, as in Sophocles. Even a comedy is funniest between the acts. He was willing to go on with the performance. The rest of it he could not face.

He had retired once more to Berg. Each morning he would leave the *schloss* in the bright, cold sun, step aboard the yacht *Tristan*, and stand at the prow, facing towards Irlonde, with a bouquet of roses, while the waters parted towards Possenhofen. It was a Wagnerian voyage. The *Tristan* was a sleek, smooth boat with a sharp, pointed prow, slung low in the water. The boat must never dock, for he refused to meet Sophie at the other end of the voyage. It was Isolde he sought. The destination of our voyages should be more noble than reality, as in Böcklin's painting.

There were so many islands of the dead, who govern

every haven of every archipelago, but with a rule so gentle that the governed still imagine they are free.

He had once read a story in which a doctor was summoned late at night. He went reluctantly, driving for miles in a carriage, until at last he reached a hooded castle. It was a night of storm. Torchbearers escorted him to his patient, whom he treated, but who died. Downstairs he told the waiting son the news, but the son only smiled and rewarded him liberally, for the man who died had been Death, and the son was now at last Death in his stead. Death was not a presence, but a dynasty, and the son was overjoyed to have attained to his inheritance. There were so many things, now, that he could do.

On rainy nights Ludwig drove to Possenhofen in a rumbling coach. Possenhofen was like that hooded castle in the story. The rain fell like tears. Footmen swarmed out of the deserted *schloss*, carrying torches. Sophie and Aunt Ludovica, hastily dressed, came down the main stairs. They were a dynasty. It was wonderful theatre. Sardonically he acted out his part. He never noticed in their eyes how lamentable his performance was.

And late at night, from Berg, alone, he could see the lights of Death glimmering across the water, furtive through the trees. The story must be dramatized. He would commission the play.

Aunt Ludovica would not let him be private anywhere but when he hid at Berg. She, too, liked the glare of publicity. There could never be enough footmen in livery or enough lights to please her. He could not go on in this porcelain world much longer. It was too brittle and too mundane. He was bigger than this.

Why did they like him only when he pretended to be smaller?

Meanwhile, Sophie's parents were insisting that the

99

date of the wedding be fixed. No matter how often he is reprieved, the condemned man will at last hear the footfall of the executioner coming down the corridor with the priest. As the time of his execution comes closer, he seems to hear those footfalls every night. At least the wedding must be put off until after May. Perhaps in the magic month of May something would happen to release him from it. He must have one more May alone. He returned to Munich, and with difficulty persuaded the relatives to postpone the wedding until August. It was a little more time.

It was one in the morning. He had not been in the wintergarden for some time. He had not been able to bring himself to go there, for it was a world which did not belong to the world he was forcing himself to live in from now on.

He slipped out the door to his apartments and stood on the cold parquet of the Residenz. There would be more women in the palace now, and even up here on the top floor it seemed to him that he could hear the echo of their laughter. Sophie, no doubt, would teach them to laugh at him. If she did not, her mother would. The halls would smell differently, too, with the sly and restless smell of women. For he knew now there would be a scandal and no heir. Apart from the horror of that much intimacy to beget one, if it were born, then it would come to be King in his stead, and so he would begin to die.

He had not remembered that story for nothing.

The palace was freezing. He moved quickly to the head of the stairs and started down. In the pale light the arches of the stair-well opened out like sullen, muffled arches in Piranesi's *Carcere*, those prisons where nobody stirs, but everybody dies in torment or has just died so. Soon he would be a prisoner for good, stifled under these arcades. He moved on. He could not rest. He could not sleep. He moved slowly, for the shadows were tangled underfoot and made his way difficult.

He went down towards the Reich Zimmer. Some of the double doors had only one wing open, some were all the way open, like the entrances to steel traps. Some were closed like the doors of private tombs. The moonlight caught ormulu and gilt, and blue and white paint, but indoors the night was colourless.

He passed into the state apartments. Once he was married he would be cooped up. They would take away his privacy, and he would exist only in these rooms. They were like the run of a dog who lives in a kennel and is never allowed in the house. He paused at the doorway and looked down the vast throne room. It seemed to him to be lined on either side with the empty, smiling, merciless faces of gratified courtiers, making a lane for him down which he could walk only one way: to the throne to dispense them favours. Once he had entered the dance would begin and it would never stop. Even when the crowds applauded, they liked him only for what he might give them. And no doubt Sophie, or any other friend he had ever had, was much the same. Wagner was a great man, but great men take only what they need for themselves, and Wagner needed only money. For the affection Ludwig wanted to give him he cared nothing. Nor did women like anybody. Women liked only things. They liked people only insofar as people embodied things or were in themselves things of value. He was a thing of value. He was a king without a queen. It did not seem to him of much value now.

Men always lost the battle between the sexes, because they saw it as a battle. They therefore gave their surplus energy to it, but no more. To them it was only a pleasant offensive game. But women saw the matter far differently. For them it was not a game, but a struggle for survival. So they dared not lose, and terror made them cunning. They must make a better marriage than other women, or lose all self-respect. Sophie would never let him go.

Again he looked down the throne room, with its ghostly, shimmering parquet that shut out the soil beneath. He then climbed the stairs back to his own rooms. If he married, this was the circuit he would describe for the rest of his life. It was too narrow. He sat in a chair and fell asleep.

Meanwhile he expected Wagner. Wagner, he hoped, would smooth out everything and make life worthwhile again. He went to await Wagner at Berg. He did not want Sophie to sit beside him forever, waving a gloved hand at an applauding crowd that did not applaud for him.

He had thought it would be easy to be a social king and so to placate everyone and keep his mind free. Marriage had seemed an amusing, slightly contemptuous game. He had not realized that for her it might be easier still, for for her marriage was not a game, but the whole meaning of her existence. Vehemence frightened him. So did cunning. She would see to it that the applause would be for her, and not for him. She would take even that away from him. She would let it be known she was neglected, so that others would feel pity for her, for pity was a reflector women used to deflect the affection felt for others to themselves.

He looked across the lake in the gathering shadows, waiting for some impossible Lohengrin, but no swan appeared. They were late in returning this year. No swan, he knew, would ever come; for dimly he perceived that Wagner had tricked him. Wagner would never live by this lake again. The great Bechstein he had ordered to ease the Master's labours was not sufficient bait. It would stand silent forever, and it would mock. They would never write masterpieces together, he realized that now. Wagner was at Triebschen. As he wrote, no doubt Cosima leaned over him protectively. Wagner had been taken away from him.

Nor did Ludwig have any escape from Sophie. Perhaps it did not greatly matter. There are more ways of dying than by death, and living inside a marriage might be one of them. He looked out the window at the glitteringly silent mountains, which in the moonlight, as though aware that they were being stared at, seemed afraid to move. When he came here in the future, it would be like visiting his own grave, where she had killed him. He did not want to see her smile the quiet smile of domestic victory.

For the women had triumphed. Wagner had written to say he could not come. Cosima wrote to say that perhaps the Master would, but Ludwig saw through that promise easily. They were afraid of his anger, for the sake of their purses, but contemptuous of his belief, for the sake of their pride. To realize such things always made him sad.

And suddenly it was already May, and halfway through May; the Master had failed him, and marriage was not so very far away. He hated to watch the doors of freedom slowly closing in his face, for they faced on a world of which he had had nothing but a glimpse.

There was no sleep for him on the night he received Wagner's letter. There would be no sleep for him any night from now on. He slept only as Venus, the morning star, began to sound in the green sky like a sonorous and distant chord, until the dawn shimmered with sympathetic sound. He did not hear it. He had no means of knowing, for he was at last unconscious, the exact approach of a never-to-be-forgotten day.

VII

➤➤🆇●🅲◄◄

That mid-May of 1867 he woke to sheets as tousled as the bedding of some Baroque saint, which felt filthy in the same way, as though soiled by some dream of ecstasy. He had abandoned all hope for May.

To be hopeless is to suffer a species of spiritual claustrophobia. He could bear the indoor world no longer, for it seemed to close down on him even at Berg. He ordered his carriage and then began to dress. For once he did not even feel the texture of the day, except to know it was one of the few left to him before his marriage closed on him like the door to a crypt.

After breakfast he went outside to wait for the familiar cavalcade attendant on his solitary rides.

The scene was brilliant, as was the light. First came the led horse. The groom handled it as Bellerophon would have handled Pegasus. Such grace was unusual and caught his eye at once. There were few people who understood the rhetoric of gesture, this young man did, and he was new to him. Behind came the carriage, in the care of two Royal footmen in blue and silver livery, their legs moving smoothly under tight white buckskins and flowing into short black riding boots.

The groom leading the horse was dressed differently. He wore a blue Eton jacket that rode across his enormous chest, as he strained for the bit of the horse. The scene entered Ludwig's mind in colour, and he saw at once that it was one of those views which for no apparent reason enter the mind complete, because they are symbolic of some spiritual condition, if only we can discover which. With a quick look at the groom, he stepped into the carriage, the groom stood back, and the carriage whirled away before anything else could happen.

Deliciously restless, Ludwig sat back in the carriage as it bounced through the woods and watched the back of the footman who was driving. He should have had the new groom drive. He watched the rump of the horse and scarcely saw the woods at all. The carriage turned automatically towards Possenhofen. He leaned forward and tapped the footman on the shoulder. He would not go there to-day. He needed to think. They headed instead farther into the dark green woods.

Why had he thought of Bellerophon? He remembered the story quite well. Bellerophon meant "slayer of monsters". He was the son of Glaucus, King of Ephyre. Like Welsh saints, Greek heroes were always the sons of kings, and it was that that gave them a nobility of bearing. If this groom were truly Bellerophon, he would in his lifetime do certain things. It had not occurred to Ludwig that salvation would come from the Greek, for Wagner had so subtly distorted German legend, that women could survive in it.

Bellerophon was handsome. So was the groom. The King's wife, Sthenoboea, fell in love with him, but he slighted her. Thereupon she denounced him to her husband, who sent him away with a letter stating that the carrier was to be murdered by the recipient. Therefore all letters of an unfavourable tendency were still referred to as the letters of Bellerophon. The King who received the letter could not kill his guest. He could at most obediently cause his death. He sent Bellerophon to kill the Chimera. But Bellerophon, protected by Minerva, did kill the beast. Bellerophon conquered all those against whom he was sent, including the Amazons.

Ludwig sat abruptly forward in the carriage, which swayed and rattled on the road. Then, aware of the footman standing on the box behind him, he relaxed and gazed at the sky. Innocence was protected by the gods. That was what Bellerophon had proved to Iobates, King of Lycia, his host. The King, being without male issue, married Bellerophon to one of his daughters.

Who would the daughter be? Ludwig did not know. The name of Bellerophon's wife was either Philonoë or Achemone. According to legend, Bellerophon attempted to reach the sun on Pegasus, but Jupiter cast him down, so that for the rest of his days he wandered the earth in greatest melancholy and dejection.

Ludwig opened his eyes. He felt oddly indecisive. He leaned forward and tapped the coachman once again. The carriage turned back towards Berg.

But when it swirled into the dusty drive, there was no sign of the coachman. The yard was deserted. Ludwig descended and went inside. All that afternoon he sat at the window of his study, watching the surface of the lake wrinkled with the little unborn waves, like the skin of a baby.

A servant knocked at the door. Wagner had unexpectedly arrived for lunch. Ludwig got up wearily and went downstairs to the Master, who still had about his clothes that tired and dusty smell which seemed to surround him like a personal signature. For the first time Ludwig entered the room to meet him with confidence. It did not matter what happened now, but there were some things he had to know.

It always infuriated him that the Wagner he saw before him was never the Wagner he wanted to know. The man's table manners were far from perfect. That Wagner he wanted to know was as permanently invisible as the far side of the moon, as though Wagner were careful to circle around him in such a way as only to expose the one bland and familiar-featured face, but never his real one.

They sat in the dining-room, at a large circular table which was much too low. On the wall hung a painting by Schwind depicting Elsa saying farewell to Lohengrin. Out of the background Ortrud peered malevolently, and the water which supported the swan boat was too shallow. It could not be more than three inches deep. The detail fascinated Ludwig. He had not noticed it before. Ortrud looked remarkably like Aunt Ludovica.

As they reached the cheese, it occurred to him that it was not Cosima who shut him from the Master, but Wagner himself. He saw the one inviolable rule of the artist, that no one must ever be allowed into a masterpiece before it is finished, for if a stranger saw how it was made, it would be destroyed. If the larva is not alone in its cocoon, it will never emerge as a butterfly. It is mortally afraid of the parasite that will eat it while it grows. It was not a masterpiece he wanted from Wagner, but the secret of producing one. And that even Wagner did not know, for the process was instinctual.

He frowned, seeing that Wagner was being patronizing only because Wagner was afraid. What was the man afraid of? He watched as the Master slowly sliced his cheese and judiciously placed it upon a wafer. In the act he saw what Wagner was afraid of. Genius is operative only when trapped in a body, and if the body starves, then genius has no way to express itself. Wagner was afraid to lose his patronage. It showed now in the easy way he contemplated his cheese. And yet the cheese itself was only a not very good Brie.

Wagner was not a man. Wagner was only a means, the miserable gross incarnation of his own spiritual talents. Let Cosima have him, then. She would never have him any more than Ludwig had. Together, from now on, their only service would be to be keepers of the flame. He did not need Wagner the man any more. That seemed to him to be the truth. But it also seemed to him that the truth was only a pack of lies, a universal process designed to level belief. He felt better, as do epileptics after a seizure. An intolerable tension had exploded and then ebbed away, all in the sight of a man eating a piece of Brie.

Suddenly a patch of sunlight came flooding across the room, and the sun was warm. He wanted Wagner to go. He wanted to be alone. He looked at the tablecloth, for the meal was as finished as that of Cana, in the room upstairs. He was now securely seated, like a man on a horse, in the saddle of another mythology. The valkyries whirled up around him, like dust caught in the rays of the sun, threw away their armour, changed their sex, and became Greek. The face that bobbed before him took on features, and the Medusa that usually haunted him disappeared. He was no longer stone. He went with Wagner to the door. It was the first time he had not felt overwhelming loss as the Great Friend drove away. The absence of that familiar emotion bothered him. Wagner was only his works. Nothing else of him remained. He would go on giving him money. Even the larva must spin its cocoon out of something. And butterflies and masterpieces are not only beautiful, but they also do not eat. We love them because they cannot hurt us or use us in any way.

He was waiting for something. He waited until late that

evening, still surprised that now Wagner left no sense of intolerable emptiness behind him. Actually he was waiting for the night. He had not much courage of his own. He could not perform any voluntary act, unless he first had the assistance of darkness.

At night it was as though he stepped through a door at the end of the hall and found himself standing, not on the same carpet, but free once more in space, with the stars beneath him and no one to hold him down.

He went for a walk down by the borders of the lake. The stars began to shine around him like a system of metaphysics which, as the night darkened, became more and more clear. They fixed in vast nets of meaning. He looked for Pegasus and found it, galloping timelessly across the sky. Only animals were honest and faithful, and above all animals, the horse. Securely seated, he could ride to his own salvation, up and up, in the smell of living leather, which was like the smell of flames. It was the special gesture of the groom this morning that had taught him that.

He felt as though he were filling in time, in order neither to be too early nor too late for an appointment. He had a sense of destination once again. He wandered a little way into the wood along the shore. As on that previous May, it seemed to stir and to grow for him. Angelic wings glittered in the shadows of the trees.

He seemed to be in a great formal park made of stone, where the allees of shrubbery rose in granite or basalt, high in the mountains, or at Sceaux or Versailles. Far ahead, at the top of the corridor, where it gave out on to space, he seemed to see a stranger. There was someone walking ahead of him in this wood, or walking towards him, he could not tell which.

Then, coming out into a little clearing like a chamber

halfway up some pyramid, he saw through the trees a distant figure and he stopped. The stars were brighter here.

As the figure walked towards him, its low polished boots snapping the bracken, he recognized it, not by any appearance, but by the way the close blue jacket rode upward on the chest. He moved forward. It was, of course, Bellerophon. The angels in the shadows drew away. He was not after all alone in this wood, and it was still May.

VIII

In August, when Wagner's work was done for the time being and he could afford to please his patron, he came to the Starnbergsee and waited to be summoned across the lake to Berg. The summons did not come. Much worried, Wagner returned to Triebschen. Perhaps this time he had gone too far.

Ludwig was in Munich. He was too distressed to see anybody. The time of the marriage was almost upon him. It gave him a bad conscience to think about it. He felt safe only when he had locked himself into the winter-garden. The boat rocked on the captive lake. He must have it taken away. He went uncertainly down the little path and into the hermitage. There he sat down to watch the flaccid water. Instead he found himself peering anxiously into the shadows of the rustling undusted ferns. He could feel the palace seething with gossip beneath him. He did not know what to do.

But not knowing what to do is not the same as not knowing what we will do. When it comes down to fundamentals the self has no conscience. It only feels it should have one, and that is the source of our agony. Ludwig was in agony now. Even the sternest samurai must reach a point at which saving his neck becomes more important to him than saving his face.

It was not the consequences of the truth which he shrank from, but the truth itself. He could face no limitation in himself. His limitations locked him in. He had somehow to convert them into merits, before he could accept them. He had formulated excuses about Sophie, but they were not genuine. It was the physical contact he shrank from. And to others he knew that would appear ludicrous. Others would laugh at him. He did not have the strength to withstand laughter. Once the truth were out all the women in the country would begin to boo.

He tried to pretend to himself that it was only a matter of putting the wedding off for a few more months. But the pretence would not work. Though he shrank from the truth, neither could he lie to himself. The truth was that he could not touch her; smell her, see her. The smell of people was not their own smell, but the odour of the bacteria that fed on them, and which migrated from body to body at the touch. He had not the capacity to touch her. That part of him was left out. Besides, he had got hope back unexpectedly. With hope for the future, he could not face her any more, for she had been part of the hopeless future that now lay dead behind him.

More than that, he thought any woman would swallow him as a serpent swallows a mongoose, quietly edging it down with the muscular walls of her throat. Women understand nothing but the making of children. Women would be a dynasty in their own lifetime. He was afraid of being engulfed in that womb, like Marius, and the ground smooth without a trace. The father of a child, once his work is done, can do nothing. He can only flit from flower to flower. Creative people can escape. They are bisexual, and can fertilize themselves. But otherwise there was only one way to remain young, and that was not to grow old. He must never grow old. Once a man begets a child, his function is over, and he begins to die. Women know this, and it pleases them. It would be better to be a Wagner, using women as flowers have learned to use bees, than merely to become the father of an heir.

It was silent around him. He could not bear it. He had no one to turn to. He thought of Fräulein Meilhaus, his schooltime governess. She might understand. He must speak to someone, even if it was just on paper, in a letter. He wanted Bellerophon. Bellerophon seemed the answer. He could not know that he was condemned to be everyone to whom he was attracted, for the ego is an endless corridor of mirrors, for only thus can it reproduce itself. Shatter the mirror, and the ego dies.

He did not think of the stormy session that afternoon, in which his Uncle had demanded that the engagement be terminated for good, and had said many other things besides. During that interview he had only thought that he need never see Sophie again. It made him feel like a convalescent, recovering from a dangerous illness, high in the Alps. It was easy enough to convince himself that Sophie would be happier without him.

Yet, though he would never have to see her again, he could not quite let the matter rest there. Writing to Fräulein Meilhaus did not help as much as he had hoped it would. She was not Fräulein Meilhaus now. She was Frau Baroness von Leonrod. That would automatically put her on Sophie's side. She had moved away from his childhood into the ranks of the opposition. He gave her credit. She would not laugh at him. But she would frown.

Of course Uncle Max would never speak to him again, but then he had never been intimate with Uncle Max anyhow. To be free of the marriage made him light-headed with happiness. It made him kind. To Sophie he

wrote that if she remembered him with sorrow and
bitterness, it would cause him deep grief. It would not
cause him grief at all, but it did no harm to be gracious.
Graciousness was proper to a king. It was a long letter.
When we have to justify ourselves, we always find much
to say. He did not trouble himself to consider that she
was disgraced, and that another marriage would be
difficult for her to make.

"I must say again", he added, "that the interference
of your mother in our affairs as they were last winter
was very unfortunate." He must have someone else to
blame beside himself, and he had never liked Aunt
Ludovica anyway. But he was sad, all the same. They
would never applaud him in Munich again. He put the
letter in an envelope. He could not be the king the
Munichers wanted, and he would not be forgiven for
that. He sealed the letter, left it to be delivered, and
slipped down his private stairs to the hofgarden behind
the palace. There he had a carriage waiting. He was not
exactly fleeing the capital. He did not see the matter
quite that way. But he did not want to come back to
it, either, until the gossip had died down. He got into the
carriage, which drove through the quiet streets. Everyone was asleep. No one knew that he was leaving. It was
proper the streets should be quiet, for he would never be
cheered again. And what sound can be more muffled by
time than the echo of applause? It soon loses its vibrancy.
He was distressed. They had driven his grandfather into
exile for falling in love with a cheap Spanish dancer.
What would they do to him? He thought that exile must
sound very like the echo of a carriage over empty streets.
It had a tired and futile sound.

The carriage left the cobblestones of the city, while it
slept, gathering energy to explode in his face next day.

The wheels turned on the mud ruts of the road reluctantly, as the horses pointed toward Nymphenberg. The ghosts of women seemed to snap about his heels, like ghost foxes.

In the starlight the great circle of Nymphenberg came into view, with its abandoned shuttered look. The carriage drove along beside the canal and swept up to the entrance, where it advanced towards the left-hand wing, where the stables were. He had had messengers sent ahead, but he had no intention of telling anyone what he was really doing. He must feel what it was like to be on a horse again. He must see if he could ride to his salvation, and if Richard could keep up with him. Richard was Bellerophon.

The carriage stopped. He jumped out and ran across the yard into the shelter of the stables. The ring had been dusted, as he had ordered. He had announced that he was departing for the Austrian frontier, and that he was going via Kufstein. The town was of no importance. The explanation was. He would rather be thought eccentric, than explain the actual purpose of his ride to those who could not be expected to understand. A groom held his horse. It was not Richard. Richard was at Berg. But it did not matter who was there, for this was only an experiment.

He leaped into the saddle, peering into the shadows of the room. He might almost be outdoors. The arena had the stable smell. After all, he was practising for the ride that he might be taking for the rest of his life.

He looked at the stupid, flaxen faces of his grooms. They were waiting for him to ride out through the open door. He stood up in his stirrups and ordered that the doors be closed. Above his head candles dripped in a primitive, circular chandelier.

He spurred his horse. Round and round the ring he

went. It seemed to him as he rode that he was caught up into the rhythm of the horse. This was indeed the way to liberation, following the circuit of the mind. The riding ring seemed to vanish and he rode into the sky itself, with the groom not far behind him. He vanished into the experience and found it real.

In that case Richard was also real. He felt the horse beneath him and glanced at its neck. The horse was obedient to him as no swan could ever be. Somewhere, as he rode by, he heard church bells ring out. Later he heard them again, he did not know how much later. He leaped from his horse. They were high in the Alps and Richard was with him. It was time for lunch. They had a picnic. They had reached Kufstein, and beyond Kufstein rose the peaks themselves. He was on Pegasus and rode him well.

He leaped back on the horse and went on until dawn. He had arrived. The groom asked where they were. Ludwig looked at him for a moment, and then remembered the pretext of this all-night experiment. He said they were at Innsbruck. The groom seemed satisfied. Give people something to gossip about, and you divert them from the truth. The method was simple, once grasped.

He was very tired. He stroked his horse's neck. He had found a meaning for his life. The sense of relief was wonderful.

He had the doors of the riding ring unlocked and went out to his carriage. It was almost daylight. He would not return to Munich, but go straight to Berg.

No doubt his ride would be thought mad. It was not mad. Nor was he. He had only to walk through madness a little way, because his destination lay that way, over the ridge, on the other side. He knew that now. He had proved it in the ring.

Nonetheless, he stood in the carriage and gazed through the trees towards Munich, saying a sad good-bye to the city he was losing. He would never feel the way he felt now again. And in that there was sadness. He hated to say farewell to any segment of himself. But the horses' heads were pointed up the other way. Below him twinkled the comfortable lights of normalcy, down in the darkened city, but he had a long way to go. He sat back in the carriage and closed his eyes.

He could not know that when Sophie read his letter, she smiled indulgently. She had been confronted with something both bigger and smaller than she was, and it had frightened her. Her talents were too domestic for a throne. She felt very sorry for him, but in the collapse of her parents' ambitions she could see that her own happiness might have room to grow. That hers should grow and his diminish made her sad. Like many people whose only talent is for human relations, she saw more than she cared to see, and much more than she dared to state.

IX

‒‒‒‒‒▸▸▷●◁◂◂‒‒‒‒‒

In the following months he avoided Munich as much as possible, for it was true: when he did not give them what they wanted, they turned on him, as he had known they would. The knowledge made Richard that much the more valuable, for now Richard was his only possible guide. He hoped he was a dependable one.

He had tried many things, but had overlooked the one thing he had always known to be true. He had tried women, the city, the small social world of the court. He had tried music and the theatre. He had even tried greatness. But he had overlooked the one group that would always be loyal to him, the peasantry. The native soil alone throbbed with life, and it stopped short at the first paved streets of the capital.

He stood on the edge of a clearing, in a sudden gust of warm wind. He watched the well-loved approach of Bellerophon, who reached up to touch the bough of a tree, with the same movement he had used on that decisive morning to hold the bit of Ludwig's horse.

Ludwig was myopic. He did not want to walk on, and he was almost afraid to have the figure approach him, for as people walked towards him through the veils of sight, they lost some of their magic. Bellerophon came out of the tangled shadows. Ludwig wanted him to stop there.

He did not want to see the ideal face fade into nothing-ness. It wounded him that what he really wanted, what he really saw in people, should be there only at a distance of ten paces, too far off for him to touch. Yet thus, on an Easter morning, must Dante have met Virgil, at the edge of that shrouded wood near Lake Albano, at the entrance to an underworld it was time for him to enter, while out of the corner of his eye heraldic beasts gambolled in the shadows of the mind.

So they met.

His name was Richard Hornig, and he was master in the Berg stables. He was a little older than Ludwig. He was a married man. His eyes were blue, his hair inclined towards the blond. That someone he had conjured up out of personal necessity should have an actual identity surprised Ludwig more than would have the solidification of any djinn out of any bottle. He did not quite know what to make of it. Suddenly there were things to do again, many things.

All his life he had been travelling, by coach, by car-riage, and by horse. Such travels were means of escape. That now he should have met the person in whose charge lay the means of that escape unduly excited him. It seemed to him to be poetry. Now he caught himself watching the movements of horses, as though there was a clue to freedom in the way they irritably twitched their docked tails. What he had wanted, now he had.

Often it seemed to him, as he lay in darkness, that he had seen night riders plunging down the sky on horses whose manes were on fire. Formerly he had allowed him-self ignominiously to be pulled from place to place. Now they would ride together, upward, out of the self towards meadows he had only glimpsed before.

He could not believe that he would ever be safe in any

one place. It was more than he could expect to be left alone with Richard, and Richard had a wife. Therefore he decided to take him upon a journey. He explained it as a journey. To himself he thought of it as a pilgrimage.

What Richard thought of all this we have no way of knowing. He was a tacit man. He left no records, none at any rate that he did not mean to leave. But he was also a loyal man. He smoked a pipe, got married, did his work, and begot children, because that was the thing to do.But he must have loved Ludwig after some fashion, for he was loyal to him, and true loyalty can only be based on love. The world's great emotions come to us one-sided and incomplete. If we have ever loved deeply, we know why. Of all those to whom Ludwig appealed only Richard answered him. Nor should this make us impatient with the nature of the emotion involved, for Don Juan was less a philanderer, than a man who never quite gave up hope. At any rate it is impossible to tell what Richard felt. We can only know that whatever it was, he felt it deeply, which is not the same as understanding, but perhaps better.

Nor did Ludwig care. It was enough for him to be able to feel at all. As long ago as childhood he had learned better than to expect feeling in return, for he had spent his life among those whose lives were so empty that they had no time left for anyone else.

So out of gratitude, he planned his pilgrimage. They were to take horse and ride to Eisenach. He was a little wary. Too many people had failed him, for him not to be. But he was happy, too. He had a reason for this trip.

For by the time we are fourteen we have met all the people we shall ever meet again, so when we meet new examples of them, we take them back to those places where we were happiest with their prototypes, to see if they fit. As women match goods, we match people to the texture of our lives, looking for the ravelling or unravelling of secret threads. If we are to succeed in replacing one person with another, then the fit must be snug.

So he went to Eisenach, to the Wartberg. Even with Wagner he had never been there. In a very real way the Wartberg was Monsalvasch, the castle of the grail. It was the invisible spiritual castle from which Lohengrin had entered upon the salvation of Elsa, only to fail, as Wagner had failed him.

The journey was agreeable. It was like riding through a painting, on the way to meet the artist. They rode through a slim forest so clean-swept that its floor might have been of stone. For the Germans have picked their woods down to the bone, which is what they like to see. The horses were restive, seeming to stumble together.

They drew rein on the brink of a hill where, as theatre curtains do, the trees parted massively and slowly with a velvet whoosh. There, across the gorge, shrouded in ground mist, on its prow of rock, they saw the Wartberg sailing out of the fog and into time, like Isolde's ship headed for Britanny.

Ludwig glanced at Richard, who said nothing. Wagner had talked incessantly, destroying illusions with the very words he used to create them. For an instant, as the mist cleared, Ludwig and Richard communed wordlessly. Ludwig felt the great ease of being able for an instant to shift the weight of the inexpressible within him to someone else's shoulders. It was the pause he needed, that made the rest of the journey possible. It was for this he had taken that experimental ride to Kufstein in the locked stable.

They went slowly through the forest and over the cobbles of a stone bridge, through the throat of the castle tower, into the courtyard within, and there dismounted.

He felt safe here in the small, high-ceilinged monastic rooms and winding corridors of German consciousness, perched high on the edge of the cliff. Through rounded arches, like the sockets of a skull, they could look back into the past to see the flesh and bones of how this present world should look. Always before Ludwig had come here with a sense of loss. Wagner had written the *Meistersinger* with this setting in mind, yet there was something else here that he knew and that Wagner did not. With Richard, who was malely quiet, he could realize that knowledge. He hurried through the rooms, eager to enter the Sangersaal. This was a world long familiar to him from the soft paintings of Schwind; but always before he had explored it alone.

The stones were damp. The sunlight here was not warm. Together they went down the four steps between the three arches that led from the royal apartments to the hall, and stood there in the half-gloom. He waited eagerly. There settled over him the Oriental silks of twelfth-century princes, and on his head the iron circlet of their power. He peered into the shadows, and saw Richard standing by one of the windows, in the glittering incised armour Heinrich IV von Hohenstaufen and Walther von der Vogelweide had worn when they moved freely through these courts. For Walther von der Vogelweide, like Richard, had been of humble birth. He had risen to royal courts only because his personal attainments had purified his blood, and made him the peer of princes.

Standing there, he thought of the love cult of the Minnesingers, who did not sing in order to be loved, but out of longing for the unattainable, which, if it is to survive, must never be attained. For a moment he felt the horror of those who, searching all their lives for understanding, find the meaning of their existence crumbles precisely when they are at last understood. He wanted to say "Sing". He did not. Instead he closed his eyes and heard a melody unlike any of Wagner's composition.

With his eyes shut, the special glint of light on Richard's armour was the glint of sunlight on high snow, as it floats above the granite. This was the visible Monsalvasch, promise in itself that there *was* a Monsalvasch beyond, of which the Wartberg was only the model. They would ride there in time.

He opened his eyes and left the Sangersaal, with Richard behind him. He vaulted eagerly into the saddle. Richard had passed the first test. Now it was time for the second.

The second test was Paris. He had spent the first eighteen years of his life reading. Now he was trying to match life to what he had read. He had not dared to see Paris before. Now that he seemed to have someone to go there with, he felt differently. He was looking for an answer to the nature of kingship, and France was the fountainhead of kings, in the person of Louis XIV. He had meditated on Louis XIV for a long time. They would go by train, journey into the past, and find an answer.

For trains are not merely vehicles with wheels, so specialized they can live only on their own track. Like horses, trains and other powerful machines give us the power we need to travel beyond ourselves. They carry us triumphantly into a country we could never reach on foot. A journey by train is a safe journey through time. It reverses the normal direction of our activities, so that the past is abruptly ahead of us, at the destination of our voyage. The train takes us relentlessly and safely through the present and the future towards yesterday, which is also now.

If Richard objected to being moved about the country-side like a parcel, he did not say so. He was protected from what happened to him by a stolid silent inner calm. Indifference can also be firm as rock. Those six years between their ages made all the difference. He behaved like an uncle with a favourite nephew. He agreed to go.

As they left the Germanies and crossed the border into France, while they slept, the steam-frosted the windows of the *wagon-lit*; the steam formed great heaving clouds, like that cloud in which Ixion planted the seed which would become Bellerophon. Ludwig lay on his side in his berth and watched the patterns of the false frost. It was like watching an allegorical ceiling. The whole large-kneed sky family glowed with a singular luminescence, rising higher and higher into the sky, until it lost all semblance to the allegorical ceilings at Nymphenberg, and became the apotheosis of royalty itself, in the person of the Sun King, Louis XIV, riding high on clouds of majesty. The train moved smoothly into St. Lazare.

Eighteen sixty-seven was the year of the Paris Exposition. He would see that, too. The Comte de Berg had arrived at last in Paris, bringing with him Bellerophon. They drove at once to an hotel. The hotel was in the Place Vendôme, from whose theatrical wings almost anyone might be expected to appear, from the dress-maker Worth to Louis XIV, with his poodle look and the scowl of Volpone. About greatness there is always something a little mean and pinched.

It was not Louis XIV who appeared, but Louis Napoléon III. Ludwig detested him. He was like the usher in a mortuary, placidly displaying the beautiful embalmment he had achieved of his illustrious uncle, on whose weary features he had superimposed the simper of the times. With his moustache and pendent beard, he resembled not imperial greatness, but a powdered Belgian gryphon, that fashionable lapdog which scented women were already learning to carry about with them like wriggly muffs. No wonder the Empress Eugénie could not learn the tune of "Partant pour la Syrie". It was not that she was tuneless. It was that she lacked a sense of humour. They were not real royalty: when they sat down they always looked behind them to see if their chairs were still there. Louis Napoléon was merely a conjurer asked in to divert the nation.

Ludwig was equal to Louis Napoléon. There are certain advantages to anonymity. As Comte de Berg, he could switch hats, so that when Napoléon reached for a rabbit of alliance, it was not there. Ludwig avoided him and turned to face Paris instead. It shimmered all around him.

Who can ever tell what Paris means to a German? For Paris is not the capital of France. It is the capital of an idea. In the history of the West, five cities have been capitals not of countries, but of the spirit: Athens, Alexandria, Constantinople, Paris, and Rome. They are gone forever, but still we walk enchanted through their streets. So the fabulous cities of the Arabian nights are only a memory of Timgad, Baalbec, and the cities of the Sahara, empty, deserted, majestic, silted up with soft hissing sand pouring through the valve of time, yet always real.

Of all these only Rome survives, for Rome is the epitome of order, that most ravishing idea within the grasp of Man. Truly she is *caput mundi*. The idea of order stands above all other ideas, indestructible, severe, and sad, its features worn by time. For order is the governess of reason. Only she can school the childhood of our thoughts.

But as the train slopes down through the undulating hills, and Paris slowly rises to the climax of arrival, like a great hermaphrodite it lies over its soft green couch of hills, the ravishingly asexual presence which otherwise is only with us in a dream, helpless and absorbingly elusive as the reveries of detumescence, or the long slanting sunlight of the afternoon.

The ostensible grandeur of Paris is tarnished, flat, skimped, tinny, and pathetic, like a toy procession under well-disciplined trees too clipped to breathe, a Lilliput of power, pleased in itself, that scurries away to nothing at the first glimpse of any Brobdignag, full of the paranoic grandeur of Racine, the distant, fretful stirring of Bellay. But the dream of Paris is an endless sleep, as though the soul of man were silk that ripples through the fingers and then snags, as a pair of silk stockings is the echo of an ideal pair of legs.

They went to Versailles. Ludwig kept glancing at Richard. He found it difficult to believe in personal felicity. He kept expecting to catch the destructive curve of a smile. He felt shy, the way children do at their first party, wanting terribly to be asked to dance, and yet afraid to disappoint. He was a king. He had never before heard anybody laugh easily in his presence.

This visit was the most important thing he had ever done. He was risking everything, and he hoped that Richard appreciated the risk. The carriage entered Versailles le Vieux.

It counted for something, it turned out, to be able to intimidate that silly little man, the Emperor of the French. Word had been sent ahead, as word should always be. The spiritual inheritor of the Sun King might go where he would, touch what he pleased, see what he must. That was good.

Yet, as they rattled across the Place des Armes and passed under the square iron gate, Ludwig realized that he had let a stranger into his secret world forever, and he trembled. The one thing no one must ever do is to allow anyone into the secret laboratory where the self manufactures its dreams, those myths essential to our survival. Thus he understood, in the moment of his fear, why Wagner would never allow him to cross the threshold of his operas into the midst of the creative act. It made him more tolerant of Wagner now that he felt the same fear.

As they passed under that gate and came before the façade, it seemed to him that they entered into the vast physical model of an ideal; for vulgar and ineffectual and garish though it be in detail, Versailles still embodies the geometry of royalty. It is a diagram of the problematical structure of the elect, meaningless except as a symbol and vastly out of scale. Versailles is not a building, but a system of logic. It is not a palace, but a labyrinth whose significance is clear to us only when we realize that the Minotaur was not a monster, but the personification of the dynasty of Crete.

It is not given to every man to walk the parquet of his own mind, or to hear his footsteps behind him in the corridor. It was given to him now, for the first time, not to pace there alone.

At the entrance to the château he turned to look back. He saw not the town of Versailles, but it was as though he were at Berg or Hohenschwangau, uneasily aware of Munich below him.

He wanted to stretch out his arms. He felt absurdly small and fragile. He wanted to say: "Look, I am King, but have pity. I am only a boy. Leave me this last companion for my guide."

As he looked down the vista towards Versailles le Vieux he seemed to see the rabble of 1789 rushing towards him like rats, so ravenous they would destroy the symbol that fed them, as one day the rabble of Munich might pour out towards Hohenschwangau for him. When the king grows weak, it is the duty of the king to die. Yet the last priest-king of Nemi was not murdered. He died of neglect. There is no one so impotent as those whose power has been forgotten.

Richard stirred beside him, stalwart, strong, and smelling of pungent brown leafmould. Ludwig turned and went inside.

They entered the Galerie des Glaces. Nothing would ever make Richard a courtier. There was something in him heavy and of the hills. His elegance, though it was there, was that of a warm animal, brown like his horses, an atmosphere wild yet gentle. He was that part of Bavaria that was born loyal to its kings. Wherever he was, he stood stolidly in mental woods.

Richard's heels echoed heavily on the parquet, where Ludwig walked too lightly, with a filigree strut that was not the walk he would have chosen for himself at all. He went down the hall, catching their staggered reflections in the squat panes of the mirrors. He seemed to see there not himself or Richard, but Louis XIV, supercilious and sallow eyed in his periwig, a man who, like Wagner, was more intelligent than the role he had chosen to play, more fastidious, but equally trapped in the wrong body.

All at once the gallery became too powdered and too futile. He had to get outdoors. Reality lived outdoors.

It had been easier for Louis XIV. He had lived in a world in which irony was still a weapon, and not an act of suicide. Behind him he had had the sunburst of personal power. There was not much power left to royalty any more.

Ludwig escaped to the Petit Trianon. He felt better at once. There it was quiet, placid, and somehow Austrian. He fitted better there, and so did Richard. He paused to watch Richard move unhurriedly across the courtyard towards the entrance, and thought that through the years he would see him move like this, unhurriedly towards a house. He determined therefore that he must have a dwelling like the Trianon, from which to watch this familiar figure approaching. He had always wanted to be able to go to someone. That someone might come to him was a novel idea.

He glanced around to catch a glimpse of Marie Antoinette. She was everywhere. Versailles Château is haunted by the ghost of majesty, impersonal, sardonic, and a little smelly. But the Petit Trianon is haunted by a woman. She still lives there. She looks out of the windows. She sits in the *salons*. She runs down the stairs, with one hand on the balustrade, to meet Count Fersen or Cagliostro in the park. And when you turn around, she is watching you with a smile. She sits outside, on the grass, under a parasol, absorbed at sketching. She laughs.

Sophie would never have been able permanently to inhabit a room in this way. She was too small to have any part of eternity. Now he seemed to see that bland, irresponsible, dynastic face, as Marie Antoinette turned to look at him.

They stood in her bedroom, looking out of the window at the park. In little palaces the furniture always seems to have gathered there by accident. A palace is in some sort a theatre, so the furniture is always stage furniture, assembled impromptu for the performance of a hundred plays. He looked around the room and saw Richard smil-

129

ing at him. It made him flush, for he had been caught out in a thought. But for once that did not make him furious. They stood rather far apart, with a table between them, as though they had been transported separately through time to meet unexpectedly in this room.

To turn to speak, and to realize that the thought has been uttered and answered already in the other mind, is an ultimate experience. It is a form of love, and the deepest intimacy there is. Ludwig did not need Marie Antoinette. They went outside through the bosquet to the Petit Hameau.

Once more he felt shy. He saw that this miniature village, which was false in France, would be real in Bavaria. For this toy town was somehow heartbroken. Looking at it, he longed to go home, where instead of this toy domesticity, there would be possible a real domesticity with Richard, his wife and children, so that by means of Richard he could enter a low-ceilinged, well protected ordinary life he could enter in no other way. With Richard's children he had discovered unexpectedly the joy of being an adopted uncle.

For the secret of the Petit Hameau is not that it is the foolish plaything of a spoiled, tactless queen, but that it is the reconstructed childhood of a girlish exile. For him that sort of exile was ended. Richard had given him back his childhood as it should have been, so that now he could return to Berg.

As silently, together, they started the long stroll through the past towards the palace, unexpectedly all the fountains began to play, the air first filled with that hushed, magical lull which comes before rain, to tell you that something is about to happen. He knew now that reality was not in this stale French air, but in the tart, crisp, lucid air of Bavaria.

Everywhere they could hear the fountains from a distance, their soft hiss to the wind, the endless, soothing, delicious sparkle as the jets rose and fell like crystal music muted by regret. Tritons and sea-horses, nereids and amphitrites, their flanks glistening, rode stationary in the same eternal spray. He listened to the sharp gasp and gurgle of the waters, forced upward in the air in one great shimmering release, to burst into a thousand glittering mirrors in the air, and his own body stirred and came alive. Freedom from the self is to take delight in somebody else, to want merely to admire them for being there, without the necessity to touch.

They reached the basin of Neptune. The screen of water spread like the tails of a choir of transparent peacocks. As he watched, his spirit exactly fitted the contours of his body for the first time, and life became actual. For the first time in his life he felt complete.

He shut his eyes with pleasure.

When he opened them, the curtains of water had parted, it was days later, and they were galloping under the trees towards Nymphenberg, which was the capital of his dynasty and inheritance, now that he was of an age to spend. It was here he had been born. It was here that he was born again.

One feels a certain sympathy for Richard. It is not altogether pleasant to be the victim of a metaphysical honeymoon. But one feels sympathy for Ludwig too. Since most of our life is spent in the nightmare of waking, in which we perceive that we are only other men's means, it is as well that we are at least permitted to dream once. And besides, a dream without waking would be no dream, for then we would not be able to remember it.

Unlike Versailles, Nymphenberg is a palace which demands no audience. Before him Ludwig saw the high-pitched roofs, the white walls, beyond which lay the magic of the gardens. They stayed together there for several weeks.

It was not Richard's fault if the experience wore thin. He had a wife, children, and a certain stability within himself. He could not be different every day. It is the tragedy of those who need diversion, that we can repeat everything about an experience except the first time we underwent it. Unless they are willing to change themselves, they must constantly change the water in their tank. It was something Ludwig never realized.

It took him a little while to feel disappointment again. They went sometimes to the Pagodenberg, sometimes to the Amalienberg, and everything they did pleased him at first.

They would walk at dawn in the wet woods. He would look down an unmown avenue, crowded with spontaneous daisies, towards the wing of the palace in which he had been born. Did he, as a child, look down that avenue towards himself, happy at the age of twenty-two, smile, wave, and coo with pleasure; and did that give him courage to survive until, now, he could look back down the avenue towards himself as a newborn child? He lifted an arm and waved towards the baby he had been, saying: "Yes, you were right. It is true."

The petals of the daisies were wetly plastered to the short black boots Richard still wore, refusing to be anything but the equerry he was. They laughed and moved on through the park woods.

How do we sweep towards tragedy? And what is tragedy? Tragedy is hope. Among the sedges of the Badenburgersee, a captive artificial lake, they stood beside the ruffled cool grey water and looked at the Monopteros among the frail trees. It was one of those circular open tempietti eightenth-century noblemen liked to scatter about their gardens. As a child he had always been puzzled that it contained no statue. Now he thought he knew why. It was not an Eros temple left unfinished, but a temple in which you stood to think about the Eros of your thoughts.

Mostly, during those untarnished weeks, they went to the Amalienberg, that small, one-story casino hidden in the trees. It had been built for a happy Princess, a century ago, and it was as a result a happy place. There one knew how rapture could be cold and smell of snow and warm linen, hot from the warming-pan. It was wonderful. It would not fail. Yet he had said that others would not fail, and they had. He felt uneasy. Perhaps he was aware of a failure in himself, for he was not built for joy. He could not bear the strain. It ripped him apart, when he would have been inviolable.

He approached the Amalienberg by night. He saw the lights through the trees and hurried on. He liked to be separated from Richard, for then he could meet him again. He was already trying to freshen up the experience. He went up the five shallow steps and into the rotunda room.

It was like an ice palace. In the centre the chandelier glittered with tall white candles, and the mirrors on the walls caught up the leaping flames and echoed them endlessly. This room was a glacial cave. The walls were pale blue, but all the plaster work was silver. In the reflections of the candles, the rococo sparkled, danced, and shimmered like a fast wave hanging against the sky before it fell. The building was full of the thin, hollow, whining melodies of ice, a grotto in a glacier, in which truth rang out along the galleries of a crevasse.

Richard had not yet come. Ludwig waited for him. To

wait for him made him feel nubile. Soon he would snuggle up to brown warmth, like a satiated puppy after its first determined toddle towards independence, when its legs gave out and it sat down surprised and weak, but on the whole delighted, with a puzzled frown, to find the world so big, itself so small.

Lying in the shadows, Ludwig caught a glimpse into the silver gilt mirror which reflected the square corners and edges of infinite rooms through endlessly open doors. The Amalienberg was a warm place in the snow.

But once one is satisfied, there then comes the gnawing hunger for something else, the nostalgia for hunger itself, and with it the awful despair of being complete, and so at last knowing that one may be nothing more. He had used the Amalienberg up. He was trying to keep his own emotions alive. He decided that they should meet, in future, at the Pagodenberg.

The Pagodenberg was deeper in the park and much more male, if only because it had before it water. Among its autumn trees, it was proper to a marriage, which also has an upper and a lower floor. It was less delightful than the Amalienberg, but more substantial, a satisfaction from which something had escaped, and yet in which something remained.

He was beginning to realize the differences between them, which delimited what experience they might share. There seemed to be less and less left. And all the time, while he felt such thoughts, Richard sat silently before him, smoking and quietly watching him, as though he were housebreaking a dog. It was unnerving.

What gave Richard the right to believe he knew anything about princes?

He was a little wrong. He thought Richard a peasant, but Richard was not quite that. Peasants do not envy those above them, for having lived for generations in one room, what would they do with twenty? A king may meet a peasant casually, for pleasure, in the stables or the Amalienberg. They are there to serve his necessity. But Richard was wilier and scrawnier than that.

The luxury of princes is to submit to the tyranny of someone else. So, at royal courts, you may catch a glimpse of the invincible slave owners, almost anonymous people no one dares to offend, because they have their finger on that part of majesty which adores to be whipped. That is what was beginning to happen between him and Richard.

Richard ceased to be the beloved friend as soon as they had moved to the Pagodenberg. He became instead the equivalent of Fräulein Meilhaus, the governess Ludwig had never forgotten. Now he had graduated to having a governor, that was all. Richard became the stern executioner who punishes us not for stealing the jam, but because from time to time it is good for us to be punished, since that pleases us, and because, though theft is amoral and meaningless, there are certain dangers inherent in too much jam.

As the Germans scrape their woods with an almost Japanese passion for *shibumi*, leaving here and there a twig or a fallen leaf, so was Richard the idea of a peasant, but neat, tidied, swept, and cleaned away from an underbrush of guile. For our ideals are also works of art. Year after year we perfect them. As one man paints a perfect picture once out of a hundred, so of the peasants with whom we seek oblivion, one may be the peasant who can give it to us. And in that case he is not a peasant, for no peasant can conceive of oblivion, since no man can ever really know the country in which he lives.

Ludwig should have been pleased. Such human conjunctions seldom occur. Yet the excitement was beginning to ebb. Subconsciously he knew that, and it made him restive. The people we love can never satisfy us, because they leave us satisfied. So though Richard stood squarely astride his mind, closer than did Wagner, and more satisfactory than anyone else, something remained that was unsatisfactory. So it was necessary for them to use the two-story Pagodenberg. Dissatisfaction needs room to move around in.

There for a moment, but only for a moment, he got the thrill of the experience back again. It was not truth he wanted, but the self-forgetfulness of demeaning himself with a stranger. With Richard he could no longer do that. When he tried, he was filled with panic. Richard was too good. Richard never said anything, but he saw much and he watched. It was like trying to bribe a judge who was also a member of the family.

So in the white-tile fantasy of the Pagodenberg, self-justification clawed at the walls and found no hold. For when we are satisfied at last with others, it is not of them we tire, but of ourselves, and that was a truth Ludwig would never admit. The ghosts in his mind were flooding back again. They could never be held back for long. He was haunted always by the image of his own executioner. As they lay in bed, it seemed to him that he could sense the executioner waiting patiently in the next room. It was only to be expected, for the executioner is that side of the self that knows the loved one will always go away, either when he leaves us, or when we leave him. The pretext differs. The separation is the same.

In the host of shadows who waited for him just beyond the bottom of the bed, while Richard slept, there would always be one face missing. The face was his own. He could join that company only by dying, and he was afraid to die.

136

Sometimes in small country graveyards, under the black trees, you become aware of the doting dead, like guests at a party, chattering in groups, but actually waiting for their host to join them. He knew who that host was. And the measure of a successful party is the extent to which the guests ignore their host. He would have to join them alone.

For he realized something. There was a part of his mind Richard could not understand, and it was the inmost part. Richard was hale, healthy, and astute. He believed the hungers of the soul could be satisfied by smoking a pipe. He was not altogether wrong, but Ludwig did not like to smoke. So Richard could never join the ideal companions. You could not have people both in reality and in the ideal world as well. The one cancelled out the other. It was only people who pleased you for a night, and then disappointed you forever, the well-loved people you could not bear to be in the same room with again, who became ideal companions while they were still alive, because they died for you as soon as you had exhausted them.

The metaphysical honeymoon was over. But as the jewels of the crown are crown jewels only in their setting, perhaps Richard and he might get their lustre back at Berg. Ludwig decided to depart at once. They had known each other for a year, and yet already he began to feel alone again.

The years were passing. He was getting older. He must never age. He had to flee from time. For as fashions in the capital become novelties in the provinces a year later, so a well-loved king of twenty, if he is to remain twenty, flees to the provinces, where the people still remember him, not having seen him alter and change, as he was when he was a child among them. The only way to remain young is to retreat farther and farther from the centre of life, where the light is merciless, into the shadow, where it is kind.

He would go on with Richard. There was no one else to go on with. Yet it was a pity that one could have joy only for a little while. It was as cruel as to introduce someone to a new vice, only to remove the drug supply that it had evoked a craving for. He began to keep a diary. He no longer trusted himself to speak. With Richard he had hoped that the world would open out. He found instead it opened like a trap in the floor, and dropped him deeper down into himself.

For time is the thirteenth labour of Herakles. There is no Atlas we may call back to carry that load. It is the test of strength we always fail. Try as we can, we cannot reverse the glass. Try as we may, it counts us out. We are alone. The clock ticks on. The landscape is desolate. The sands run out. And yet we try. There is beauty in that. It was only a pity that there was no one left to see it.

X

He had always known the outward forms of fear. Now he was beginning to learn its inner meaning as well. In 1869 he had been with Richard for three years. To be near him he stayed chiefly at Berg. The gossip about Sophie had long ago died down, but he wanted nothing to blow it into life again. He avoided Munich as much as he could. Yet he had to go there sometimes.

He tended to forget that he was not only a suffering animal, but also a king. As a king, he had certain duties to perform. They were not the duties he would have thought proper to a king, for by the nineteenth century kings had already shrunk in function to social secretaries and keepers of a rubber stamp. But whenever he forgot them, he was reminded of them soon enough, by the correspondence on his desk.

And among his correspondents, a certain Elizabeth Ney had recently become the most annoying. It was impossible to evade her. It was equally impossible to see her. Every time she wrote, it was like receiving a message from the Mafia in the morning's mail.

When he did have to go to Munich these days, he took Richard with him whenever he could. Richard was with him now, as at his desk he idly pawed over the morning's correspondence. He no longer had the energy to conceal

139

that sincere part of him that others took for eccentricity. And among these eccentricities was a growing terror of publicity. He could not bear to be seen by anyone. He had his reasons.

For there 's nothing more disturbing than a mirror at the end of a shadowy corridor, for then the man walking towards you is the man you are walking toward, though because of the mirror which permits you to see each other, you are never allowed to meet. That was why he did not want portraits of himself either executed or displayed, and Fräulein Ney was a sculptress.

To judge from her letters, she sounded not so much like a great artist offering him physical immortality, as a fashionable tailor soliciting his trade. She sent a list of the eminent great whom she had turned to stone. It was not thus that the Medusa was wont to advertise her powers. Nor would he be set up for the public to gawk at, merely that this woman might earn her competence.

On the other hand she was extremely insistent.

He said to Richard: "What shall I do?"

It was not Richard's sort of question. To answer that kind of question he merely took his pipe out of his mouth and left you to watch his silence. One went away with the same feeling one would have on leaving Delphos on a day when the oracle had refused to speak. The wisdom of horses, and Richard was a groom, is limited. They only know the world standing up. They cannot know that great weariness of the self which makes us long to sit down to rest for a while in the portrait or bust someone has made of us.

It was a turning point, but he did not know it.

He refused to see her. He was afraid to see her. A woman does not and cannot hold the keys to immortality, for it is her biological function to fill in the unknown.

140

Into the great hole of unconsciousness to which men erect monuments, she throws children of flesh and blood, as one throws earth into a bay, to make more land and so be safer from the sea. A woman exists to diminish what man would make more vast.

And Ludwig did not know that some women can be of neither sex, and so like Janus face both ways. He had built a cage for greatness once before, only to find that Wagner moved away, since greatness does not create in rooms, however beautiful, but in the mind. Immortality must be spun out of ourselves, if we are to pupate into eternity. Ludwig did not know that, either. Artists pass down to immortality only what they see of us, so that we arrive there incomplete, with our essential self long lost, and their essential self permanently imposed upon us.

"Who is this woman?"

Richard did not know.

Richard, he saw, would always try to limit him, not from evil intent, but out of his goodness, which could not conceive that goodness, far from being a unique virtue, was merely the smallest, if only humanly inhabitable, planet of a cosmos of vast extent. Goodness was not freedom. Freedom was far out there, where being habitable was not a virtue, but only the unique quality of a trivial and unimportant sphere; for suns burn where no worlds are, and who is to say their warmth is lost?

There are virtues of which we do not even know the name, attributes of the macrocosm of the self, where we are at last free in the world of the plus geography, only whose minus is visible to us, in the parable of our native hills and heights, but of whose actual value we can never be cognizant.

Yet he needed some new experience outside himself.

His own experience with Richard had been blocked. It is dreadful to cross several countries on the way to freedom, only to find the last border shut because of a technicality. He had wanted to lock Richard in with him, and now he found himself shut out. It had never occurred to him before that what was of paramount importance to him might inspire merely indifference in others. It was all very well for him to hide in the country outside the capital, but also it was terrible to live unknown, die, and leave nothing behind. Perhaps he could at least send his image down through time.

Perhaps the Ney was not a spider woman. Perhaps she was another saviour come to wake him up, and he was tired of sleeping. Perhaps she would give him the other thing he needed, that he could have with no one person and did not even know the name of.

"I will see her," he said, gazing at the litter on his desk.

Richard looked up. "See who?" he asked, and smiled. The smile made Ludwig feel better. Try though he would to help it, if he no longer trusted Richard's love, he still sought his approval.

"The Ney woman."

All the same, he was uneasy. Portrait painters and sculptors, like diarists, smile at us and then do what they will to us, beyond our power to stop them. They send their personal opinion of us forward into time, without our permission, and though they assure us they have been flattering, who is to know what they have really said?

Certainly she addressed him fulsomely enough when she wrote. She called him "Thou King of the Realm of Ideas". He decided to let her prove that he was. He ordered the Odysseus-Saal of the Residenz Palace set up as a studio for her. Then, for a week, he worried and bit his nails. In the end he went to the sitting only because he was disgusted with his own indecision, and felt that he had to force himself to perform some public and determined act. Richard he left at Berg. He wanted to see if he could face her, and through her the world, alone.

When he came into the room she was already there, at her modelling stand. He was relieved. It meant he did not have to speak to her.

The room was lit from high up, and he sat under the converging rays of light, in a gilt arm-chair on a dais, and was glad he could not see her clearly. Yet he was curious. He had not met a stranger for some time.

He was vaguely aware of an efficient blur, moving in strange, long robes, which were certainly not ordinary clothes. He did not bother to look at people any more. It was safer not to do so. Instead he waited to be summoned out of himself by a voice, though he did not know what the tone of that voice would be.

The portrait was to be a bust, so he was at liberty to alter the position of his body as he pleased. Still she did not speak. He was aware instead of small creaks and whisperings in the room around him. Sophie was happily married now to the grandson of Louis Philippe. Gossip should be dead. Yet the palace seemed to be stirring. It knew he was there. Very faintly, and not altogether joyfully, he smiled.

Still the Ney woman did not speak. He began to be annoyed. Out there, flitting in and out of the borders of his sight, she was like the ghost of a moth, or something worse, and he longed to know what she was turning him into. The thought of a head slowly being built up in clay was for some reason more terrible to him than the thought of a skull. He shifted his knees.

The sounds in the room were louder and dangerous. He wanted very much to move his head. He did not like these public rooms. He should have brought Richard with him.

> We are not empty shades.
> *Mark well my words. Collect thy scattered thoughts.*
> *Attend. Each moment is of priceless worth,*
> *And our return hangs on a slender thread*
> *Which, as it seems, some gracious fate doth spin.*

The lines came to him from nowhere. He half turned his head, afraid of an auditory hallucination. It was the voice of the sibyl, the voice he had been expecting to hear.

> *I have not learned deception, nor the art*
> *To gain with crafty wiles my purposes.*
> *Detested falsehood. It doth not relieve*
> *The breast like words of truth: it comforts not,*
> *But is a torment. . . .*

He realized the sound came from in front of him. Slowly Elizabeth Ney swayed into his field of vision, tall, with a handsome, sexless head like that of the sibyls of Michelangelo. It was a voice that should have come out of one of the Great Friend's operas. The lines he recognized now. They were from Goethe's *Iphigenie*. He settled himself in his arm-chair to listen. It was as though she were speaking to him from the safe distance of a theatre, a woman in a play, who comes to wake the conscience of the hero. Also he had heard she detested Cosima von Bülow, which could do no harm and did not displease him. She stopped reciting. He waited for a moment.

"I will see the bust now," he said. He rose, as one would rise during an intermission, and walked towards the modelling stand. Behind him the high light converged on his vacated chair. Elizabeth Ney stood aside. He looked at the bust. After all, the Wittelsbachs had always patronized the arts, from the days of Dürer down to Kaulbach and Wagner. It was the family thing to do. He stared at the bust for a long time.

"No," he said. "I will not be like that." He was profoundly shocked.

It was not his own face, but that of Otto, smooth, implacable, unreal, a little mad, someone two-dimensional enough to sidle out of time and become a shadow, a man in a mental iron mask peering at the present through fanatic and despairingly gentle eyes. He felt responsible for Otto. He had been afraid of him ever since that day when they were children, playing Maria Stuart near the greenhouse door. As he looked at the bust, he could hear time tick to the metre of his mind and life slow down. It was a face that never had and never would wear a crown, before which the flimsy curtains of insanity were drawing together like the curtains of an upstairs window in a transient hotel. Otto was sequestered. Reports on his brother were laid on his desk twice a month, and he hated to read them. To do so was like reading one's own obit in the morning paper, at breakfast.

He turned to Elizabeth Ney abruptly.

"You will do me full length now, in the robes of St. Hubertus. You will see. I will be different."

The bust had upset him profoundly. His resemblance to Otto was something he tried to keep at the back of his mind. He strode out of the room, without dismissing her. He had at last found someone to torture him. To pose for her was to be slapped awake, in a shower as cold as the marble she would turn him into.

145

The sittings went on.

"Your Majesty has no faith in humanity."

"How can I, after so many disillusionments?"

They often talked like that, while he posed.

"Contact with reality draws ever farther away from your Majesty. Already it has, for you, almost escaped into formless distance."

Why did she speak in that ridiculous way? Did she expect him to write it down, or did she write it down herself? But what she said was not quite true. He began to explain himself to her. It was a luxury to do so, for she had to listen. As a sculptor turns about the platform on which his armature rests, so slowly he turned his life about, revealing now Sophie, now Paul, now Richard and Fräulein Meilhaus, but never Otto. As the easel swung back, the shifting light changed them into Marie Antoinette, Louis XIV, the woodsman in the clearing, Maria Stuart, and the figure of his executioner. It did not matter. But about Otto he would not speak.

"Choose now," she exhorted him, "before your Majesty has surrendered to the self-destroying tortures of solitude."

Where did she find these phrases? And what could she know of solitude? The choice was already made. He was Prometheus, strapped to the Taurus of himself, and the eagle came and tore him open every night. It was cold on Caucasus.

"Is there any man in whose generosity and high-mindedness I dare to believe?" he asked her, thinking of Richard, in whom he did not dare to believe.

She was a clever woman, and also a little more than a woman. She had the instincts of a man. "Yes" she said. "Yourself."

"I have no self."

146

He watched her face eagerly, to see what she would say to that. She said nothing, but accepted the truth of it with an impatient nod. She was not Sappho now. She was Egeria. "God made you what you are. You did not create yourself. Therefore you may admit freely what you are."

That he could never do, for God has also made critics, and critics, being unable to create anything, are dangerous to life. For though there may be those who will not betray us to others, they will still manage to betray us to ourselves.

"What would you have me do? I am not Louis XIV."

She was politically minded. He had given up politics. These exhortations were irrelevant. It does no good to tell an eagle in a cage to use its wings.

"Louis XIV is not King of Bavaria. You are."

It impressed him. He had not thought of the matter in that way, ever. But of course she was right. The noble hero, outcast, rejected, living in exile, still comes back when his people are in danger and leads them to victory. That was his role. He had forgotten. He had tried to be creative, but music, the stage, sculpture, painting, architecture, even friends, these are the materials of a creative artist. He was not a creative artist. He was a king, and the raw material of a king is politics. He had sought salvation in the wrong medium. Now he would be architect of the State, and so saviour of his people. Again he would be loved.

He was a Wittelsbach. From his line had sprung consecrated emperors. And she was a sibyl. Unfortunately she was a sibyl in the wrong time and place. Later she would go off to rot in Texas. Nonetheless, she had helped him find his role.

XI

————————⟫⟫⟩⟨⟨——————————

It was perhaps just as well that the experiment upon which she launched him was mercifully short. By the time it was completed, she was far away near Galveston, dreaming her own dreams. At least his ruins were his own.

But she had so fired his imagination, that he did not even conceive of ruins. He conceived of triumphal arches, bandstands, bunting, and parades. The time was unpropitious. She had left him on the threshold of 1870, and in the contention of great forces there is no room for the neophyte.

But he did not know that either. He did not realize that each generation must learn its own wisdom. He thought that wisdom could be inherited, like the crown.

After leaving his last sitting with the Ney, he received shattering but by no means unexpected news. It only confirmed him in his new resolve. Wagner had married Cosima, so that at last the bronze doors on to the creative world he had coveted were firmly shut in his face, like the doors of a bedroom on the guests at a wedding.

So it was time for him to conquer the real world and to force its respect, since there was nothing else he might have. He took his thoughts to the wintergarden, where he could think them best.

Who was there to tell him the system of the present world? He was a constitutional monarch: they brought him only yesterday's newspapers, never to-day's. He must see for himself. He would need vision, which is the only valid yardstick of political greatness. It was a pity that to achieve his ends he should have to stoop to the tactics of his prime minister. Like Christ, the Wittelsbachs had been given their crown only when their temporary power was gone. That power he must re-establish. It was a matter of *amour-propre*.

For what did people now think of him? The Great Friend thought less than nothing. He had scooped up his gifts and drifted away. Our family never thinks much of us, but the Empress Elizabeth liked to laugh at him, and to spread gossip about him besides. Richard was already disappointed, and wanted him to be firmer. Sophie he knew better than to trust. She was safely married, but she would always hate him, because he had embarrassed her. His governess, Fräulein Meilhaus, behaved too patiently and understandingly to have anything but secret doubts. The Cabinet thought they could do as they pleased with him. They even made it a practice to sigh anxiously in his presence, with exasperation, as though they were in actuality the regents of the child they obviously thought him.

If he entered politics, he would have to deal with Bismarck and Crown Prince Friedrich of Prussia. Bismarck had no respect for anyone, but only feigned it. Crown Prince Friedrich was a bumptious toady who despised everything that was not Prussian. If Ludwig wrested power away from his ministers, what would the world think of him then?

What would they say? Wagner, for one, would be delighted, and attribute everything to his own influence.

A stronger Wittelsbach would make him sorry he had fled such patronage. He would pretend to recognize Parsifal and Lohengrin again. Sophie would be so consumed with envy that she would smile at him whenever she saw him. And Richard would be gratified. It would be pleasant to see a warm glow of respect in Richard's eyes. The Empress Elizabeth would have to pretend not to snigger at him from behind her barricade of spurious affection; and the Cabinet would be put in its place. Bismarck would be courtly and sardonic, as always. He would also be furious, for only Bavaria stood between Prussia and the unification of Germany. Crown Prince Friedrich would have to strut his Prussian superiority at some small court in Pomerania.

It was a delicious dream. Like Louis XIV, Ludwig would rule and unite the country. Even Fräulein Meilhaus, Frau von Leonrod, who asked nothing of him, would feel that her loyalty was justified and be pleased with him. It was so long since anyone had been genuinely pleased with him.

But why was it, hurrying down the corridor to meet the Cabinet, that he remembered the words of someone now a total stranger, of Paul who had once called him "a wild little brain"? Perhaps because the words were human and direct, and gave him the same pleasure a dog feels, when someone strokes its ears after it has retrieved the mallards. Words lost their warmth. We all have these treasured phrases, which we take out from time to time, when we feel cold. Words could not warm him. Therefore only power was left. He would rule supreme in a cold country, or not rule at all.

When one knows people have two faces, like Janus, and turn whichever is the more suitable to the weather, particularly when the emotions stand open in time of war, one feels nothing but contempt for them. One is flattered then not by their praise, but by their meretriciousness. Yet if he could not have the dangers of love, at least let him have the security of being feared.

He opened the door at the end of the corridor, and stepped into the Cabinet room, a shabby tiger among professionals. It would perhaps be more decent not to say what they did to him. Dishonesty was their career. To him it was only a desperate measure. How could he win?

The delicious dream became a nightmare soon enough.

To the aristocrats of the nineteenth century, the political figures below them moved with a jerky and inevitable precision, like the statues of the hours on some marvellous blue and gold medieval clock. After the hour, and the figures whirl by out of sequence, but it did not occur to Ludwig that he was attempting to set the clock back. To him the principle of monarchy was self-regulating. He could not see the politicians in the works, the cogs both large and small, nor did it occur to him that the mechanism might wear out.

Instead he saw the face of the clock, both waking and in his dreams.

It was the time of the Franco-Prussian war. The Cabinet had explained that to him patiently. So eager to act was he, that he had answered someone else's cue. Prussia hoped to squeeze Bavaria out like a blackhead, in the pincers of a war, and so to rule the Germanies alone. He should contrive things otherwise.

As the hands of Germany met at noon, the door to the left snapped open and out leaped the statues of the current hours.

First came Louis Napoléon, a figure with neither a past not a future of his own. The arrangement of his facial hair gave him a superficial resemblance to Charles I, but the rest of him moved with the abrupt gestures of Tom Thumb. He was the son not of a dynasty, but of the brother of a great man. He was astute, but like so many virtues that are French, his astuteness was too miserly to be practical. On the first stroke of noon he vanished back into the clock.

The second figure was in better repair. It must be the Empress Eugénie. She had many years ahead of her, most of them a little mad. With a soft click she pivoted away from her dressmaker and took the road to Sédan.

Immediately behind these out whirled three figures chockablock. One was a brisk old man. One was placing the crown upon his own head. One was packing a bag. Who were these? The future kings of Bavaria, but Ludwig could not see them.

The seventh figure was more majestic, a great black eagle with gilt wings, leading by the nose-ring a dancing bear with the face of a woman. Behind them stood an enormous figure in white chalked buckskin, knee-length black boots, and a spiked helmet, carrying a whip and a hoop. His eyes were fatherly, but shifty. His gestures were oddly supple, as he moved along after the others, flowing down the track. He nodded and smiled. It was Bismarck, leading Bavaria in chains.

Down in the square those who watched the clock raised a shout, for immediately behind Bismarck rode Lohengrin in the guise of St. Michael, patron of Bavaria, his foot upon the dragon Prussia, his sword upraised against the conqueror in front of him. Peering deeper into his dream, Ludwig recognized himself and sat upright with the agility of decision. Like the bear, St. Michael was his patron. He would liberate the bear.

He had waked from his dream too soon. He did not

see moving on the track behind him the statues of the future kings of a united Germany, unwilling William and William the untouchable. The clock stopped chiming. The tourists moved away, unaware that when they returned another noon the figures, though the same, would have different names and a different order of precedence. They did not care. Tourists have no patience to see any marvel more than once.

To Ludwig, as he became caught in it, the dream became obsessive. He had it almost every night. He shook his head and slipped out of bed, for he always waked at the same point. Below him on the cobbles a carriage rattled by. He went to the window and glanced at the closed doors of the Theatinerkirche. Time was going too rapidly for him. He could get no hold upon it and no leverage. Politics were more difficult than he had supposed; and it was often thus with a well-contrived war. He was foolish to suppose that in anything so self-centred as politics his mere appearance could tip the scales either way. He was uneasily aware of that. Kings did not make history any more: it was merely presented to them for signature. Even the kings of Crete did not know the plans of Daedalus. No more could he fathom Bismarck's designs.

His interviews with the Cabinet ministers did nothing to help. At first he was cautious, like a man who has not played cards for a long time and is afraid some of the rules may have been changed. Then he decided to call out the troops on the side of Prussia, and to march against the French before they could march against him. It was a decisive act, and he admired himself for it. He did not realize that Bismarck had manoeuvred him into it, and did not admire him at all.

Each of us has a portrait gallery in his head. In moments of ambition, which usually come at night, we saunter barefoot over the cold parquet, holding aloft a torch, peering at idealized likenesses of ourselves.

Here was the *portrait d'apparat* showing the defender of Munich, invaded by the French. The overpainting faded out. Here was the King fleeing his capital.

And here, in a triptych, were the friend, the conqueror and the dupe of Bismarck. Closed, the wings of the central panel showed a king sitting in an empty room, a slide rule and a compass on the table beside him, the architect of Germany, deaf, ugly, forgotten, and ignored.

Here was the commander of Bavarian troops, insignificantly lost in a cloud of Prussian advisers. And here Füssli's *Nightmare*, the figure of a young man thrown back on a rumpled bed, while the Crown Prince sat on his chest, digging spurred heels into his ribs, like a monkey with saucer eyes, and there peered out from the draperies the enormous presence of Bismarck with a horse's face. As a matter of fact there had already been a newspaper cartoon of that scene.

It came out quite suddenly, the day after the war was won. For in war, as in everything else, the only real victory is that which the allies have over each other. That is not something that can be learned on the carpet with a set of lead soldiers. It can be learned only at school, and later, among men.

It made no difference that Prussia had won the war. It made only slightly more difference that Bavaria had been defeated in the course of it, and that Prussia now controlled the Germanies. What mattered was that he had been made to look a fool. What hurt was that he was one.

The armies were coming back, almost before they had had time to set forth. He stood at the window, watching the parade ground below him. Bavaria was no longer a sovereign state outside her own boundaries. The matter was over as soon as that. The nightmare was over, but so also was the dream. There would not be many more.

At the ends of columns of Bavarian men down in the square rode Prussian officers, hedging them in and ordering them about. As a reward for such a spectacle, he was hailed as the saviour of German unity. That was what the crowds shouted, anyhow. He did not bother to listen. Instead he seemed to hear the warning voice of his grandfather, Ludwig I, he who had lost his throne. "Don't give up any rights of the Crown. For a short time you will be praised for it—but the loss remains. How changeable the *aura popularis* is. Your grandfather has had his lesson."

So had he.

When he drove through the cheering crowds, these phrases turned in his head in rhythm with the turning wheels of the carriage. His grandfather was quite right. The crowd would applaud anything, but never the same thing twice. He remembered how, at Versailles, with Richard, he had turned to see the rats pouring towards the palace from the town. Applause is like the warmth of the sun. But like sun that breaks intermittently through heavy clouds of disapproval, it is gone before we can settle ourselves to receive it, making us feel colder than ever. It comes out somewhere else.

He knew now what had happened. His hand had been forced, so that he would play the wrong card. He felt as though he had seen the flag of Bavaria fly for the last time. At the moment the crowds were shouting their enthusiasm, but this applause would dwindle away like any other. Berlin would siphon it off. If the crowds did not know that they were applauding their own destruction, he did, nor did he wish to hear what those for whose admiration he had craved would now say of him.

He decided to leave the capital. He could not bear to remain there. He would go to Hohenschwangau, for after every defeat he moved farther and farther from Munich. The cold waters of the Alpsee beckoned him. Slowly they lapped round his consciousness, full of the odd consoling gentleness of the inanimate, that would have us join it if we could.

So he sat in his carriage with the shades drawn, as it headed for the hills. Only up there was kingship an ideal and not merely a factitious reality. It was only among archetypes that he could move, for he was one himself.

At Hohenschwangau he whipped himself into a fury. He decided to abdicate, for one thing he would not do: he would not give his crown into the hands of the Prussians. Let someone else do that. He would not, like Cleopatra, make the long sea journey to Rome in order to keep his crown at the precise moment that he had begun to lose his country. Once he abdicated, he would rule the hills. No one would ever dislodge him there.

It was something he had threatened to do before, and he must have known that he really did not mean to do it. He would be king of the Alpsee, as sunbathers in the course of time, because they cannot tear themselves away from the sand, become the recognized *jerifes* of the beach.

Therefore he sent for Otto. That turned out to be a mistake. One look at Otto was enough to show him why. When Ludwig told him what he proposed, Otto turned a pale, groping face towards him, like that marble face Elizabeth Ney had carved, but much farther away. As Ludwig watched, he seemed to see the sands of sanity slip out from under Otto, as the latter found himself in a sudden surf of events. Otto could never rule.

The light in the room was dim. Ludwig turned away, flinching. He did not want to see Otto sitting like Cnut in the surf of his own madness, stubbornly, until at last there would only be an empty chair to show where he had been, against which the returning waters faintly washed.

"Speak," he said. "Say anything, but speak."

Otto did not want to speak. He looked frightened, but compliance was part of his nature. His voice, when it came, dubious to answer any question, was the thin, furry, bloodless shriek of a bat, too tired at evening to find a place to hang.

"No," he said. It was the only word he could be induced to say any more, as though he were the negative of himself, but a negative dusty and cracked and impossible to print up any longer. He was not quite mad yet. Yet for long afternoons he would sit with his forehead pressed to the glass of a window, looking out at the rain, repeating that one syllable over and over to himself.

Ludwig did not like to see him. It was like looking down unexpectedly into one's own fresh-dug grave. That woman should not have made that bust, for in so doing she had made something real that otherwise could have been held off a little longer.

Ludwig sighed and tried to explain the situation. Otto only smiled. It was the smile of apathy, the smile of saints. He sat in his mind like the figure in a child's snow toy, as the artificial snow more slowly settled and everything was still around him. Ludwig twitched his hands. There was no escape from the crown he had himself destroyed. All its jewels sprouted into thorns, the emerald spikes, the diamond flowers, the ruby blood. Everyone has a cross to bear, but only now did it occur to him that he was himself his own. Golgotha, too, was a mountain of sorts, towards which he had to drag his way, while the crowds began to jeer. He had had no idea the way could be so long.

157

Very well. It was quite obvious that he could not abdicate. But he could send Otto to Versailles, where his pale, blinking withdrawn face would show how far Bavaria must be reduced, to yield her sovereignty to Prussia.

When he heard that, Otto looked more frightened than ever. As gently as he could, Ludwig got rid of him. Meanwhile he would return to Munich, briefly, to face down the conquerors.

They might have defeated him, but they would not see him flinch. He would show that for so long as he lived, then Bavaria would have a king. And after that, he would show himself no longer.

He remembered the Galerie des Glaces at Versailles, that interminable room with its mirrors, in which the Germans would be so uncomfortable, yet secretly so pleased to exalt themselves in France. He had not liked that room when he had walked there with Richard. It was strange, but typical, that with Richard he should have been so happy precisely in the halls of his next defeat. It was not a hall, but a corridor. Ludwig had no liking for corridors. They led nowhere, and the doors along their walls were always locked.

The Germans lost no time in parading through Munich. Ludwig defiantly wore black. What else could he wear? He stood at a window of the Residenz and watched the German troops deploy through the streets like toy soldiers, their crests waving gently as seaweed in a tidal pool. He saw Crown Prince Friedrich at the head of them. He knew he would never abase himself before that man.

Yet he would have to ride in this procession, his first ride as a vassal, and see another man at the head of his own troops. Applause meant very little now. It rippled like laughter and sounded much the same. He let the curtain fall. As soon as he could he would leave the capital for good. There were too many mirrors in the rooms of the Residenz. He did not want to see his own face any more. He did not want anyone to see it.

He would grow a beard. There would be no more of the wild little brain, so extolled by Paul, and there had not been for a long, long time.

He had to find a mirror that would not break and that would not distort his features. He could not find it either in people or events. It must be some otherwhere.

So as he rode alone away from the city in his closed carriage, he said farewell to events, as he said farewell also to people. There was no room for him in the world of outer events. He was too big for it, and yet too small.

He could sense Bismarck behind him, like a stern father, gathering up the broken toys of statecraft and putting them away for good. Everything was a toy to Bismarck, even the arts. But the arts were not merely divertimento toys. Like the Spiritual Exercise of St. Ignatius Loyola, they were a discipline designed to prepare us for wisdom.

But the preparation was a long one. He was twenty-five. He had almost sixteen years to go. Still, if he had known that, he might have felt better, for the Wittelsbachs were long lived. He himself thought that he would have to drag his way through fifty.

XII

When a king loses his employment what is he to do? It was to Ludwig as though he had lost the power of speech. The years began to scurry by, like mice in an empty house. He was growing older, and the older we grow, the less alterable become our acts, particularly the distant acts of our childhood, whose momentum drives us forward into space, out of our own atmosphere, into the void where nothing exists either to stop us or to slow us down. As though our goal were a planet, we are impelled relentlessly towards a destination that will not be there until we arrive.

There are certain faces which, like those of Phocion, the Buddha under the green fire of the Bo tree, or Alexander flushed before the fires of Persepolis, we see very clearly even though no image of them exists to aid our memory. So it is with the face of the ideal, which hangs before us in our dreams, a Medusa which turns not only flesh to stone, but stone to flesh. We can never see the features of the ideal. Yet when it smiles, we are warmed by the familiar expression of a well-loved friend we have known all our lives.

For Ludwig the features were still those of Richard, but only when Richard himself was not present. Only when Richard came into the room did the face begin to fade.

It was to that face that his diary was addressed, in the hope of catching some expression of approval or remorse in those eyes. If we could see our own faces when we were sleeping, we should know much more about the nature of eternity. As it is, we search the face elsewhere.

Yet the human face ages; and it is only the face as first we saw it that we continue to love; so that all the people we know and love and see every day are only the souvenirs of themselves as we first met them, precious to us only for what they remind us of.

And to Ludwig his diary was the only escape he had from loneliness.

The times when he sat down to compose himself before making an entry were the only moments he had to himself any more, for it is only when we order our thoughts that we realize our identity. Absorbed in them, we are apt to forget that we are less than they. Day after day he sat before the book and looked at the volume before him. If his diaries were to hold his thoughts, then they must be put together with the same expensive care as some reliquary from the hoard of Liége.

These tall, bound volumes were his good intentions. Anything written in them was written for good.

They were bound in royal blue, richly stamped, and set in the covers, like medieval jewels with magic properties, were porcelain plaques of the woodsman he had seen with Paul. Often, at night, now, he reverently turned the pages of himself, found a blank sheet, and began to write. All around him his world had begun to die. There was nothing for him to do but to take its image as he watched it fade.

For certainly his retreat from life had been rapid. He did not live in the 1870's as he had lived in the 1860's. He had taken refuge from himself, as much as from the world, in a dreamlife that pullulated around him, beyond his strength to control.

Now, in the winters, under the male moon, he would glide swiftly through the snow in his sleigh. The sleigh was like something out of a landscape by Boucher. As he rode, the moon always followed him over the trees, like an indifferent and yet kindly eye, so that merely to be seen by something bigger than himself was to survive.

If Richard drove him, then he wrote it down. Under that moon they had the only privacy they ever got.

But when he rode in the cutter, its gilt glittering against the blue shadows of the snow, wrapped up alone in a fur robe against the cold, with a gilt goddess holding aloft her lantern to the path ahead, then Richard was not there, for he would not have him like a footman standing on the step behind him. The bells jangled as the swift cutter swerved through a black wood. It was like returning to the Christmas of childhood. When he came out of the cold Fräulein Meilhaus would give him tea. Of course she never did, but still, he wrote it down.

These rides took place in and around Berg, and at the site of Linderhof, the first palace he was to build. His private name for Linderhof was Meicos Ettal, an anagram for L'état, c'est moi. Once he had thought that was the motto of kings. Now he began to perceive that it had another meaning even more disdainful. It referred to the country of the self, to which we are always pushed back, when we try to invade others. The self is a defeated country that tried to rule the world and lost. So he drove through the freedom woods of long ago. The breath of the horses rose like an offering. The rides might be freedom, but they ended always in an empty room. Therefore he tried to stretch them out.

Even when Linderhof was finished, at night, with all

the candles crackling down to stubs, he would take a walk through that palace and come eventually to the State Bed in its awful room. He would not get into the bed, but he would look at it.

Standing there, in the garish light that was worse than any darkness, he would begin to tremble. He could feel violence course through his veins like a poison, and knew that when eventually it reached his fingers he would do something unspeakable. Thus, finally, does a man in solitary confinement beat the walls, so that when the gaoler at last comes to free him, he assaults him brutally. He does not do so because he resents his solitary confinement. He does not do so because darkness has driven him mad. He does so because the walls are too high.

Often Ludwig would stare at that empty bed behind its sacred railing. He would feel too tired to dare to sleep. At midnight he would summon the sleigh or cutter and go out into the solemn wisdom of the moon. If the sleigh went fast enough, he might be able to catch up with laughter once again.

Others can trap affection into marriage, and keep it by them, even after it is dead. But to people of his temperament, the end is in the beginning, so that emotion becomes a certain sad tenderness and nothing more.

In the centre of every maze stands a pillar bearing a reflecting globe. The reflecting globe, like the eye, sees many peer within it, but retains the image of none, for none can see the hollow centre of the heart. The globe is deserted. It has no message inside.

Such were his thoughts. Steadily, year after year, he wrote them down. So did those caught in the Kraken toss out a bottle with a message to the world, only to see it enter the maelstrom before or after them.

There were not so many events in those years which

163

succeeded the Prussian war. Such as they were, he treasured them. For it is dreadful to live in a world without events. Like the world of the deaf, it is haunted by voicelessness.

In May of 1873 he called Richard back to him and took him to the Amalienberg and the Pagodenberg. But no revival is ever a first performance. It has not that excitement. Its interest is merely historical. It was as though they had both arrived at Verona, on different errands to Juliet's tomb. Richard was married. The essential part of him belonged to someone else. Richard would always be indulgent. Richard would always forgive him even his physical necessity. But Ludwig did not want to be forgiven. He wanted to be enjoyed.

When he stood now in the long daisy allee at Nymphenberg, it was alone, and the baby no longer looked out at him from the window of his birth. That self had died. Nor was Richard beside him in the tall, wet grass. He wanted to escape. There was no escape. It made him feel violent, but violence he did not yet dare give way to.

For though political violence excites the applause of the masses, personal violence frightens them, for that endangers their own security. People fear the madness of others only as a danger to themselves. Of that true madness that sits alone in a room they neither know nor care, nor understand until they, too, come to sit alone in the room of themselves, and by then it is too late.

He had before him the example of his brother Otto to prove it.

Those years were very long. Those years were like walking down a narrow circular staircase, deeper into a crypt, and never to know when one would reach the bottom stair. The air grew stale. The walls grew damp. Then one heard the first cries from the dungeons below,

164

but did not dare to turn back, for the weight of darkness above.

Once one entered upon that narrow stair, so like the disused stair between his apartments in the Residenz and those prepared for Sophie below him, it was impossible to turn upward again. The steps spiralled relentlessly down, past iron rings set in the wall. He would gladly grasp at any of those rings, to rest a little while. It took all his energy to remain where he was.

Every repeated act was another step below him, offering itself deceptively to his foot. After each sexual act, each cloudy white outlet of the self, he was down another step. At the bottom lay the Procrustean State Bed, and he did not want to see the figure stretched out there.

After each step down, he swore to his diary that he would never take such another. But there are times when the body does not dare to be alone. So after each oath he reached down another stair and grasped desperately at another rusted ring on the accelerating wall. He turned another page of the diary.

In 1873 Wagner returned to Munich. It was another event to write down. But Wagner was no longer the Great Friend. He had changed masks: now he was the Great Man. Ludwig went in to Munich to see him, but as soon as the meeting took place, he sensed the difference at once. Wagner entered the room to meet him as a man would enter a bank, glancing around for a favourite cashier. Fame had made him impatient and his clothes had a cleaner smell.

Before this apparition Ludwig felt helpless. Thus must a sculptor feel, his model finished, when he comes back to see the enormous marble copy made by the journeymen, coarser in feature, made of an inferior material, almost unrecognizable, but undeniably his own work.

There seemed little to say. The meeting was a failure.

He wrote it down in his diary. He wrote it not as it had happened, but as it should have been. It was not exactly a lie, for lies are as absolute as the truth they seek to emulate.

At last, he wrote, he had seen the adored friend after a long separation. Unfortunately he could not adore the Friend. We cannot adore that which refuses our adoration: we can only praise it. No man is our friend, either, who accepts our emotion as a phoenix gathers kindling for its nest. Blessed embrace, wrote Ludwig, but it had not been a blessed embrace. It had been the embrace of a potentate accepting tribute from a state unknown. World fame had made Wagner an emperor. He treated Ludwig as one would an inferior.

The truth did not matter. The diary mattered. Happy hours, he wrote, faithful unto death. Unfortunately Wagner was faithful to no one, except perhaps to Cosima for taking care of him so well. Does our desire to retain a good servant prove we feel affection for her? Not at all.

Besides, no artist is faithful to anyone. He is faithful only to voices we cannot hear. An artist exists only in the work he has not yet written, which to others remains unattainable: he takes refuge from us there.

In the restless way he sat, the pompous movements of his hands, Ludwig could see that Wagner would never belong to him. Yet it was still agreeable to write in the diary that he could.

When Wagner had gone, Ludwig went to Berg. There on the lake he seemed to see not the swan of Lohengrin, but the ghostly creaking ship of the Flying Dutchman, condemned to search for a faithful woman, the ropes and rigging hanging like spider webs. Moonlight made the boat almost visible, as it sailed farther and farther away from him. The boat had no crew. It sailed of its own necessity. When it returned, if it ever did return, it would bring only the vampire body of Nosferatu, a creature once human, who now valued human life only as a source of nourishment. Nosferatu was himself. Opening the diary, he wrote down his farewell from shore to ship. From ship to shore there was no signal, nor was there apt to be.

The circular staircase wound through sleep. Clutching his diary he took another step down. The dungeon came closer. Down there lurked the figure of an executioner, waiting for him. If we cannot have reprieve, then the executioner becomes a welcome figure. But even he will not come when he is called.

As Ludwig looked down the long line of his own dynasty, he saw that sweaty, yellow-booted executioner capering before him. With Richard he was still sometimes safe, but only for a little while. Richard had no real power to save him. Richard could at most console. There was no one else on that stair. Or rather the only figure on it was someone going down ahead of him, whose identity he did not wish to know, but did know. Otto.

His life hung before him like a torn web. Had Richard and he been man and woman, they would have whirled off in the arms of time, in a liberated waltz, a vision of tulle and pale pink roses, like his cousin, the Empress Elizabeth, who danced through experience towards her own death, but safe in the embrace of marriage. It was not fair. There was music, too, in his own soul, that leapt and bubbled like a dying fountain, even as leapt and fell the fountain in his bedroom at Hohenschwangau.

His music piped furtively under the leaves and in the random ambling of powdered snow, moved this way and that by the wind. In his mind he heard the piping, plaintive murmur of an almost inaudible procession that fifed him always out of every welcome town. Sadness is all the happiness we know. In its centre sits the soul that longs to smile. Two must dance, if dancing there may be.

Beauty is always sad, for beauty alone knows beauty is fugitive. Beauty is what we would do together, if we could be together. Out of the crysalis of any true meeting, unfolds the winged creature of memory, who can neither eat nor drink. There is no dance so heavenly upward bearing as the dance of those who cannot dance, and close their eyes along the wall.

Yet some music still came to him. There was an echo from the Alpinglow of the highest peaks, the music of the spheres, as one who touches a wineglass with a wet finger after it has been drained. That is true music. That is the last we hear.

Ludwig found it horrible.

At Bayreuth Wagner laid the cornerstone of what he called the Music of the Future. Ludwig refused to attend. The Great Friend sealed in the cornerstone of the opera house the telegram Ludwig had sent him. That seemed to him dreadful. It was not right that he should survive only in the cornerstone of another man's fame, on a flimsy scrap of paper. That telegram was lodged now in the wall of the circular stair, so that others might see that he had passed that way down towards defeat.

Below him Otto reached the bottom stair. That was in 1874. That was the year when Otto's complaint became obvious. It was also the year that Otto hung before him like a mirror in the morning, to show us the worst of which we are capable.

Faced with Otto's nature, Ludwig could not sleep. He got up and drove to the Halbammerhütte, the latest of his small hideaways in the woods.

It was only a little hut. He had furnished it with gifts from his governess, Fräulein Meilhaus, collected through the years. To him it was the nursery of childhood, that prepubescence which is the only refuge we have from self-contamination and from sin.

He sat there in the cold in the middle of the night; but Fräulein Meilhaus was not there and he was not six. She was Frau von Leonrod now, and he was twenty-nine. He sat there behind his beard, which if it hid him from the world, also closed him off from the hairless world of infancy. There was no refuge here. He was too firmly wedged into the past, either to go forward or back. It was not his fault. He had been forced to live too soon, so that he outstripped himself.

Somewhere, even as he sat in the Halbammerhütte, Otto was also awake. Otto did not sleep any more, so they said. Otto lay with his boots on for eight weeks, screwed up his face at the future, and barked like a dog. He, too, had retreated, but to another part of the garden. The dog Doppelgänger, who had been there at his coronation, sat in Ludwig's memory, and Otto barked at it like a puppy, refusing to leave the only source of warmth he had known.

Otto would blink his eyes and peer out at the present like a mouse through a grating. Then he would relapse and bark again, the way dogs bark at ghosts which mercifully we cannot see, but they can. Sometimes in his madness Otto must bark at him: Ludwig did not find that a comfortable thought.

He wandered about the Halbammerhütte, feeling the stuff of the curtains, afraid to part them lest Otto be out there, looking in, with those great serious eyes that saw the other side.

A mask must hang in Otto's mind also, the features of

169

the ideal, a Medusa already turning him to stone. Ludwig remembered that when he had gone one day to Fürstenried, to take Otto for a drive, Otto had waved to the people only after the carriage had passed them. For Otto was farther ahead on the journey than he was. The thought was horrible.

And now at last the time had come for Otto to be locked up and sealed into his silence for good. How far off was the time when the same would be done for him?

It was not an agreeable experience, yet Ludwig had to be there. He was not only Otto's brother, but his sovereign. There were papers to sign and people to conciliate.

Otto would still walk, if there were attendants to guide him. Ludwig waited below in the hall. Otto came slowly down the stairs, dressed more neatly than usual. On either side of him was a footman. When Otto reached the bottom step he turned to Ludwig and from very far away, from an immense distance, he smiled beguilingly.

Ludwig instinctively drew back. It was a smile of invitation from a dangerous stranger. It was as though Otto had said: come with me. Escape with me.

The doctor was also waiting in the hall. Gently he took Otto's arm, motioning back the attendant footmen, and together the group moved towards the front door and the waiting carriage outside.

Otto had a new doctor. Ludwig had not met him before. He was a short, rotund, prissy, unreal man, full of his own importance, with a bad breath and an overweaning peremptory manner, in a professional black suit. As the procession moved out of the door, Dr. Gudden, for that was his name, seemed to hesitate, and then he turned back to the hall with a smile very like Otto's. He was an alienist. It was his business to find everybody mad. It was the smile of one who seconds an invitation.

Then he left and a footman closed the door behind him. No doubt the second smile had been meant to be reassuring, but Ludwig stood motionless. It had been the smile of someone who knows you will come, because you have nowhere else to go. Dr. Gudden's had been the face of the executioner who haunted his dreams.

He was badly scared. He had remembered something.

Several years before there had been a procession through Munich on the Feast of Corpus Christi. Fearing something untoward, Ludwig had not attended nor had he allowed Otto to take part.

The procession wound through the streets to the cathedral, between lines of soldiers stationed to hold back the crowd. Ludwig stood at a window of the Residenz to watch. Below him he saw someone break through the cordon of soldiers. It was Otto, dressed in hunting clothes. Otto rushed into the cathedral. Ludwig drew back from the window.

He had the news of what happened soon enough. Otto had flung himself before the altar and shouted that he had committed the sin against the Holy Ghost.

And so he had. If he could not be saved, he had shouted, then he would be damned. He would refuse God's grace. If he could have nothing in his immanent world, then he would refuse compassion from the transcendent next. He, too, was royal. He had no choice, before silence closed upon him, but to refuse pity. If God would have no part of him, then he would have no part of God. Thus Otto. And thus, at some moment in their lives, all men capable of pride.

All those in the cathedral heard and saw him, even as the attendants hustled him out of sight. Otto had had no choice but to go mad. Others had impinged upon him. Rather than bear their touch, he had thrown himself away. And indeed, even for Ludwig there were few choices left. He had to proceed cautiously.

For converts may think of their religion every day, but for those who are born to a religion, God fails them only when they need His presence most. To see Tolstoi with God, said Gorki, was to see two bears in one den. And two bears cannot live in one den. One of them must leave. One of them must be the weaker, and go down to his defeat. If we cannot accept our limitations, then it is God who must go. What do we do then? For it is no victory after all. When He goes, He takes the world we fought for away with Him. He breathes it in and out. The sound of that respiration keeps us awake at nights, for the sound of the death-rattle is the worst ghost there is.

Otto was not mad. Otto was damned. Otto had reached the bottom of the circular stair.

Ludwig would do anything to escape that fate, yet found nothing to do. He had worn out Richard's love. It was as threadbare with much twisting as was the iron ring on his finger that Richard had given him. Suddenly he was thirty-two. It was ten years since he had first met Richard, three years since Otto had been carted away to his perdition. If he could not abdicate, then perhaps he could leave Bavaria. He must find another kingdom.

For Otto was shut up in the castle of Fürstenried. Otto was now a mirror in which he did not dare to look. The executioner was not alone any more. Otto barked. The executioner had a dog swift on the scent.

As long as he was in the same country with Fürstenried, Ludwig would never be safe. He had not forgotten Dr. Gudden's smile. Nor had he forgotten Otto's. The two echoed each other, like directional lamps on the roof of a low passage, telling us which way to go.

It drove Ludwig to desperation. He sent one of his

servants in search of an ideal country. He sent him to Venezuela, Egypt, Afghanistan, the Philippines, Columbia, Chile, Samos, and Rügen in the Baltic. He presumed that the trip was really carried out, though he did not ask too closely.

What would he give in exchange?

He would give Bavaria in exchange. Let someone else live with the unvisited nightmare at Fürstenried, with its eternally yelping dog.

The mission was not a success. How could it be? The servant Burkel returned with the message that of all peoples, the Bavarians were loyalest to his Majesty.

What nonsense.

It only meant that they would never let him go. That nocturnal vision at Berg had been accurate. The boat of the Flying Dutchman sailed into the moon, and now it was returning. The only passenger, as he had feared, was Nosferatu, the vampire of the self, come to suck him dry. He could not love himself.

He must have love, for only love could save him now. Yet there was no love. He was thirty-three.

XIII

———————▶▶▷●◁◀◀———————

For what is the nature of love? It has no nature. It is only a process, such as chemistry, which follows the same course wherever it occurs, no matter who conducts the experiment. It is the inherent and unalterable movement towards release, nothing more.

If years after we have ceased to see someone, we think: this is an experience I would like to share with A, because it would enrich him, and his enrichment would enhance me, then that is love. For love exists only beyond the barriers of the self. It is not an emotion, but an experience. It is to go through the great door with someone else. Since no one exists beyond that door, then love is to know that nothing exists, and to be satisfied with that.

The process is catalytic change. We have it with many people each time a little weaker, each time the same, until we reach the great door by stasis, instead of by volition. Love in that sense is to become unchangeable through too much with many people, for change cannot exist within a single body.

And what is the door? The door is time, which has two leaves. Shut, it is the present, which is compounded of the past and the future. Open, it is timelessness. We think we open it in the death of the body. Alas, we find it only in selflessness.

What more beautiful delight is there in the world than that, at some time, somewhere, in some manner, we should, as Man, be able to enter into a world where Man does not exist, and where all things rest potential yet complete in the great *néant* which is: that we should, like a tired engine, put on a final burst of speed, and as we attain to insight, burn out utterly or fuse? So we pass beyond our point of greatest consciousness, and at last reach the unconscious to which we properly belong.

Mercy, stars, pretensions, great estates, self-abnegation, the pride of Saints, all these are vehicles. All these are nothing. And when, like kings, like the immortal sacred prototypes of Man's humanity who die, but live forever in our minds, we die, why then we live.

The man who lives alone is not alone. But the man who thinks he finds understanding with another, experiences in this world that felicity proper to the world beyond, where there are no worlds.

Yet Man is worthy of all admiration. He is nothing. But in the short history of his reign temporal, with that clammy, grey, convoluted mass with which he comes into contact with the ideal, he has this triumph: that sometimes, when his mind burns out like an overcharged battery, he perceives that he is part of a vast felicity. Then for a moment he *is*.

Then he is loved; then he is beautiful; for only then can he believe in love. We are but an inferior part of that vast impersonal design. But that we are, gives us equality with rocks. Sometimes, when we turn our heads at an alarming, unfamiliar sound behind us, accidentally, we have insight and so are made whole before we die.

As long as the mind of Man can conceive of nobility, then nobility he has. We are only precursors. We exist only for the benefit of those who come after us. Our love

175

is what we have to say to them. They will be much larger than we are, much more noble, much more fine, but that much of us they will understand. Such is our monument. Such is our love.

Sometimes it lasts an impersonal twenty minutes in a tousled bed. But sometimes it lasts into eternity. We are not. Yet knowing we are not, then we know we are. Our greatness is that others will be, who without our having been could not be. In this we approach that which created us.

This Ludwig knew but could not say.

But at least, to give him credit, when he dismissed Richard by accepting him, he knew that in this man, unlike other men, there was a fragment of truth, and was only sorry that the fragment was not more. At least in his lifetime he had loved someone, and who of us can say as much and say it truly?

Yet dismiss him he must, for he must enter eternity alone. That was his damnation. He could not escape it, elude it though he would. Every life is a parable: this is the way we should not go; it is also the way in which we must. Only in death are our souls what we would wish them. Ludwig was merely a man, the poor ruins of the self. Yet ruins know what buildings ought to be.

And what is our nobility? That we should prepare the way for some being that will see nobility more steadily, until there is nothing but perception of felicity, and beyond that state, even felicity will cease, and there will only be union with what is; and beyond that, merely Is. We can follow greatness only a little way, into the universal wood, beneath the sighing pressure of the rain.

But within the wood there are also steps spiralling down. We cannot elude them, for we are the entrance to them. Ludwig saw them and was badly frightened. Otto

176

had gone ahead down into madness, down these stairs. He himself was going mad and knew it. Yet there could be consolation in that, for madness is more than a disease. Madness can also be good company, when no other company we may have.

Where do we go, when there is nowhere else to go but down? Ludwig did not know, for he was not mad yet. He was only driven to the frontiers of madness, knowing we may safely cross that border of the mind, given we have a *laissez-passer* to get back. Somewhere there must be somebody to sign that document, as Richard and he had signed his diary so often that now he no longer dared to keep it, lest they have to sign it again.

He must love in order to be. Without love, how could he die?

PART TWO

XIV

———►►➤●◄◄———

But love may take peculiar forms. With him it took the form of the family sickness, which was a mania for building. This form of madness is not unknown. Some of us build monuments to those we love. Others build traps to catch them. From 1869 until 1886 he built incessantly. He only stopped when he could build no more. Even before he was first defeated, he began to construct a refuge against defeat. Even the most victorious of armies is wise to retain a strategy of retreat.

So he began to build, as the pharaohs built, compulsively. Such buildings are like trousseaux which; he no longer marriageable stitch away at with such confidence. And who is to say they are wrong, for as they sew, they smile. They know that if the trousseau is sufficiently perfect, then the ideal husband will appear.

Building was the passion of the family. All the Wittelsbachs built. Each one of them clumsily evoked a dream. For Ludwig I, his grandfather, it had been the dream of Italy.

It was his grandfather who had given him building blocks on his seventh birthday. Perhaps it was an early lesson in a system of consolation he would find useful later, for Ludwig I was a wise and tacit man. In any event the lesson took. There are times when the events of our childhood can be the salvation of that adult world which is without events.

The first shrine Ludwig built was Linderhof. He began it at the time of the Franco-Prussian war, as though sensing he might need it very soon.

Always he had liked the site, below the medieval monastery of Ettal, and twenty miles from Hohenschwangau. Even as a child he had thought it a magic spot. In its little glades spotted with flowers was the perfect place for a Knight of St. Hubertus to encounter the holy stag, symbol of salvation in the magic world of nature. He was, after all, a Knight of St. Hubertus, and he had never been able to find salvation anywhere else. It was a pretty vale, intimate and yet not too far from the snows. He had always meant to build there.

Two years before he and Richard had sauntered down the allees of Versailles and entered the Petit Trianon. He remembered how they had shared each other's thoughts. He attempted to reproduce the Trianon. He attempted to reproduce that one room where they had once stood together. Perhaps they might share such a moment again, he and Richard, if he built the surroundings for such an experience properly.

Certainly the palaces he built are tense with an atmosphere of waiting, the atmosphere we feel in an abandoned temple, when we stand in the empty shrine, half believing the gods might suddenly come back. He half believed it, too; but only half.

Linderhof was to be a very private place.

He went often to inspect the site. In winter the weather was so severe, the bark of the trees so tough, that the deer had to be fed by hand. To put a summer palace in a winter landscape was an ultimate act of faith, yet are there not legends that deep in the Himalayas there is an apple valley, where the blossoms are perpetual and no one is ever old? And in the Antarctic are there not narrow open lakes, on whose fringes yellow lichens grow, as the first plants left the sea long ago, to sway on the borderland of life? And what Empress of the Russians was it, who gave orders out of caprice and malice, so that there stood on the Neva an ice palace, to discomfort the wedding night of a former favourite? Linderhof should be as glittering, but warmer than that.

Ludwig sent a commission of architects to Paris, to find inspiration. Linderhof should be French. When they returned, and the building began, he shut the site to the world. Like Wagner, he would create alone.

He spent a lot of time there. He lived in a small hunting lodge nearby, that had belonged to his father, and every day went to a hummock from which he watched the foundations rise. He liked to see the workmen. He liked to talk to them. They liked him. They knew who he was, but they did not plot against him. They were loyal. That reassured him.

Sometimes he would drive through the surrounding forest in a gilt coach, with plumed lackeys around him, like the magic prince in a fairytale. For the farther we retreat from the capital, the closer we are to the truth of any country, and it was the truth he sought. The peasants believed the life he led, far more than he was able to believe in it. He took reassurance from them. He would step from the coach into the woods and there talk to the stonecutters. They did not seem to mind if he admired them. They saw no advantage to themselves in his admiration, so they relaxed. The smell of sweat in brisk woods, like the smell of a sauna, is the cleanest and most male of smells.

Near the site was a small woodsman's hut he had

ordered to be built. There he could wear lederhosen and silly hats, and for a moment be a woodsman or a stone-cutter, too.

On the pine needles there lay wood shavings coiled like the fronds of ferns. He could pick them up and play with them, to feel growth within the spring of the shaving, like the tensile strength of a fernball. The smell of wood freshly planed is like the smell of babies freshly washed.

Before and below him the idea of Linderhof began to spread out like blueprints on a table. Already was installed on the hill behind the site the Moorish kiosk he and Richard had bought during that brief springtime in Paris. To enter it was to enter Asia, whose morals are not ours, so that for a moment, conforming to theirs, we are free of our own.

Buried in the grounds there would be a grotto invisible from the outside, and blue, above whose water would flow a yellow moon, and on whose narrow shores there would be feasts for the traveller, not so much a Venusberg, as the interior of Virgil's cave at Posilippo.

Linderhof took many years to build. During those years Richard seemed to draw farther and farther away from him, even while the building became more actual. In these rooms, at least, would walk an experience not quite lost, for it could be felt in all of them. He had only to hurry down these miniature allees to recapture the ghost of it.

When winter came, the basins of the fountains had to be drained, and an ice castle hung from every faucet and jet. The garden statues wore snow on their shoulders like epaulets. Then the place became real. Its baroque garden front stood up like a water organ, and all its springtime youthfulness was frozen immutably in the cold.

Then he loved it best. Then there was a crack in the air, and one might ride perilously through the night, by the lantern of the sleigh, in search of events.

It took ten years to finish Linderhof. They were the years during which he was beaten back farther and farther from the world other people live in, into that world which has but one inhabitant. Only a child, a madman, a suicide, or a genius lives in a single world. His choices narrowed down.

And ten years later, when spring slowly unfurled the garden he would stand enthralled among the trees, peering out, until against the forest which was still black with winter he would hear a noise, lean against the bronze back of a crouching lion above the *schloss*, and wait, excited. Then, with an almost inaudible rumble, as of great powers first released, the fountain would charge out of its jet, rushing up like energy out of a triton, shoot forty feet into the air, and blow in the wind like separating mist. Then the world was truly renewed. It was like the bursting of a fig. In that great white seminal rush that meant for him the birth of spring, hope would be renewed, and everywhere in the palace and the grounds, night or day, he could hear it playing above him, like the leitmotif of *Tristan*, carrying him irresistibly towards the climax of the act.

And yet it was not satisfactory. It could not be. It was built for someone who was not there, in memory of someone who once had been. No one should build a monument to the living who is unwilling to alter his plans, for only the dead are beyond change. Only the lost love lasts. The others all decay.

He took a walk through those empty rooms.

Instead of solitude, he had been fobbed off with loneliness. The only sleigh to jangle towards the *schloss* was his own sleigh when he returned. No man should ever finish what he builds, for once a thing is perfect it allows us no way in, perfection being jealous of itself. The creator is forever barred from his own works. They outgrow him as a child outgrows its parents.

He went into the dining-room. In the dining-room he had installed a hydraulic table, so that he should not be disturbed by the servants while he dined. When he pressed a button, the table sank into the kitchens. He would gaze into the hole with horror. It was like the opening to that circular stair down which he moved. It led down to the cellars and it yawned like madness. Then it rose, set with his dinner, and sealed him in again.

Nor was the bedroom any better. He had built the wrong dream. He would never stay in it overnight, lest it turn into a nightmare. To live alone at Linderhof was to wander through the overstuffed rooms of a well-loved mistress unexpectedly dead, who has taken her personality with her. It was true. He could visit the past only if he shut his eyes. Wait how he would, it would never visit him.

The workmen were gone. Their hammers were silent. There were no more wood shavings underfoot. He could not sit and watch the carpenters, and they were the only audience he had. If he must live, then he must build again. He realized that. Reality was always somewhere else, in the next room. So in order to capture it, it would always be necessary to build more rooms.

"Damned be the blinding apparition which oppresses our senses," he wrote in his diary. But he did not write the truth. It was he who was damned, not the apparition. For Eros was not merely a charming boy who wounded us in ecstasy. Eros was also the wilful boy who shattered Jove's thunderbolts to bits.

186

Nor could he bear the gallery of mirrors at the garden front of the *schloss*. It was as futile as that similar gallery at Versailles, where Bismarck had robbed France of its king and him of his kingdom. He had to do something about that gallery. It seemed to him altogether natural to smuggle in a chamois and set it loose in there. He had already gone that far into wilfulness.

The chamois faced the walls of glass and smashed them. The glass fell tinkling to the bottom of a depthless nightmare, but as it fell it set his spirits free. He stood at the door, watching the chamois butt its way to freedom. When he could bear the sight no longer, he opened a window and it scuttled on the parquet, looked at him uncertainly, and launched into space, sailing for an instant against the incessant mockery of the fountain outside.

In the empty room there fell one more piece of glass. It splashed against the silence. He moved to the window, stood on the balcony, and gazed down. The light streamed out across the white gravel towards the pool of the fountain. The orange trees stood motionless in their urns. There was no moon. The chamois was unhurt, but it was gone. He heartily wished he could go also. Already it would be toiling up through the woods, and so in a little while it would reach the safe peaks of its habitat. He had no habitat.

XV

So in 1878, in his thirty-third year, he began to build Herrenchiemsee. He must try again, but he was warier now. If his own past could not give the present back to him, then the past of another might.

For he had given up all hope of finding understanding or wisdom in any living face. He looked now to the faces of the dead, and in particular to the faces of those dead who live immortal in our minds because they epitomize a principle. In the gallery of time there are certain portraits which tell us salvation lies within our heads; and this truth, though terrible, is also comforting.

Alone in his library he drew out an engraving of Louis XIV. It was a wily face. There was not much wisdom in it, but much animal cunning and a stubborn will to survive. Louis XIV struck a bargain with mortality and won. Yet it is difficult to know how to make use of another man's wisdom, for wisdom is an end-product, and it is the technique we need.

It was an intelligent face, but a poodle is intelligent at the end of a leash. Among that breed, only Charles II had a warm spaniel intelligence, and so we forgive him anything. But Louis XIV could be forgiven nothing, so he did not dare to be wrong. His is not a face that teaches us how to live, as the sad, weary, intentionally merry face of Charles II does. It is a sharp face, telling us only how to survive. Ludwig had need of such wisdom.

He studied the engraving. Linderhof had failed, and no spider ever repairs a web: she makes another, for she knows that once a thing is touched, then it is gone. Ludwig would reproduce Versailles. He set about the task at once.

There are those who would say that Herrenchiemsee is more beautiful than Versailles, by which they mean more moving, and who is to say they are not right? For Versailles is a stage set, but Herrenchiemsee is an ode, perhaps a threnody. We go through Versailles as we would go through the Maginot Line. It is mighty and splendid and damp, but as a system of defence it failed. Herrenchiemsee is full of quiet pathos. It enshrines an emotion, where the other is merely the monument to a will. The windows of Versailles are always watching us. Its allees are a text-book on strategy. But the windows of Herrenchiemsee are blind and introspective, like the eyes of the Virgin in a Piétâ.

Yet Herrenchiemsee is strangely without joy. It is not the work of a man, but of a dreaming white-skinned boy trapped in the body of a man. Linderhof was an ex-voto. Herrenchiemsee was only something to do.

It was built on the isle of Herrenworth. There was a reason for that. The most a king can do, in disenfranchised times, is to rescue something from the greed of his subjects, an act for which only the future will thank him. Speculators had bought the dense, living forest on that isle and threatened to cut it up into kindling. There is something in the soul of city men which rejoices in the death of a tree. Ludwig bought the land out from under them. So Herrenchiemsee was begun. He would build nobility in the woods, where it belonged.

Yet of this building he enjoyed only the model and the plans. He even went incognito to Paris in search of designs. From a world he could never touch he brought back the souvenirs that would make it visible. It was his determination that now sovereignty should have its symbol, even though sovereignty was no more, as once emperors carved their deeds so high on rocks and obelisks that even their descendants could not destroy them.

And yet Herrenchiemsee is beautiful, in the same way that autumn is beautiful, when the world is going to sleep. It is the palace of a somnambulist.

For he was decided that though outwardly the palace would present the idea of sovereignty, orderly, extensive, yet concise, inwardly it should reproduce those state chambers in Munich through which, years ago, he had moved inexorably towards the mockery of a throne.

In the great hall of Herrenchiemsee he placed a statue of Louis XIV, not as the object of his admiration, but as a warning to the impious, as before any sanctuary there was once placed a guardian statue of the God within.

The building of the *schloss* took years. But he took no pleasure in it. It was empty. As he limped facelessly towards his descendants, he heard behind him only the vacant footsteps of himself. He would rather have had the sound of one human voice to speak to him.

Now the only voice that spoke to him, told him he was not a man, but a principle, and that to maintain that principle he could neither touch nor be touched by anyone. He was self-immured for a principle, like Antigone; yet noble as she was, what were her last thoughts underground? Truly they must have been terrible, down there in the permanent, mortal dark.

He found Herrenchiemsee like that tomb. He felt that no one must ever see it. And he did not wish to see it himself. He visited it only in the daytime, and slept elsewhere. He had not the courage to stay there overnight.

And the aimless years went on.

One day in autumn, the Empress Elizabeth, who was staying at Possenhofen, rowed across to Berg, when Ludwig was not there, accompanied by her daughters. On his desk in one of the rooms she placed a sealed envelope addressed to him. She did not quite know why. Perhaps pity moved her. Perhaps, she, too, was consulting an oracle and afraid to hear the answer.

When, days later, stopping at Berg, he picked it up, he thought for a moment it was a message from someone who had yet to appear, the person for whom he waited. He opened it eagerly and found a poem. He was deeply hurt, as though rebuffed to find only a familiar hand and not that of a stranger.

The poem upset him. It seemed a warning from the dead, for since he did not see Sisi any more, she was dead to him, as dead, no doubt, he already was to her. It was another token that his only escape lay within.

He came and went, between Berg, Linderhof; Herrenchiemsee, and Hohenschwangau. He had nothing else to do with himself other than to move from place to place.

Yet there was one room at Herrenchiemsee he avoided, and when he did appear there, it was only in masquerade.

Taking Richard and a few lackeys, dressed in costumes of the early eighteenth century, and himself robed in the ermine and plush of Mignard's portrait of Louis XIV, he would enter his carriage and whirl up to Herrenchiemsee. In its rooms he would stalk the corridors as Louis XIV stalked, like a rat-catcher hunting down the nobility. But there was no truth in the impersonation. It was not real.

Tall torches would illuminate the garden. The candles

reflected the bright colours of the pilasters and the twinkling of the chandeliers which, unlike stars, could be let down on a pulley and replenished when they guttered out. But the robes hung round him like a shroud. He tore them off. Like the shirt of Nessus, they would burn him up, for he had raped the wrong ideal. The image was no doubt a little mixed up, but then so was everything.

He was growing older and he had no heir.

Yet some of his family would supplant him. They were fecund enough. Prince Ludwig Ferdinand, his cousin, had married the Infanta Paz of Spain. They were in Munich now. They were together. They were safe. The nightmare did not stalk their bed. They might even have his heirs, now that Otto could have none. They had asked to see Herrenchiemsee.

He decided to let them do so, but they should not see it while he was there. They should see instead how cold, unyielding, and inexorable was the royalty they might, perhaps, inherit.

So, when he had removed himself, they arrived. Silently, and maybe even tittering, with those significant glances which the middle classes love to throw back and forth like balls of yarn, they moved through those horrible, bright rooms. They saw the nightmare of a dream left unfinished. They saw the Salle du Conseil, the Chambre de Parade, the Salon de l'Oeil de Boeuf, and the whole jiggerypokery mockery he had wanted to lay out before them. He never asked to know what they thought of it. He did not want to know.

But a day or two after they had gone, at midnight, he approached the *schloss* himself, and unwilling to enter it, stood in the moonlit garden, gazing through the trees towards the façade. In the garden the statues of hounds

192

and stags seemed to shift and move, but were too small to do him damage. At last, while the lackeys held up torches, he entered the hall, skirted the statue of Louis XIV, and looked to see what his royal visitors had left of themselves there.

What they had left was a little of their life. They had even left their laughter, which melted into silence like snow crystals on the floor. But it was not laughter for him. For him they had only pity. It was another reason to avoid them.

Abruptly he gave the order that the great hall of mirrors was to be illuminated. That was the room he avoided, but now that they had been there, he felt that it was safe for him to see it.

One by one, the chandeliers leaped into life, and, as the lackey released the draw pulleys, sailed up in a chorus of crystal to their natural height. There they trembled and swayed in a breeze off the lake, as though a presence were entering the room through a window carelessly left open. He frowned. The windows should never be left open, for there was nothing beyond them at all.

Then, half fearfully, he entered the room, alone, and could feel their passage through it a day ago, in a gregarious perambulating huddle, and their voices soft with pity. Their pity was not what he wanted of them. He glanced towards the doors, which were obediently closed. He stood by himself, as invisible to those who had been there as now they slowly became to him. They faded away. He began to stride up and down the room. They could have children, and a king does not even begin to exist until he has produced heirs, who are his memory, in which he truly lives. He would have no children. He was thirty-six. How could a boy of twenty-one be thirty-six?

As he walked up and down that endless, fatal hall, the square panes of glass in the mirrors made huge prisms. In the spluttering light above him, which lighted nothing, from a thousand panes, at different heights, he saw bits and pieces of his own enormous body, staggered across the panes of glass which, as he approached closer, snapped into a single image, until, going very close to one of the panes, with the wind from off the lake like the tap of a finger on his shoulder, for the window still stood negligently open to the park beyond, he saw not his own bearded face staring out at him, but Otto's.

As he turned and backed into the safety of the centre of the room, from every panel he seemed to see Otto's face, beckoning and smiling to him half-gaily and half-sadly, with the wisdom of the truly mad, who, like the dead, cannot tell us what life is like upon the other side, yet seem to know.

Otto, sealed already in the lead casket of himself, flickered in the mirrors, repeated endlessly, and raised a forefinger to his lips, as though there were a secret between them that not even the empty room must know. Ludwig turned and ran.

Outside, in the hall, leaning against the door, he reached out, touched an orange tree in a pot, and plucked off an orange, as one would hold an orb, which is not only a symbol, but a weapon. But the orange came away in his hand. He turned it in his palm and even it was without life. It was artificial. There was no life here, but only madness.

A king must have heirs. If he has heirs, then he can live. A little of his responsibility drops from him, and knowing that kingship will not die, then he has done his duty and he can believe in life again.

Once more he ordered his carriage. He waited outside

on the lawn until it arrived. Stepping into it, he did not once look back, but behind him the windows of Herren-chiemsee grinned in the moonlight like the eye-sockets of a skull.

He went immediately to Nymphenberg.

The Prince and the Princess Paz had been staying there, but for the time being they were away. In the carriage he dozed. The journey seemed to go on forever. When he awakened it was almost dawn. The carriage was rattling over the winter leaves of Nymphenberg, as the horses methodically chewed away the roadway snow.

The *schloss* was in darkness. It was better so. He directed the carriage towards the west wing, and taking only a lackey with him, ran across the snow and into the building, afraid to be seen by the relentless stars, so like those spluttering chandeliers, but higher, which in the swaying ice-decked night seemed to make the same derisive music.

He fled up the stairs, following the lackey. At last a serving woman opened the door, wearing a flannel wrapper and with her hair in plaits, to receive him. He paid her no attention, but told her what he wanted. She looked startled, but he forced her to obey.

More slowly now they moved through the empty, silent rooms, towards the other end of the wing, which faced the park, as did the windows of the room in which he himself had been born.

With a warning shrug, the woman opened the door to the nursery.

Stepping lightly across the floor, he told them both to wait for him outside. Something in his manner forced them to comply. He stood in the centre of the room, blinking his eyes, and then moved towards the cradle under the window. Prince Ludwig Ferdinand and the

Spanish woman had lost no time in having a son and it was ten months old.

He looked down for a long time at the small red face, wrinkled with sleep, in the light from the window. There was no likeness either to himself or to Otto in it; and as for Otto, he would never have the chance to gaze down at it with his solemn, beckoning stare. This much of royalty, at least, was safe.

As he left the apartment and went down the stairs, the face of Otto hung before him in the darkness like a mirror, luring him on to the latent image he knew he must not see.

XVI

He built again. There was still one more refuge, which he had prepared for just such a disaster as this. There was still Neuschwanstein. At Neuschwanstein he could still be safe. Or so he preferred to believe.

Of course Europe is scattered with the medieval castles of nineteenth-century kings. They stretch from Miramar to Cintra. To us they offer only the shelter of a toy, discarded as Man outgrew his monarchy. They have the quality of those long-coveted dolls little girls are given only at the moment when suddenly it is too late for dolls, and which they keep by them when they are young women as precious mementoes of a world long lost. But nineteenth-century monarchs took the matter differently. They were quite serious about their fortresses.

Neuschwanstein does not have this dolls'-house atmosphere. It seems to be the dreamer, not the dream, so it still has the power to renew itself before our eyes. It is not a building, but an offering left at the naked foot of an alp. For a moment, in the evening, as mists curl round it, it might indeed be Monsalvasch. It is not Monsalvasch, but it is built on the site of all those places where Monsalvasch was thought to be. At Neuschwanstein the Emperor, rising naked, wears for the first time his new clothes, and there is no one to tell him they are other than they are, for there is no one there at all.

Of the three *schlossen*, it had the deepest roots in time. Rather, an anemone, buried upside down, twisted and turned its white way through the sub-conscious, to break the surface with this one white phthisic bloom at the end of summer. It was better so. Neuschwanstein was to be the last prepared defence, should Herrenchiemsee fail or Linderhof stand too long empty.

Here as the walls rose up around him Ludwig felt safe. Here he had a joy in watching the workmen again. The castle was to be long but narrow and to rise directly from the rock. He had simple rooms over the keep. They were austere yet intimate, like a workman's rooms. From their windows he could look out to see the towers rise against the Alps. He could look the other way, across the shaded forests of Bavaria, standing on their hills like a loyal army, waiting to defend him.

He was in a fever to get it done.

The workmen sweated to put the blocks of stone in place, like lumps of sugar gone to build a fairy tower. It was a sweet experience. He paid the workmen, therefore they loved him. He could walk among them and never hear a murmur or a sneer. With them he could relax. Sometimes they would accept him as an equal and let him lay a stone. That gave him excitement. It made him feel that he was a part of it, having built himself in. He had designed that Neuschwanstein should be difficult of approach, and he slept over the keep, like the guardian of his own slumbers.

Often he sat at a window in the moonlight and watched the shell, rising in white stone like an unfinished dragon's tooth. Buildings should be built by troll magic, all in one night, for otherwise we are tricked by the gap between conception and realization. That is the period when we are most vulnerable. It is the period of danger.

Never did a hermit crab seek a shell under the pressure of the sea more assiduously, for in 1878 he had only eight years left. He could not know that, but perhaps he felt it. The work took too long, and until it was finished anyone might get at him.

He stood in the lumber of what was to be the Romanesque throne room. The pictures that should be on the walls were not there yet. The painters worked slowly. He urged them on. They splashed the walls carelessly, and the paint fell roughly into the right shapes. He did not care so long as the shapes were there. But it must be complete, for at Neuschwanstein he should be free in the manner of the old German kings, not by holiness, but by might.

There was no time to waste. The building must alter magically every night. It must be complete. Every patch of wet plaster, every empty wall, was a weakness. The emptiness must be plugged with paintings, to hold out the loneliness: the wet plaster must be reinforced against the cold. He must insulate himself with images.

From his windows in the keep he could watch the rooms multiply like the cells of a hive. At last the towers went up against the sky. Then the screen of the façade rose between him and the rooms beyond. At one or two in the morning he would pick his way through the debris of the forecourt, lurching and stumbling, hold his breath, and then enter the tall shadows of the throne room like that cave in which Barbarossa sleeps with his men, or that Byzantine hall in which Henry IV Hohenstaufen was Holy Roman Emperor. From under the arcades shadows beckoned him. They paced the corridors and spoke to him. He could speak to them.

High above him, as the building rose, the masons were approaching the walls of his own rooms on the third floor. He turned and went back to the keep, aware of the derisive whiteness of the mountains and the steel breath of the mountain air.

Each morning he would feel better. In the mornings, when the workmen were back, he would walk among them like an ordinary man, searching in their faces for the face of a disciple, or the face of the woodsman in the glade. He never found that face, but he still hoped to do so. In their eyes he read that he was truly King.

There was such need for haste. The building became more and more complete, yet the more complete the emptier it was. The older he grew the more he needed help. He decided upon another test.

Between the platform of the *schloss* and the ravine there was a thin iron bridge, leaping across the chasm above a stream, in one single span. He stood watching the bridge for a long time. Then he summoned Richard, as he had once summoned Paul, not because he had any illusions about Richard's being the true friend, but because there was no one else to summon. He would let him enter Neuschwanstein, but first he should do so by riding a horse along that thin and narrow swaying span. Thus they had entered the Wartberg once, riding together.

He stood on the bank, watching anxiously. He forced Richard to cross. There was no danger. If the magic knight is strong enough to reach the magic castle, then everything is true. Richard looked at him strangely but said nothing.

Breathless he watched. Richard kneed the horse gently on to the bridge. The horse trusted him and stepped precisely, making the neat, artificial movements of a medieval charger in a painting. The bridge trembled. Slowly horse and man inched their way across it, while the sound of ravenous water came louder from below.

Ludwig frowned. He could see no armour. It was futile to attempt the impossible.

The horse, lowering its hind quarters, pawed and scrambled on to earth on the other side. Richard turned, waved, and moved on through the keep.

Ludwig dusted himself off and went rapidly across the bridge after him. Lohengrin had come, and Parsifal. He blinked in the delusively bright sun and entered the shadows of the keep. There he stopped short.

It was as though there were no one there at all. There was only the Richard he knew now. He sent him away. When he had gone, he would have called him back, but that he could not do.

It was later afternoon. He sat on the dusty dais of the throne room, for the throne itself was neither ready nor paid for. He wanted to cry. The light entered high from the windows, making impalpable pillars of its own, until he was surrounded by a hall of pillars. He watched the motes dance up and down like dusty steam. Far off he heard the hammering of the workmen. In his mind a door closed like the door of a vault.

Then for the first time in daylight, he deliberately summoned the invisible company and held levee in the throne room. Slowly they stepped from memory and from the ikons on the walls, all the admired figures with which he consoled himself. Walther van der Vogelweide, Tannhäuser, Lohengrin, Parsifal, Elsa of Brabant, Maria Stuart, Marie Antoinette, Louis XIV, the Emperor Henry IV Hohenstaufen, Fräulein Meilhaus as she had been, and the woodsman in the wood as he always would be. With a sudden rustle they became actual. This was his kingdom. These were his subjects. And there was Richard as he had once been, hovering on the edge of the crowd.

But at the outer fringes of the throng he saw others; part of the Palace Cabal, whom there were no guards to arrest, those courtiers who had destroyed Byzantium: the Flying Dutchman, Dr. Gudden, Sophie, Bismarck, Louis Napoléon, Crown Prince Friedrich, those who were loyal to Otto, not to him. Their party gained adherents. He could see in their eyes what it was they wished to do. Even though he could not see their faces, he could always see their eyes.

Somewhere in the depths of the unfinished building the hammering stopped. It was as though a heart had stopped. The workmen were through for the day.

He rose to go in search of them. They must never stop. He must keep them here to build. They were his only loyal guards. Behind him, with a sigh, the invisible company dispersed, except for a few, who stepped behind pillars, whence he could hear their whispering.

It was absolutely essential to go on.

But it was not so easy to do so. He was running short of funds.

Down in Munich they cabaled against him, for the middle classes would never leave the monarchy alone. They were too eager to rise themselves, to understand the nature of the holy: they saw the spiritual only in terms of material expense. They would build churches, but never enter them. The monarchy was already built for their use, they were ready to move in, and they were thrifty. They wanted to strip it of everything of value, in order to adorn their own pride. It was not enough for them to be received at Court. They would not feel safe until they had the monarchy itself safely in receivership, for money, being their only faith, was their only security.

They tried to cut off supplies. He evaded them. He must borrow money. That upset them. Money was the only holiness they believed in. The situation grew desperate, but build he must; and though the loyalty of the workmen was beyond doubt, he knew well enough that in our age loyalty has no credit, but must be paid for in advance. No one understood why he must build.

At last he learned that a loan of four hundred thousand marks was available, on a condition. It was not enough money, but it would help. The condition was that the guarantor demanded to be raised to the nobility.

That amused him. It was as though rats, having eaten the stores of the ship, then demanded to take the wheel. But after all, why not? The nobility was already infected and disloyal. It aped the middle classes half out of envy and half in self-defence. Why not let the reverse process operate as well? He granted the letters patent and took the money. He need not see the man. Indeed he did not need to see anyone. When he could no longer build, then he could no longer live. Like a man pursued up the winding stair of a tower, to live he must retreat always to a higher room. He had already had that higher room prepared. When Neuschwanstein was done, he would begin Falkenstein. There must always be a step beyond the last stair.

But again he was wary. He would tell no one the purpose of Falkenstein, or what it was to contain. He knew better than that now. So he commissioned the plans and told no one what they were for. If there were oddities of detail, then let others make of them what they would.

Falkenstein was to be very high. He could see it already. He laid the plans in secret, like a fuse to powder. It, too, would rise, like Neuschwanstein, from the ruins of an ancient castle, but it would be closer to the apex of the Alps, on the edge of a deep gorge. It would look deep into the heart of things. It would be huge and unapproachable. It would be inviolable, as a shrine should be.

Slowly, as he wrestled with the architects, the plan took form. When he saw it drawn out across a vast sheet of paper, he knew it would be the ultimate secret of his building. It would defeat even Otto. He would return to Herrenchiemsee and show the ghost of Otto how futile it was to beckon and to smile.

So once more Herrenchiemsee was opened. When he arrived with Richard, the gallery of mirrors was already lit. The candles blazed defiantly. This time there should be no shadows. In the chandeliers roared two thousand five hundred lights. He entered the gallery at six.

There he told Richard about Falkenstein, not because he trusted him, but because he must have an auditor, so that Otto should hear. The gallery was damp, but the warmth of the candles soon removed the damp. He paced up and down, glancing nervously in the mirrors, but saw only the clean surface of the glass, reflecting himself and Richard, but no one else. He walked there until three in the morning, for Richard must understand. Richard must keep him company, during this vigil in the knightly sense. As he talked, Falkenstein took shape, for Falkenstein still lay in the future. In remaining unbuilt, it would be perfect forever. It would defeat Otto utterly, for only the perfect can capture the essence of the real.

As he paced, talking more and more rapidly, lurching across the slippery parquet, he seemed to pace through Falkenstein. As he passed back and forth, he looked again and again in the mirrors. There was nothing there.

But towards morning, as the candles began to sink lower, and shadows leapt up in the sockets instead of flames, it seemed to him that he did see something. He stopped in mid-sentence. Then he went on. On the way back, walking closer to Richard, he checked that particular mirror. There was nothing. Then something caught at the corners of sight, and he took a step back. The mirror there was cloudier. It seemed to him that he saw the echo of a smile, and though he saw only his own reflection, something was certainly beckoning. He called for more candles. He watched carefully as the lackeys lowered the chandeliers. But there were not enough candles. The shadows grew darker. He could stay in the gallery no longer, and Otto had not heard, nor was Otto defeated. The glass grew blacker and had deeper images. He left the room and had its doors locked behind him. He stood with Richard in the hall and gave a little sob. It was not safe to be alone with images. To-morrow night he would go to the theatre.

He dismissed Richard, but he could not sleep. Not even away from Herrenchiemsee could he sleep, for Herrenchiemsee was always there, a door to Fürstenried. There was something waiting in that gallery of glass, and there are some doors that will never lock.

Build he must. He must build Falkenstein, before too late. He felt the urgency of those too weak to control events, who see them pour through their fingers as though our life were a rope in a tug of war with destiny.

Nor was Richard asleep either. Instead he sat in his house near Berg, his wife and children asleep, and wrote tersely in his diary that the King now never slept until 4 a.m., as neither had Prince Otto in the old days. Then he paused to think, and his thoughts filled him both with relief and with an almost uncontrollably acid sadness. After all, he had once loved Ludwig deeply, and there are some battles of which we know the outcome well in advance, though not necessarily the strategy. But he had a wife and children. There was nothing he *could* do but watch. It was 1881. They were getting close to the end.

XVII

From Herrenchiemsee Ludwig had gone to the theatre, but he had not told Richard why. Just as he had given up hope, the world seemed to open up again like a great submarine shell. He could not know it was only to capture the diver for the pearl. He sat alone in the Court Theatre in Munich. The play was Hugo's *Marion de Lorme*.

He was excited, for only in the theatre can we participate in the possible. That is the hold the theatre has on us. Tired of the improbabilities of everyday life, where events begin to die as soon as we enter upon them, we turn for reassurance to the stage, where we may watch things happen in our brains, the way they do before we act. On the stage we may enjoy the consequences of actions we no longer dare to undertake. There we can repeat our mistakes without penalty, for if we grow bored we may always leave and come again, whereas if we grow bored with life we may leave it only once. We may come and go as we wish, for only the actors know they are condemned to repeat themselves night after night. They bear the burden of self-knowledge for us, so that as we watch them every experience becomes unique, as it should be.

Sitting alone in the theatre he thought all that.

The theatre was dark, like the night, safer, and more conveniently mysterious. He preferred it empty, for others should not see our life as we would live it. As he sat in darkness, as the footlights suffused the curtain before it parted, it was as though he stood on the shores of the world, waiting for the first life to appear from the sea.

The Court Theatre connected with the palace. When the emptiness and alienation of the Residenz became too much for him, he had only to open a door in a side room, step along a quiet corridor, and open another door behind the royal box, to rediscover magic once again. If he knew the play by heart, he could drop in as he pleased. On this 30th April 1881 he was particularly anxious to be there on time. In the connecting corridor he looked out of a window and down to the deserted cobbles of the street below. To-night might be important. Unexpectedly he felt hope, even though he was tired. He hurried on. The whole year had felt strange. It might be black, but it would not be grey.

For his excitement he had a certain reason.

Wagner had returned to Munich. Ludwig had not particularly wanted to see him, but he had given him use of the Court Theatre for two months. Sometimes we have certain friends for whom our affection is undiminished, but whom we can never bring ourselves to meet again. We write to them. We exchange gifts. We speak well of them. But there was once a moment, perhaps trivial, but never to be forgotten, after which seeing them became impossible, because they did something so blindly wilful that we could never see them as they were before again.

He had to agree to meet Wagner in the wintergarden, but he dreaded the meeting. He sat in the Indian hut and watched the artificial moon in the water. Wagner was announced at five. Ludwig rose uncertainly. When our friends have become famous, something personal goes out of them. Now he and Wagner were rival kings in different countries, each coveting the conquest of the other. Between them there could be no ease or trust. He looked up anxiously.

Wagner came down the path among the ferns. Time had made him heavier. Yet absorption in the arts gives us a curious youthfulness. It was like the meeting of two lovers, after many years, when neither can remember which one failed the other, yet each remembers very well. They had much to talk about, but nothing to say. In Wagner's eyes shone the defensive youthfulness of the artist suddenly grown old.

They talked for three hours. They did not talk with each other, however, so much as at each other. Ludwig felt far away from his own words. Wagner still reeked of tobacco, as he had at that first audience, years ago. It reminded Ludwig of his youth.

At eight o'clock on April 29th they slipped into the theatre for a performance of *Lohengrin*. Ludwig sat there, hoping the work would make it possible to communicate with the man.

There is a strange tenseness about an artist who sees some work of his own after a lapse of many years, the same tension one may observe in parents as they watch their children receive the baccalaureat, a sense not of accomplishment, but of loss. Ludwig stirred uneasily. It occurred to him that Wagner saw in *Lohengrin* what he had seen at Linderhof, a beautiful cage for something that had flown away.

He saw in the way that Wagner hunched forward to watch as Lohengrin sailed away that he, too, still searched for an embodiment, not in his life, but in his works. The man who finishes his life work before he dies, dies twice. Wagner was full of plans. He would do an opera upon the life of the Buddha. But they were only plans. He was ripe with accomplishment, but the public had stolen all his fruit. New works might grow from the seed of *Lohengrin* and *Parsifal*, but new works by Wagner never.

The curtain fell. They rose. Wagner watched the darkened theatre expectantly and then sighed. Ludwig understood. So, too, must he go on with Falkenstein, even though it would never be built. The visit had made him sad.

When Wagner was gone, he went back to the wintergarden. There had been some letters for him. He held them in his hand and then put them on a table.

At last the stillness became too much for him. The water of the imitation lake had lapped too often at the shore. He pulled his letters to him and began to open them, putting on glasses to read, since there was no one to see him wear them.

There was a note from the director of the Court Theatre, who enclosed two photographs of a new actor. Ludwig was not too interested. He opened the envelope and slid out the pictures. He had been reading Victor Hugo recently, and had taken a fancy to *Marion de Lorme*. Two lines in that play fascinated him. The Marquis de Saverny, the chief character, somewhere said: "If I found adventure in a passing encounter, then the heart of illusion could still be broken in upon."

It could never happen in life, but Ludwig longed to see it happen on the stage. He had ordered the play to be performed on April 30th.

He turned the pictures over and stared at them.

He found himself looking at a young man whose hair was parted in the middle and fluffed out at the sides. The face was heavy and the hair untidy. Yet the features were fine. The mouth was delicate, and its upper curve echoed the concave curves of the nostrils. The eyebrows were well drawn. The eyes looked out sensitively from far away, seeing everything and full of power. He was not only looking at the ideal face he had always sought. He took off his glasses. He was looking at himself.

He sat there for a long time and then picked up the pictures once again. There was no doubt. It was himself. If he had been born of the people, he would have looked like this. He might even have had this power.

He was startled and disturbed. Of all the people we see every day, seldom do we look at a stranger only to find ourselves staring back at us. The young man's name was Kainz. Ludwig ordered that Kainz was to play Didier, in *Marion de Lorme*.

What was to happen? He must find out.

April 30th was a Saturday, on the brink of May. That night Ludwig slipped eagerly and unseen into the darkened theatre, taking his place in his box. The performance was a little late in getting started. The orchestra was repeating itself.

As the curtains began to part, he sat very, very still, uncertain, terrified, and poised to flee.

The stage was revealed. The scene was the bedroom of a château at Blois. The Marquis de Saverny was discovered importuning Marion de Lorme to become his mistress. Her heart was given to another. Saverny departed in disgust. The actress who played Marion de Lorme was pleasing, but had a piping voice. Ludwig could not abide high-pitched sounds. He sat forward and watched the window at the rear of the stage.

A figure scrambled over the balustrade to enter the room. It was dressed in black and wore bottines. The costume was abominable. The lighting was worse. Ludwig frowned. He could see nothing clearly, but he would not wear his glasses in a public place. The piece was badly directed. Didier had his back to the auditorium. He flung himself at Marion's feet. He was graceful, but in an oddly discomfited way. He must be young. When he spoke his voice was deep, controlled, and beautiful.

"Who am I who crawl with the base herd?" he asked Marion. Yet some commoners did not seem to be commoners. When, later in the scene, the truth emerged that he had been born a foundling, Ludwig relaxed. It was an ancient rule that foundlings, because saved by the grace of God, were enrolled among the ranks of gentlemen, and therefore might consort with their peers. So that was all right. Perhaps the woodsman in the glade had been a foundling, too.

Didier was young and his movements had a certain helpless vigour. Ludwig sat back in the shadows of the box. The voices rose to him out of the theatre. Saverny entered. There was a brawl with street robbers. Didier saved his life. The two men found they were rivals for Marion's hand. Didier spoke again. His voice was better now: he was getting the feel of the part.

"Your road lies that way. This is mine," he said. The two men separated and left the stage. But this was a play. They would meet again. Ludwig felt no real anxiety about that. The curtain went down. It seemed a long time to wait until Act II.

Act II took place also at Blois, but outside, at the doorway to a wineshop on a public square. The scene was excessively tedious: neither Didier nor Saverny appeared for many, many minutes. Ludwig closed his eyes. His left leg had gone to sleep. The scene was designed to build up audience tension. Ludwig waited, anxious and bored. He could not remember how Didier looked. A wisp of dialogue caught his attention.

"Of what use is the King, I pray to know?"

At last Saverny entered. He was in search of Didier. He spoke frankly to his fellow nobles:

> *"Didier is he called.*
> *Many of nobler race, who strut and boast,*
> *Have greater names, but no whit greater hearts."*

At long last Didier entered. His manner was pensive and noble. Assuredly he was no mere commoner. Saverny, not knowing him, provoked him to a duel. It was thrilling and tragic. Ludwig hunched forward. The King's guards entered and arrested both men for duelling. Saverny shammed dead. Only Didier was hauled off to gaol. The penalty for duelling was death. This was not life, he was watching, but optimum reality. Marion entered and mourned. The curtain fell.

Ludwig paced up and down at the back of his box. He was hungry. He wanted sandwiches, but the footman had not supplied them. He did not ring. It was better to go hungry, than to be disturbed.

At last the bell rang and the curtain rose. The third act took place in the grounds of the Château de Nangris, a gothic building with modern additions. The scene was long. Didier did not appear until the end of it. Saverny was present in disguise. At last a troop of strolling players entered to seek shelter for the night. Didier was with them, also in disguise. He had escaped from gaol. He was certainly both noble and handsome. His eyes were bewitching. Ludwig drew back into the shadow of his box. The eyes seemed to stare directly at him.

It was a pity Didier had so small a part, yet perhaps it was better at first to catch only a glimpse of him, for a glimpse was sometimes better than a view. The figures we see over our shoulders or flickering on the borders of the eye are not always terrible. Sometimes they are angels of the annunciation, full of joy. They comfort us until we turn to them, then they disappear. Didier spoke.

> *"O let me drink oblivion from thine eyes!*
> *God willed, when mingling with my clay a soul*
> *that throughout life an angel and a demon*
> *should wait upon my steps. But Blest be He*
> *whose wondrous mercy doth the demon hide*
> *and let me see the angel face to face."*

Ludwig nodded as the words came up to him. He felt the same way. He strained to hear some edge of the personal in that voice. He would save Didier. He would save himself.

> *"Do not, I pray, deny my thirsty heart*
> *the bliss of having thee,"*

Didier ranted from the stage, and it was a cry from the ideal self. It should not go unanswered. Didier, too, must know what loneliness was like.

> *"Alas, when this sad journey's at an end,*
> *when I am weary, then the ice-cold bed*
> *that waits for me, is narrow, there's not room*
> *for two."*

Ludwig frowned. It was not a problem of two. Didier was himself. The theatre seemed to stir. His attention strayed. The play dwindled away into plot mechanics. Didier was discovered, arrested, and carted off to gaol. Saverny could not allow him to go to his death alone. He revealed himself, and together the two men were incarcerated.

Act IV took place in the King's apartments at Chambord. The King had been rendered impotent by his ministers. He no longer had even the will to act. He refused to intervene to reprieve Didier and Saverny. The act was endless. Didier did not appear in it. Probably he was resting in his dressing-room. What was his face really like? Would he be Didier offstage as well? The action went on and on.

"I have enough to do to live," exclaimed the stage king, "without the care of reigning."

That, too, was true. Ludwig waited for Act V.

At last it came. The scene was the *donjon* at Beaugency. The plot ground on relentlessly. Marion spoke:

> *"Even to save your life, my Didier,*
> *I cannot be again the shameless thing*
> *I was! Thy breath did elevate my soil.*
> *Besides thee naught of my old self remained,*
> *and thy love gave me back virginity."*

It was true. The play was very true. Didier could change his whole life. The executioners arrived. Didier and Saverny embraced for the last time. The play was so directed that it was Didier's face Ludwig could see, over Saverny's back. Didier was clearly moved. The two men were led off to their execution. They would always be together. The curtain fell.

Ludwig sighed and did not stir. He felt an immense gratitude. After a while he went back to the wintergarden to savour the experience alone.

It was like *Tristan and Isolde*. Love was always the prelude to death. So it was in the *Aida* he had seen the previous afternoon. If we must immolate ourselves, we should not have to do so alone. Lohengrin had given Elsa a ring. Richard had given him a ring, made of iron.

214

To Didier he would send a ring also, but it should hold a star sapphire, like a star of hope. It was difficult to remember that the man's name was Kainz. He was eager to hear what Didier would have to say.

An answer to his gift came on May 1st. Once more, after so many years, May began auspiciously. The letter was in a fine, bold hand. It spoke of humility.

It made him eager to see Didier again as soon as possible. He scheduled a second performance of *Marion de Lorme* for May 4th. When the fourth came he sat watching the stage anxiously, but it was indeed Didier and indeed himself he watched. This time he sent a gold chain, with an enamel swan dangling from it, like the Order of the Holy Ghost in Hugo's *Hernani*, that order only those of noble blood might wear.

On May 9th the play was to be *La Marquise de Pompadour*. He commanded that Didier should be present to watch, in a box below his. He did not dare to meet the man, but perhaps he could establish contact in some way, in the dark of the theatre, watching a charade together, as those at mass watch the altar.

So Ludwig sat alone in the royal box. He sent an equerry to Didier with opera glasses and a copy of the libretto. All through that interminable performance he sat motionless, listening for sounds from the box below him, the sounds not so much of movement as of shared emotion. Sometimes he thought he caught the stealthy turning of a page. At least their eyes were both watching the same spectacle, bifocal to the same experience.

As the performance went on he thought less of the stage and more of the box below him. It was terrible not to dare to come closer, and May was wearing on. He commanded another performance of *Marion de Lorme*, and got no sleep until it took place.

It must be almost dawn. He bit his lips. If he could love no one, at least he could protect himself in another. But would that other understand? Was Didier, despite the resemblance, really himself? The darkness of the theatre was deceptive. The illusion was not on the stage, but in the eyes of those who watched.

Yet he could not be mistaken. He had seen the man's bearing. It was noble. For there are certain truths the knowledge of which is an inherited or intrinsic privilege. To know them is to be that special hermetic sort of aristocrat, the autocrat. Autocrats are born at random, whereas aristocrats issue only from their own house. What the one inherits from a family, the other derives from genius itself. Few of us have the strength to be absolute in ourselves and to ourselves. Yet only spiritual autonomy can pull us through.

The third performance of *Marion de Lorme* was less a performance than a sacrament. He watched eagerly. When Didier was led off to death, Ludwig arose and clapped twice. He had never done that in the theatre before. Afterwards he drove straight to Berg, opened his diary, and permitted himself to quote from the play. "So unseparated we died, eternally united," he wrote. It was a promise to himself.

Didier wrote to him at Berg and May sped by. It was not right that they should not meet. Didier should appear in other parts. Ludwig sent him a copy of *Hernani*. He wanted to hear more of that immortal voice, and in *Hernani* it was possible to die for a principle. He wanted to listen to the great speech in the tomb scene, in which we learn of Hernani's origins:

> "*Since heaven made me a Duke, and exile,*
> *a mountaineer . . .*"

He was agitated. Berg seemed emptier than ever. Once a week he visited Richard and his family, at their home nearby. He needed their reassurance, for he was about to do something of which he felt afraid. On the way back he always walked by the lake, escorted by a footman to act as linkboy. The footman annoyed him, but he needed a light. He was finished forever with menials such as he.

Along the shore of the lake he watched, catching glimpses of the mountain peaks. May became unendurable and drew to its close. He could not bear to spend all of it alone. That was neither right nor necessary. Yet he hesitated. The weeks went by, narrowed down, and opened out of each other, like a series of tunnels through which he drifted in a boat, now with head room, now not. He could stand isolation no more.

So on the 29th he sent a messenger to Munich, and knew he had done a fatal, an irrevocable thing. That made him more restless than ever. He had sent for Didier. But of course Didier was not entirely Didier. He was also a man called Kainz, and of the man Kainz Ludwig felt mortally afraid.

Had he taken another step down in the circular stair, or had he not?

XVIII

———————›››❯❮❮‹‹‹———————

When Kainz received the messenger, he was nervous, too. Knowing what he would some day be, he resented how people treated him now, knowing how they would change their opinion of him later, and thus losing future friends in a foreknowledge of their hypocrisy. An actor is someone else only in the evening. He cannot be another man all day, for if so, then he is locked up in one role, and that is madness. Nor did he know that it was Didier who had been summoned, and not Kainz, for he was still young enough to take pride in being himself, so it was of himself he thought when people praised him, not of his roles.

He had not seen the King, but the King had watched him. Kainz did not know whether to expect a demigod or a monster. He thought he was being summoned as an attractive boy, not as a budding actor. He did not know that love, being inexorable, would demand both.

He thought that kings were merely actors, too, but born out of the trunk on to a permanent stage. He was right: they were; but he forgot the sacred origins of the drama. He forgot that at least to himself the priest is still King, the King still priest, even though the audience no longer believes it. And now there was no audience.

A carriage called at his lodgings. There was something unreal about the whole experience. He liked to step out of the theatre into the world, not into another play. He did not yet know that the performance is continuous, and that if we are to survive we can never cease to act.

Being patronized by the King made him feel uneasy and vaguely Greek. Unfortunately he did not look Greek, and to the Greeks appearance was everything, since it was the mirror of their thoughts. Rifling in his mind through all the roles he had ever played, he could find nothing to give him so much as a hint how to behave in this one. Even the stiff, formal, passionate poems of Count von Platen did not help much. He was oddly excited. He was Kainz, going to visit the King. It was something a little wider than his life so far.

The carriage was a small closed calèche, suffocating and very uncomfortable. He wanted very much to sneeze, though that would not have been respectful. The view flashed by the square windows like a stereopticon. He managed to catch a nap, but ached all over. The journey went on for hours. It began to be dusk and the horses were climbing. The air became pure, which jerked him awake. He rubbed his eyes. Something had changed.

It was only that they had turned off the road, having reached Linderhof. Whether it was seemly or not, he hung out of the window, squinting in the gloom.

Linderhof glittered among the trees, a frosted wedding cake, trimmed with silver leaves. There was a restless movement to and fro somewhere, like the rustle of silk or leaves shifting in the wind along an abandoned, ruin-ated corridor. As the carriage swept up to the entrance, he had a glimpse of the fountain, weaving hypnotized back and forth under the moon like a giant, impalpable cobra, the one thing in that landscape heartlessly and inimically alive. Then the door of the calèche was opened and he was ushered to his room.

It was such a room as he had entered only in plays. It was also transient. It contained no bed. He was told to change. He must have seemed bewildered, for the servant told him he would sleep in a châlet on the property. No one slept at Linderhof, not even the King. There was some constraint here he did not understand, and a certain fearful mockery as well. He was brought hot water and asked to hurry.

Obediently he plunged his wrists into the water. After washing, he changed into an evening coat and white tie, trying to get his bearings, but without success. A lackey came to the door and beckoned him outside.

To his bewilderment they went not into one of the state rooms, but downstairs to the garden floor. At the foot of the stairs the lackey paused. His name, he said, was Burkel. He did not smile. The two men stepped out on to a terrace. They were going into the garden. This close-to, the fountain hissed and spat. It cast its spray everywhere into the moist air, and it seemed to follow them as they skirted the basin, as though it could see them. Almost, in an abrupt gust of wind, it lunged at him. It was tall and utterly malevolent, glittering against the shadows.

They stepped off the gravel, on to a narrow path. Kainz stared while the fountain drew back and then lunged again, splattering poisonous drops close to his face and eyes. The lackey Burkel lingered ahead, like a confidant in some muffled melodrama. With a wary eye on the fountain, Kainz followed, feeling the gravel pop under the thin soles of his evening shoes. The fountain still watched above them, the top of its trajectory oddly like a flattened head. He had not known that water, the source of life, could show such venom.

The air was so fragrant as to be oppressive. It smelled of mummy. He hesitated, seeing the lackey stop once more ahead of him. This was it. He would be asked either to undress or to recite, and his career had reached such an impasse that he did not greatly care which, except that he was tired. In the circumstances he was only too anxious to do what was expected of him. But what was expected of him?

Before them was a large granite rock. The rock slid away. He was startled. Beyond was a small vestibule. He could hear Burkel's torch spluttering. The walls were damp. They walked a little way and came to a wider place. He found himself standing once more on gravel, at the edge of lifelessly lapping water. The lights were blue. Under them two swans perambulated the pool. They were the colour of blotting paper. They had been indoors too long. Kainz grunted with surprise, but was not heard, for beside him a red, blue, and yellow waterfall gushed from the wall.

Burkel made an odd movement and set off towards the left. The torch he carried smudged still more a ceiling already much smudged. Bewildered, Kainz followed him along a strait path which curved around the water towards the other side of the grotto. They came to the entrance of a gazebo built of silver-painted shells. Steps to it were concealed by rocks.

Behind him Burkel moved rapidly away, but not before Kainz saw his smile. The reflection of his torch fled across the water, where the swans sailed angrily away from it. There was a movement within the gazebo. The grotto was chilly and evening clothes are far from warm. Kainz went up the steps, as Burkel disappeared. The waterfall gave a convulsive spurt and shifted colours.

Inside the gazebo was a supper table, laid out with such things as one has at an after-theatre party, of which only a dish of *glacé* trout ornamented with anchovy rosettes caught his eye.

If he had been anywhere else, he would have smiled. He had spent most of his youth in the green room, and he recognized what he saw. It was the usual arrangement. For talent and genius mean nothing. They have a certain survival value once we have arrived, but they will never allow us to scramble to security unaided. Platonism is meaningless in the theatre; and we are lucky to attract attention at all, so we cannot afford to reject any sponsor who appears. If attention comes from someone of the sex we prefer and is not too ugly, that is more than we can possibly hope for. Kainz did not smile. He was too puzzled. He knew that this sort of thing happened, but it had not happened to him before.

Where was the King? A man stood at the other side of the table, half hidden in shadow. He stepped abruptly forward. He was tall, and he swayed slightly, his fingers flexing with impatience. His face was very white. It was a chipmunk face. His hair was parted in the middle, and his mouth was muzzled by moustaches which flowed down on either side into his beard. His chest was enormous, and it made him swing like a pendulum upside down. It was the sort of face you expect to see waiting for you at the end of a corridor, in sleep. His eyes were penetrating, disappointed, and warm, even though angry. He sketched a gesture.

"You are late," he said. His voice was choked.

Kainz knew he was late. He felt miserable.

The figure was too angry to be imposing. It stared at him. As it stared, Kainz could feel himself growing uglier. He felt soiled.

"You are smaller than Didier," said the King drily. He moved back behind the table and made a vague motion towards it. Kainz could think of nothing to say. Behind him the swans grew irritable at each other in the lake. Time suddenly prolapsed.

Ludwig was shaking visibly. Kainz scarcely noticed. The King quivered like a fox at an empty burrow. Kainz tried to speak, and saw the words wither in front of him in the air.

"You had better sit down," said the King. He did not sit down himself. He eyed Kainz narrowly. Kainz could think of nothing to lessen the tension. He could not help it if he was a small man. He felt himself dwindle.

The King began to pour champagne, but suddenly put the bottle down, as though he could not move. Kainz did not dare to look up at him. He looked instead at the glasses. The bubbles rose slowly yellow through the stem. They would never break the surface.

The King drained his glass. "This is unforgivable," he said. He backed away from the table and left the gazebo. Kainz sat rooted where he was. The swans hissed. The waterfall spat. The lights flickered. He had failed. He had had his chance and lost it. He was not what the King wanted after all.

Someone bent over him. It was Burkel.

"He expected Didier, you fool," said Burkel. "Who cares about an actor? Recite!"

Kainz sat up. Burkel's round, smooth face was staring down at him. "Act," repeated Burkel, and winked. "We all act here. Stand up." He drew away.

Kainz stood up. He looked out over the lake. He could not see the King anywhere on the path.

With desperation, he scrambled back into the only safety he knew. He cleared his throat. On the water the swans waited motionless. Shadows came and went across the ceiling.

He began to recite. He chose Didier's scenes in the last act of *Marion de Lorme*. They were the longest speeches. The roof of the grotto cast back his voice distorted. Automatically he shifted his voice production to obliterate the echo. He felt the part take hold. The swans raised their heads. The speeches rolled out into the air before him. He did not feel inadequate any more. He launched into the fifty-six lines in which he renounced Marion de Lorme in order to die with Saverny. On the stage he wore an open silk shirt for that. Automatically he began to undo his tie, standing with his feet planted wide apart on the floor of the gazebo. He closed his eyes. Somewhere he heard footsteps. The executioners were coming. There was a special trick he wanted to try out of halting for a moment on the noun, before rushing on to the dependent clauses. They would never let him use it in the theatre. He used it now. He reached the end of the speech, paused for breath, and opened his eyes.

The King was standing before him at the table. He was watching him with hungry eyes, but they were not hungry with lust. Kainz understood. It was not Kainz the King wanted, nor even Didier. It was the power to speak such noble sentiments. The King handed him a glass of champagne and Kainz drained the glass. He gave a sudden smile and felt much better. The corners of the King's mouth twitched and he poured again. He leaned forward intently.

"Go on," he said. He seemed larger and more commanding now.

Kainz went on.

He was puzzled, but he felt much better. Now he was doing what he knew how to do. So long as he followed his own voice, he was safe in this labyrinth. He decided to let it out, though warily conscious of the acoustics of the grotto. He tried all the tricks he had worked on for so long, that in the theatre they would not let him try. Before him he could see his voice, curving, swooping, flying, dipping, a glider hypersensitive to the controls. He went on and on. The grotto vanished.

There was a creak. The King sat down.

"You must rest," he said. He dug out the side of the *glacé* trout and served it upon a plate, passing it to Kainz. "Have you learned the role of Hernani yet?"

Kainz nodded. He was happy and he was perspiring. Few of us are ever loved for our abilities, especially in the theatre. "In act one," he began, and even to himself his voice sounded different. Dimly he realized why. He had dropped the Viennese accent and was speaking instead with the accent of authority.

The King's eyes now snapped with enthusiasm. They were alive. Kainz saw for the first time that they were beautiful. Desire did not matter, if only there were something to admire. The King sat forward eagerly on his chair, and Kainz did the same. He began to recite with his mouth full. They sat there together until well past dawn.

Kainz was no longer nervous. He began to see the eager, white-skinned boy behind the beard, and something inside him that was older than he was felt oddly moved. It felt exultant too. He was a success.

The visit could go on.

It went on for twelve days.

Each day they took long walks, or else went for carriage drives. Kainz had never before been treated in this way. It was fantastic, and he began to be worried about his voice. Burkel brought him an atomizer and throat spray every morning. He seemed as anxious as Kainz himself.

Some things bewildered him. He could not be Didier every day. He began to sense something of the nightmare of the actor who is allowed to play only one role. They read Byron, Hugo, Grillpartzer, and Caldéron, but always he must be Didier. In these parts he should not be Didier. And who was the Didier the King thought he was?

One day, while they were walking down a hillside towards the lake, the King took his arm. He had the feeling that Ludwig had not wanted to do so, that it was something he had tried not to do, had wanted desperately for days to do, and was half ashamed of having done. Kainz became very still inside and abruptly the King broke free. Kainz surprised on his face a strange, half-haunted look. He did not understand it. What did it matter, one way or the other, any more? Yet he could see that to the King it mattered a good deal. Kainz knew that physically nothing could happen between them now, for they had passed beyond that point where it could, since now they knew each other too well to be able to discover each other.

One day they went to Berg, and drove beyond the *schloss* to a small farm. It was immaculately tidy, like the toy village of Marie Antoinette.

They went there for lunch, and though the King did not tell him why, he could tell that the visit was important. It had the feel of trying out for a new part. He met the King's master of the horse, his wife and children. The time passed easily, and yet there was some kind of constraint he did not comprehend. The King kept watching the master of the horse, whose name was Richard Hornig. Kainz felt instantly that Hornig did not like him. Hornig watched him closely. Yet as the afternoon went on he could feel that hostility slowly melt and change into something softer and more equivocal. Hornig watched the King with disturbed, faintly indulgent, faintly apprehensive eyes. And as they left, Hornig seemed to wish to speak, but then to think better of it.

The King seemed happy and relieved. Together they drove back to Linderhof. Ludwig half spoke; half hummed, half sang as they drove along. It was as though some obstacle had been removed. Kainz wondered what sort of test he had passed. It was very like the theatre. There, too, one never knew exactly why one had been chosen or rejected for a role. Merit seemed to have nothing to do with it.

His visit drew to a close.

He was sorry it was over, yet no doubt it was just as well. He had grossly overtaxed his throat and it was sore. The King deluged him with gifts. It was strange. The last day the King had seemed both embarrassed and sad, almost as though he were frightened. Almost as though he were saying a final good-bye. Kainz was apprehensive. He did not want it to be good-bye. On the other hand he could not walk around the woods spouting poetry forever, either. He found it good to be back to the theatre.

Once back in Munich, and he wrote to the King. The gossip at the theatre was worse than he had expected, and he did not like the amused glances that now followed him. They were the worse to bear in so far as they were incorrect. The matter was more complex than his fellow actors could be expected to understand. He shrugged his shoulders. He was used to envy, and it was less dangerous if it was also tinctured with contempt. It did not matter. He had a patron now.

He waited to hear what the King would write in reply.

The King wrote nothing. Kainz became alarmed. He had taken a step up. He could not now take one down. Then, at last, there was a letter. Its tone surprised him. It mentioned that occasion on which the King had taken his arm, and it was furious. Kainz did not quite see why the King should be furious, but he wrote to apologize anyway, though he did not know for what. He could not afford to lose everything now, just as everything was within his grasp.

There was no reply to his apology. He went on with rehearsals of *Richard II*. His position had become far from enviable.

Then the King wrote proposing a visit to Spain, in the form of a pilgrimage to the home of Caldéron. Kainz was relieved. Yet only when it occurred to him that the visit would fall through, did he accept the proposal, for he was to open in *Richard II* very soon. He could not leave the theatre and his career. He had some anxious moments. Yet if consent would please the King, he did not mind. It was pleasant to please the King. There was something innocent and touching there that evoked affection, even if it could not receive it. As he wrote the formal, flatteringly adulatory phrases which Court etiquette demanded, he realized that he meant them. Pity and affection are almost interchangeable. When he visualized the King now, it was not as a man with a beard, but as a little boy. It was most odd.

Richard II was the best role he had had to date. It was to be the cornerstone of his career. He could not give that up, and he would not, but he was sorry about the projected pilgrimage. It would have been enjoyable.

Another message arrived from the King. He quite

228

understood about the performance. Wagner had been so. But the play would only run for a week. Kainz was to be ready to go to Switzerland on June the 27th.

Kainz hesitated. Something held him back. But for the sake of his career, it was imperative that he should obey, so he obeyed. This time the leave of absence from the theatre could be arranged quietly with the manager, and no one need know where he was. He began to perceive that it was not altogether an agreeable thing to be a royal favourite. At the same time he felt anticipation. After all, in its own way it was all rather grand. He supposed he would have to be Didier again. It was a role he had already left behind him, but he would always remember it. It had given him his start.

XIX

He was wrong. The part assigned to him was Tell.

He was to join the King not in Munich, but at a small railway station close to Berg, where the train would pause long enough to allow the King to board it. As the train began to slow down for the station Kainz felt within himself not exactly affection, but a great tenderness to oblige. In his heart of hearts the interpretive artist, to whom are entrusted the sacred creative thoughts of others, must always feel a little sorry for those who cannot express themselves through others. The King was locked up in himself, and Kainz would gladly have let him out, if he could have done so. To tell the truth, he felt rather magniloquent, with a condescension natural to the stage but which had now begun to grow in himself, as he felt his new authority.

With a final snort of steam the train stood like a waiting pack animal in the station. It was dusk and there was a thin indifferent rain.

Kainz felt silly pretending to be Didier, for an artist is never interested in what he has done before: he is only interested in what he is going to do next. Once he has breathed life into a part, the life goes out of it for him. Everyone is the same. The inner self is bored by what the outer self may do, and views it with detachment, for it has thought the action before the action becomes apparent, so it hurries on.

He was not quite easy in his mind with the King, for it was difficult to face him as an equal. If he had been more successful, it would not have been so difficult, but his success was yet to come. He looked out of the window. A line of men approached the train. They were the porters of the safari and comprised cooks, valets, a hair-dresser, and an equerry. Beyond them a figure stepped out from behind a van. It was tall and weighted oddly at the bottom. Its hat was dripping with rain. Deliber-ately it raised its hand and broke into a smile. Kainz waved in response. It was the King out there. Didier waved, not he.

Soon, very soon, Ludwig bustled into the compart-ment with a shuffle and stoop, the train shook itself, and they were off. Kainz faced him. He had the role down pat by now. He wondered what he would be asked to recite. It turned out to be Byron.

"Off to the Tell country," said Ludwig genially. Unpacking his memory, Kainz lurched into Childe Harold and scarcely listened. He had no idea what he was in for.

He soon found out.

The King talked enthusiastically like a little boy, his hands on his knees to steady him. The King proposed to cast him for one of his own favourite roles, not so much to see him act in it, as to be able to act it through him.

They slept that night on the train and woke up on a siding at Lucerne. Kainz had never been to Switzerland before. It was certainly invigorating to be so high up, but the country was too tidy, too overinhabited, and he cut himself shaving. Ludwig was impatient, as though he had

231

an enormous secret to impart. They left the train and went to a steamer. It was draped with blue and white bunting. Ludwig muttered under his breath and went aboard. The lake drew away around them.

Everywhere Kainz must recite. Any role is endurable for three and a half hours, but this one went on forever. Even in moments of contemptuous self-doubt, he could not have thought of a better punishment for his dramatic aspirations.

When Schiller wrote *Wilhelm Tell* he had never been to Switzerland. Kainz began to realize why. At Brünnen they stepped from the boat. The King wanted to show him the landscape of Schiller. Kainz began to be grateful that the character of Melchthal does not enter the play until the fourth scene of Act I. At least he was not forced to row across the lake in an open boat during a storm, as Tell had done earlier in the play. There are advantages in being cast for a minor role. The King would surely have made him do so, if Melchthal had done that, rather than Tell.

Kainz was not deeply moved by scenery. It was something he liked to watch while sitting down. Considering the limitations of the stage, Schiller had chronicled Switzerland alp by alp. But at least on the stage the floor was level. The Alps were not. At Brünnen Kainz climbed the hill and delivered Melchthal's first speech. All told he did it rather well, he thought, and the pines made a superb backdrop. The King was not satisfied. Several scenes of the play take place at night under the moon. Kainz was exhausted. He was not used to climbing. They went back to the hotel for a brief snack, to wait until the moon rose. The King was in a trance. When the moon appeared, they went out with torches. The night was bitterly cold, but you cannot act in an overcoat. The torches spluttered against the trees, as they climbed higher and higher. Even that did not satisfy Ludwig. He now wanted to see the scenery that Schiller had not been able to depict in the play. Kainz was drugged for sleep. The equerry came to rouse him at dawn. Kainz stared at him. He thought something must be wrong. He dressed hastily. The equerry told him to put on hunting clothes and cleet shoes. A suit was already laid out for him. Kainz thought perhaps something had happened to the King.

Outside he found a corps of sleepy guides and Ludwig, fresh-faced and eager. The King scarcely spoke to him. Instead he turned, gave a curt nod to the guides, and the party was off. Kainz had had no time for breakfast.

In Scene 2, Act II of *Wilhelm Tell*, Melchthal speaks to Stauffacher. He has just been to see his father, whose eyes had been put out at the order of the Austrian tyrant. The spectacle so enraged him that he left the old man and crossed the mountains to join the rebels at Uri.

> *Through the Surenen's fearful mountain chain*
> *Where dreary ice-flelds stretch on every side*
> *And sound is none, save the hoarse vulture's cry,*
> *I reached the Alpine pasture, where the herds*
> *From Uri and from Engelberg resort . . .*

It is one of the great setpieces of the play, and describes in minute detail Melchthal's journey, which Schiller had been unable to show on the stage. The King was waiting. It was to be shown now.

Kainz looked at the mountains and gasped.

"Yes, it will be magnificent," said Ludwig, and glanced at Kainz, who was shivering in leather shorts. They clambered into a carriage, the guides following them in another. It was cold and misty. The sun had risen, but gusts of steam rose from the fields. They drove rapidly. Kainz was seriously distressed.

The King did not speak again. He seemed to be in some kind of suspense. He wanted Kainz to recite. To Kainz, it was as though the King did not think he was there unless he recited. He was sleepy and his throat was sore. Driving towards the mountains, the carriages breasted a rise of ground.

"Engelberg," breathed the King. The town was pleasant and small. Kainz wondered what they would do there. It sat in a flat green meadow, the site of a huge convent. They whirled past the convent walls in a shatter of dust. The carriages did not stop and Kainz was hungry. He knew it would be useless to explain that he was not accustomed to the altitude. He had to go on talking. The carriages bumped down a dirt road to the end of the valley, into timid woods. The woods thinned. The mountains rose abrupt and blue on every side. The carriages stopped. Ludwig did not stir. The guides got down to the ground, joking among themselves, while they glanced at Kainz.

"Now you will climb," said Ludwig. He sighed. "I wish I could go with you."

Kainz stared at him with disbelief. He was helpless and penniless in a strange country, and if he refused, Ludwig was quite capable of leaving him there alone. Something in the King's eyes told him he would not refuse. It was a lost look and distrait, but it had command in it. He turned to face the rock.

The guides were waiting for him. He went to join them. Once he looked back. Ludwig still sat in the carriage, gazing up at the peaks ahead. His face was baffled, yet victorious, as though he had somehow defeated them and was surprised that victory had brought no change in him or them.

They toiled wearily upward for half the morning. Far below lay the valley of the Engelberg. Kainz's legs were already dead below the knee. The guides were not talkative. They were constrained, almost as though the King were there, leaping ahead of them, with that ponderous agility of his that could be so surprising.

Higher they climbed. The sun was merciless. Every once in a while Kainz straggled too much and turned round, as though to see the view, but actually to rest. The guides spoke some kind of dialect he could not follow. If he asked them to turn back, they would merely shrug. They were stolid men who had received their orders and looked forward to receiving their pay. They would not allow him to turn back.

Higher still they went. The snow glare was unbearable. The sun was a burn in the sky. At last they reached a tarn so elevated that part of its surface was still rimed with ice, even in July. The rocks were naked. There were no plants. The mountains danced in the air. In that desolation something stirred. Kainz sat down on a rock.

His heart pounded and his temples hurt. The height made him giddy. When he opened his eyes it seemed to him that Ludwig stood there, just beyond the edges of the eyes, staring at him, bitterly disappointed and somewhat frightened. It seemed to him that the King said: "It is not much farther."

"I can't make it."

He saw that the guides were staring at him. Reluctantly he rose to his feet. He, too, was frightened. He gasped for air. He thought he would die. The guides clumped uncertainly and looked at him over their shoulders.

The King seemed far ahead of them now. Perhaps it was imagination. The height was vertiginous and the guides often stumbled. Kainz closed his eyes and prayed, but prayers did not help. There was nothing to pray to. The brandy the guides had forced into him made him sick at his stomach. Over him the sky tilted and teetered, as the guides led the way.

Far ahead he seemed to hear a shout. His eyesight seemed to shimmer as much as the landscape did. The guides had stopped. They stood on a grassy knoll, across which ran a rough path. They must be very high indeed. The air was unreal and illusionistic. It seemed as though the King were behind him now, struggling to get into his mind. He knew the King must never get into his mind. He staggered and the guides caught him.

Ludwig was standing a little way away from him, looking across the ravine. The guides nodded. The ravine was perhaps thirty feet deep, rough rock, and on the other side, across a narrow patch of ice-coated rock, stood the crests and ridges of a miniature vestigial glacier, locked in the snow but swirling up to the rocks and peaks beyond. He could tell that the King was very angry. He wanted him over by the glacier.

Kainz gasped and put his hand over his eyes. He was trapped between the guides and the King, and he was furious. He scrambled into the ravine, driving himself forward. He tore his hands on the rocks, but managed to stumble and slip over the ice-filled patch. There was something there he had to see. The King drove him to see it.

He was not going to be beaten at this game, whatever it was. The best way to get even with the King was to give him what he wanted, but Kainz was mortally afraid. His heart was ready to burst and his legs were no longer any part of him. The whole expedition was unbelievable.

The King was already well ahead of him and stood by the glacier, waiting. Kainz was so angry that he derived strength from his rage. He passed the ice rime and stood on solid rock. Then he looked down. He saw traces of a path. It was Melchthal's path, but that could not be true, for Schiller only imagined that trip. It had never taken place. Or had it? He was horrified.

He looked around him dimly and saw the face of the King, outlined against the ice, waiting for him to speak. He tried to do so. The glare was unspeakable on his eyes and no words would come. The King stared at him, wide-eyed. What was Ludwig trying to do to him, or to do with him? If he could not speak he would die. Was that what the King wanted? He opened his mouth again, but nothing came out. He knew Melchthal's speech by heart and could not remember a word of it. Something came out of space and shoved him to his knees. He pitched forward on his face. He knew nothing more until he opened his eyes and felt himself being placed in an empty carriage. It started off at once. He closed his eyes.

When he opened them again he knew instantly that they had descended. There was something different about the sky that told him so. Lying on his back against the horsehair of the carriage, he felt disoriented and unreal. He wondered not where they were going, but why they had stopped. He heard voices. The door opened and a giant got in beside him. His eyes were hard with snowglare. He could neither blink them nor change their expression. He merely looked.

He saw Ludwig. Ludwig looked concerned, yet eager. "Sit up," said the King. He pulled Kainz up on the seat and then banged the door closed behind him disapprovingly. Someone else clearly should have done that. The

carriage went on again. Far ahead of them glimmered
the waters of Lake Lucerne.

Kainz sat like a rag doll. He knew he should pull himself together, but he could not make the effort. Ludwig
bent over him intently.

"What was it like?" he demanded. His lips were parted
over small, sharp white teeth.

"Horrible."

The King drew back. What had seemed an amiable
expression vanished. He stared straight ahead at the
horses. Kainz lost consciousness again. Dimly he could
feel his body being bumped about.

Once more the carriage stopped and roused him.
"Where are we going?" he asked. The King did not
answer. Two grooms heaved him up by his armpits and
walked him towards the little steamer. He shook them off
and went up the gangplank. The steamer pulled away
from shore almost as soon as he was aboard. The lake
was quiet. The boat crossed it as a fly icing. Even so
there was a cool breeze. Kainz shivered, but he could
feel himself recovering. He got up and went in search of
the King.

He found him standing at the prow, watching the peaks
beyond Rütli with impatience. Kainz did not go to join
him. From the back there was something defeated, yet
determined about the King, hunched over the prow railing like an exile being ferried between two countries.

Kainz could still see before him the figure of the King
at the glacier, shimmering through snow blindness, yet
in some way really there, by act of will. The thought
sobered him. For an instant the King had been at his
brain and in his body, with a sad desperation to get in.
Ludwig did not turn around. Bewildered and frightened
for his own security, Kainz turned back and sat on one

238

of the side benches, also watching the hills above the Rütli hut. He had his own reasons for not wanting to go there again.

When the boat docked the King was nowhere in sight. Going down the gangplank, Kainz saw him already standing on the shore, that grotesquely bottom-heavy body tugging at its feet. There were times when Ludwig seemed an apparition, the more terrible for being flesh and blood. The King was talking to the equerry Burkel. Burkel came over to Kainz and seemed disturbed.

"Where are we going now?"

"Up the Brünnen. He wants to hear Melchthal's oath again," said Burkel. He seemed to check Kainz mentally, not out of concern for him, but out of concern for the King's wishes. He shrugged. "Make it if you can."

Kainz felt that if he did not make it, something dreadful would happen. He sighed and forced himself to move forward. Fortunately the guides had been dismissed, and it was to the interest of the servants to help him on. Ludwig moved at the head of the procession, in and out of the trees, and would speak to no one. It was as though, having lost one tower of his defences, he was hastening to repair the other.

The gradient was not so bad as it looked, and the servants managed to help Kainz out when he stumbled. The sun was still hot and he felt filthy. His throat was completely dry. He was more worried about his voice than anything else. For two hours the party wound through the thin forest. Kainz was slightly drunk with the brandy that had been given him. The King had not spoken to him once.

He knew the reason for this trip: if Ludwig could not have the one thing, then he must have the other. Kainz even wanted to give him the other, but it was too late for that. He could scarcely keep awake. Only by cursing Schiller rhythmically could he keep his feet in motion.

At last they reached a grassy meadow, open on one side to the lake. It was filled with late spring flowers, still blooming at this elevation, but somewhat dry to the touch. The King had gone into a patch of trees, no doubt to compose himself. Kainz sat down on the grass and tried to ignore the dull throbbing in his legs. In a moment the King would want Melchthal's speeches, and mentally he began to search for them, rooting out the key phrases that would open memory. He found one, and then another, blinking drowsily, and then he could not find them any more, for memory opened down into sleep.

From time to time he felt himself prodded, but with the best will in the world he could not respond. No more can the chicken in the egg emerge until it is strong enough. From an immense height of blackness above him he could see the King against the glacier, weeping bitterly.

When he woke it was dark. The grass was damp. He sat up quickly, scrambling to his feet, but he was utterly alone. He blinked, fearful of the wild darkness, and of the velvet sky above him. The air seemed suspended. He knew at once what had happened.

He stumbled down the hill. In an hour he reached the shore. The Rütli hut was closed for the night. He had only a few francs with him. At last he managed to find a boatman to row him across the lake. It was like Tell after all, but Tell, Act I.

Two hours later he burst into his hotel room. It, too, was empty, but with the special emptiness of a room which people have left for good. The King's light was on, but he did not dare to intrude upon him. He sank wearily down on the bed and went to sleep again.

When he woke he knew at once that he was alone. He shook his head, scarcely able to move in the bed. It was terrible. The room seemed dingy and the light hurt his eyes, but it was the sensation of being utterly alone that troubled him most. He wondered what had happened, only half realizing that he was still alive.

The door opened and an equerry came over to him. Through half closed lids, he saw the man move on tiptoe about the room, checking the louvers of the windows. He felt like a boy who has done something wrong, helpless and resentful at the same time.

"Does the King wish to see me?" he asked.

The equerry turned towards the bed. "The King has gone," he said. He gave a crooked smile. "If you are well enough, we have got you a seat on the evening train."

Clearly the equerry knew he was penniless. Kainz closed his eyes. He had not the strength either to feel angry or ashamed. That would come later. He took the train.

Staring out at the rain through the coach window, he realized that he had known this would happen, for the climb was not the cause of it. The climb was a substitute for something else.

Two days ago they had crossed Lake Lucerne to re-enact the scene on the Brünnen from Schiller. Afterwards they had gone to the Rütli hut by the lake. It was a Swiss national shrine, and accordingly well kept up. There were tables outside, and the footmen had brought along refreshments. Ludwig had stationed them about the grounds with torches.

Together, he and the King had gazed out at the lake in the twilight. Kainz had been very tired. Then he had felt a pressure on his arm, but a different pressure from that he had felt there before, at Berg. This pressure was timid, ashamed, and yet imperative. It was too late for that sort of thing, and Kainz had shaken the hand off. No man can use another man's body as the vehicle of his own escape. Escape in that sense is only transient, illusory, and mutual. Yet even so he wished now that he had not been so brusque.

In Munich he found waiting for him a favourable contract to appear in Berlin. With Court favour gone, even had he wanted to, he had no way to turn back. He signed at once. The day after he signed he received a large box. It was from the King. It contained eleven bottles of champagne. In the twelfth, wrote Ludwig, he had drunk his health. Kainz looked at the empty cradle and wanted to cry. He thought he understood. He went to Berlin all the same.

To reach fame we must travel very light and go alone, and he saw fame ahead of him now, down the road, with her smile of the Sphinx. All famous people have that smile, rapacious, yet sad. He would never play Didier again.

Yet the King was not mad. He was only ill from loneliness. Kainz shivered. The King had been born with an identity. But what happens when, after years of struggle, hardship and terror, at last you earn the right to say, *I am*? Where do you go then? Do you sit alone and drink a twelfth bottle of champagne? It was better to be an actor. At least an actor has an audience. He does not beat against a closed door, in an empty cell.

XX

——————▸▸➤◉◄◄◂——————

Ludwig felt badly about the matter. It was 1883. It was too late for delights. With Kainz the failure had been his own. With one gesture at the Rütli hut he had damned himself for good. Once more he sat alone in the tower room at Berg and opened the diary.

"On this day a year and a half ago, I saw the unforgettable third performance of Didier," he wrote. The only freedom we have is our memory of past events. But was the performance so unforgettable as all that? Now he was not so sure. It seemed to him now that he forgot a little more of the unforgettable every day. It was dreadful to live in a world without events, silent, still, and dead. There was no sound anywhere. Wagner was not there. The speaking voice had failed, and there should be no more music. He could not bear to hear it any more.

Insomnia yawned beneath him like a pit. He could no longer sleep, yet did people realize that to lie awake all night long was not to be awake, but that sleeplessness was a parody of sleep? In some ways the Greeks were a primitive people. They recognized only the twin gods Mors and Thanatos, born of the night without benefit of a father. They did not know that awful boy who masquerades as both, in a stern mythology without women. Mors was a woman. Who was it made death male? But

243

sleep is masculine. It is a wiry, hooting boy, stalking our labours. Sometimes it is the erotic child, luring us on to bed. There, with a crooked smile, it vanishes.

In our waking life we steel ourselves to live alone. The stoics never slept. But there are some men who can never sleep alone. When life is so cold, they need another body to keep their bodies warm, otherwise they lie awake and shiver down the night. Insomnia is one of the diseases of unrequited and unrequitable love. It is a deficiency disease. We lie awake, not because we cannot sleep, but in the futile hope that at last, as the body ebbs towards dawn, someone will come to make sleep possible.

When we lie sleepless, parody of our desires fits over us like a lid and we are buried alive. We have no choice. The sleepless are too tired to make a choice. The choice makes them. For the sleepless do not really lie awake. Instead they are cataleptic, but their minds are alive. One by one, as the hours ooze by, they are exposed to all the experiences which sleep alone makes bearable. They feel their body ebb, their metabolism approach the threshold of death, their limbs grow helpless and their breathing slow and shallow. The nightmare sits on their chest, they sweat, and they hear the tinkling rattle of that sistrum which in consciousness we call the death rattle, last music we shall ever make, inferior to the music of the swan.

Slowly the rats swarm up from the hold of the unconscious, and ravenously begin to gnaw the living body of the self. A plague has driven them to this. The plague is sleeplessness.

We lie awake until dawn. Vigilantly we watch the shadows. For if we lie awake until dawn, we have the chance to find in the daytime someone who will make the next night endurable. We can never lie awake long enough, however. The nibbling rats reach the heart, and we fall asleep convulsively, with one last captive heave of the chest, to unseat the nightmare. When we wake we are tired and it is afternoon. It is then too late to find a companion to make the next night endurable. The shadows on the grass are already long.

And sleeplessness makes day and night the same. Everything has a like grey texture. There is not light enough for hope. We think of suicide, but we are too weak to act on the thought. Yet the idea is consoling. Then we could sleep. But that too is a delusion. What is the use of sleep, if we cannot know we sleep? The self says yes. The body says not yet. The self says now. The body says too tired. The self says yes. The body then says no. We are too tired. At dawn we fall asleep.

For the world is utterly empty. There is no one left alive to tell us we may sleep, and the bird at dawn is too far off. Her song to wake another world, in our world says good-bye.

Berg was a station on an endless route. Linderhof had failed. Herrenchiemsee was dangerous and unfinished. Neuschwanstein was emptier each time he entered it. There remained Falkenstein, which would be the perfect grail to house the ideal of purity. It would rise upon its rock like an organ prelude, in great buttresses of sound. It was what he believed in in Wagner, and if Wagner was gone, at least the belief remained.

But to build he must have money, and there was no money left. He summoned Richard. Richard's face seemed numb, yet under its features there must be somewhere the Richard he had once known, who was capable of understanding what it was he needed. Richard must be made to realize that a loan was essential, no matter

245

what its source. He did not quite know how to make him realize that, for though he could explain what Falkenstein was to be, he could no longer explain, even to himself, exactly why he had to build it.

He paced up and down through the halls of Berg, with Richard beside him, talking endlessly. It was something to do. It occupied the nights. It kept him from self-indulgence. At the end of each corridor he would turn to look at Richard, but no communication was any longer possible between them. Richard was not intelligent. Richard was only tired and loyal. He had somehow to make Richard see what Falkenstein was for.

What was it for? He glanced round him. He looked out of the window to the quiet surface of the Starnbergsee. What was Falkenstein? It was the shell of an ideal, which is all we have left when the ideal has died. Yet from the configuration of the shell we can at least tell what the ideal was like when it was alive, and how what we believe now had some such remote living ancestor, frozen like a trilobite in the pressure of a rock.

To raise money was impossible.

"You must raise it. What are you for?" shouted Ludwig, and was immediately sorry, for Richard blinked. That was enough. Ludwig did not want to hurt him. He did not want to hurt anybody. He only wanted his help. Perhaps that hurt most of all, yet surely there must be somebody to help.

Richard looked at him curiously and said he would try to raise yet another loan. Ludwig was only mildly mollified. The promise was merely a crust stuck through a grating. We are never rewarded for what we do: we are only punished for what we have not done. Munich hated him for loving what Munich hated. There was nothing so implacable as ignorance. The blind hate those who can see. The captive do not want liberty. They want the destruction of the free. The walls of our prison topple down on us very slowly. We have plenty of time to watch them fall.

He would bring Wagner to Falkenstein when it was complete. Then Wagner would see what Ludwig saw in him. If Ludwig could not create himself, he did at least have the power to make creation visible and possible. At any rate he had had that power once. Now he must have it again, or silence would stifle him.

Somewhere Richard raised 40,000 marks. It was enough to break ground for the foundations. If the tough soil was once broken, then the shoot might come up. Why do we have to have money in order to thaw the heart, when the sun thaws the ground so easily? Is the sun life's money? As far as Ludwig was concerned, if there was no love, there should at least be understanding, even if he had to build it on a mountain top. He ordered the work to commerce. Everyone else had turned to dust. If he could not have Wagner back, at least he could have the emotion he had first felt for Wagner embodied in Falkenstein. Perhaps when Wagner saw it he would feel differently.

But in this life it is impossible to trick the executioner. He is wilier than we and he waits. In Venice Wagner died.

At Berg the torches burned all night. Ludwig sent Burkel to Venice at once, to help bring the body back home. He had seen others die. They were strangers. But Wagner was part of himself. Wagner was his noblest work, which he had coddled, coaxed, and paid for. To have Wagner still was to lose the power of speech. A part of him died.

247

If we must sit in the shadows, as we must, then no amount of light can ever help. Day after day we fight against little men, who are afraid to grow. We lose and there is nothing we can do then but to defend ourselves. That they kill us with their misunderstanding and neglect is not so bad: what they do to our bodies after we are dead is worse than indignity. Maggots secrete a fluid to make death edible. So do men. They call it grief.

None of us is defeated by death. At the last moment we can go over to the other side, accepted as were the crusaders by the Saracens for our prowess and our valour. Without loss of dignity we join the ranks of those who fight the living. To cross the threshold is as trivial, though as painful, but as meaningless, as circumcision, which is an act in its very nature clean. But the living desire to make all things like themselves, and the revenge they take upon the bodies we leave behind us is equivalent to the sack of a town too long brave under siege. In that sense only is death horrible. The Greeks did well to burn.

The revenge of those who hated us in life is to deify us dead, for that way they obliterate the fact that we were human. Burkel brought him a complete report. The Master had died at his desk. Cosima held him for many hours. Then he was laid out. He was catheterized. His body was painted with arsenic so poisonous that Cosima could no longer approach it. When she was allowed in to see him, he had been taken away for good. Only a tinctured chrysalis remained. His features had been twisted into a smile and a death mask had been taken, to show that no one had ever made him suffer. At least we have the power to make the dead simper with our own bland indifference.

He was placed in a lead casket and the lid sealed down. The body was taken to Beyreuth. There it was eulogized;

248

for no ideal, no aspiration, no grandeur, no nobility does Man admire until it has been immunized by death. The obsequies, wrote Burkel, were dignified. Burkel was a fool. Of course they were dignified. They were graced by the silence of relief. Man fights insight every day. We canonize the illustrious dead in the same spirit in which a hunter cuts a new notch in an already well-notched gun.

He avoided the funeral, but to Beyreuth and Wahnfried he must go, to see if anything was left. He arrived late in the afternoon, alone, leaving Burkel in the carriage outside on the road. He was a pilgrim now.

Wagner was of Saxony, and Wahnfried, his house, had a naked, cold, northern look that fitted oddly in Beyreuth. It had the winter smell. He opened its gate and stood on the gravel path inside. In front of the house, surrounded by shrubs, stood a bust of himself. It shocked him. It showed him in youth, when he had first met the Master. It was as though there were two graves at Wahnfried, not one. The bust seemed to usher him in to witness the greatness of a stranger. With a glance at the curtained windows, Ludwig moved round the side of the house, towards the garden at the rear.

There was still snow on the ground. It had been snowing when the coffin was brought here. Perhaps it was the same snow. Over it some dull minister had spoken some empty pious words. They could have had nothing to do with Wagner. Christianity is meaningless, for we are at its ebb. It is merely a salt *étang* left by a receding sea; for the spirit, like faith itself, is tidal. It can never be captured inland, in the lake of one religion only, and that evaporated past its flood.

He had almost reached the rear garden. He paused and then went on. Before him was the monument, crusted with snow. Had it snowed in Venice, too, as the black gondolas bore their burden to the station? Why, when water is the source of all life, together with the sun, is it that it is in mist the great barque of death flows smoothly towards us down the stream, hiding with drifting curtains of snow a figure we cannot see, a shadowy presence which floats away on the waters of life, but which is more than life? Must all our meaning go away with us? As the gondolas paraded sadly down that last lagoon, did they take the world away with them, or did they take us to the world? Somewhere did a snub-nosed boat put out to sea, even while the coffin was being loaded on the train for Germany?

It had been snowing. He did not know.

He looked at the great slab of stone there in the garden. Beyond it lay small mounds in the earth. These were the little graves of faithful dogs, of Far-Frisch, Köchel, Wolf, Gremmie, Froh, and Marka. He remembered Marka. In his memory there also started up and stretched the black dog of his childhood, the dog Doppelgnäger who would follow him now, eager for an affection he could not give it. Dogs, like people, are ambiguous. When they follow us, how can we be sure that they do not pursue?

He sat for a long time in the garden, in the snow. It was peaceful there. But Wagner was dead. The great star had fallen, that had given him the means to plot his own course against the sky. Yet there was still a long way to go. The walls of Falkenstein dissolved.

Wagner had been mean and presumptuous, and had used him badly. He had known all that. It did not matter. All men were mean in some things, and he had done with men. But Wagner had also been truly great. Even our reliable beacons must be built by human hands, and though the contractor cheats, we do not mind, for beacons we must have, to cut the gloom.

The time had come to enter the pyramid. A ship had sailed over the horizon. If he was not to lose that guide, then he must hasten to cast off his own ropes, in order to be free to follow. He would enter loneliness for the last time, like a voyage or a monument, and who is to say the two are not the same? Anthony was dead.

Burkel was waiting. He would return to Berg. He got up and left himself behind. If he was no longer himself, it did not matter what he chose to do. When there is no one left whom we can love, what then is love? He knew the answer now, but found it frightening. It was more than he could face.

Back at Berg he searched for something that he could still give up. There was not much.

He still liked to go to Richard's house once a week. It was only a half an hour's walk from Berg, a fragrant stroll through the trees towards warmth and some humanity. There, if he could be father to nothing, at least he could play uncle. He brought gifts to the children, so he was sure of his welcome there. The house was clean and airy, and for once he did not have to stoop in rooms too large for him, nor stand erect in those too small. It was only a performance, but it was a performance of which he was fond. He must give it up.

He did not want Richard to see what would happen now. We should never be seen as we are by those who once knew us as we were. That is indignity, whether we have risen or fallen in the interim, either way. Besides Richard had left him in spirit long ago. Now he dismissed his presence as well. Even as he did so, he could see in Richard's eyes that there is a point beyond which no one can be saved, and that he had passed that point long ago, almost without knowing it.

He heard Richard's footsteps retreating down the

corridor for the last time, rustling like leaves. It was odd to realize he would never hear them again. They had always been back before.

With Richard gone, he was at last alone in a world that contained only objects. That is the last world, the world where men, being merely a commodity, have no souls and so become inanimate. Silence dripped around him like water round a tap. Except for panic, he was not sorry.

It was 1885. It was fifteen years since he had made his first experiments with this new soulless quiet world, rowing round solitude like a man in a boat, on a lake too small to have a shore. Yet the years were very long.

He had done such foolish things. He had eaten dinners at which the plates were laid for guests who never came. How could they come? There had been no one to invite. He had picked water lilies on the lake of the wintergarden at the Residenz. He had seen the table rising through the floor at Linderhof, into an empty room. He had taken that ride to Kufstein long ago, to pretend Richard was with him. He had not come to silence unprepared. He had long ago learned the rules; and if life was to be a parable, it should be a parable of the past. Wagner was gone. Kainz was gone. If there were no men to match their voices, then he would hear no voices. He would communicate with the world by note. And that is what he did. It was a nuisance to scribble them, but they saved bother.

Even objects now moved against him by stealth, like figures on a board of chess. How does the King feel, watching from the castle corner the strategy he alone can do so little to defeat? He sees his queen throw bishops, knights and pawns across the board, not to save him, but to destroy the enemy. Only the enemy is concerned with his defence until it is too late, the queen is lost, and he has only two or three moves possible to evade defeat, for the board is swept clean. Only the pieces of the other side remain in place, their strategy planned too early in the game for him to defeat now. Given all his guile, without more pieces back he can only achieve a stalemate. He can defeat his enemy only by constructing for himself a prison so strait that he cannot leave it, or the enemy enter.

He knew perfectly well that the court and his ministers cabaled against him in Munich. They always had. As his own pieces were swept off the board, he saw their strategy, and Otto standing in his own castle square at Fürstenried, safe from the moves of the game. He had not the power left to defeat them, except in so far as he made his own prison strait. His brain worked clearly. That much he could do. He could retreat to Neuschwanstein and there be safe. But what is safety, to be motionless? When a man sits still his body goes to sleep. His circulation fails.

So he communicated by message only. He would speak to no one. Sometimes, all too rarely, a message reached him from outside, in return. Of all those he had ever known or ever taken into his favour, only Kainz and Wagner wrote to him afterwards. Was it because they had a life of their own, whereas the others had had merely the life he had given them, which they lost when they lost him? It was possible. Twice in his life he had touched something alive. His fingers still tingled from the shock. For a letter from Kainz he was always grateful. It was a message from the past, which he had thought could send no messages.

But even the past grew silent in time. The messages from Wagner had ceased. Those from Kainz would do the same. These last years tightened around him like rope around a winch, when the anchor is too heavy.

He watched the outside world grow narrower. Stalemate would be soon. That filled him with relief.

It was a pleasure to appear in public now, for every appearance might be his last. Only once was he disconcerted. He met the Infanta Paz again, the wife of his cousin. She seemed almost real. When he spoke, even of Kainz and *Marion de Lorme*, she appeared to understand. He could feel her waiting to enter his imagination, was touched, but pushed her back sadly. It was too late. Yet he was moved. She really did seem to know what he talked about when he spoke. He found that a curious sensation. But she could be no more than a spectator. Everyone was a spectator now. He sent her flowers. Why should the actor not send the audience flowers, if for once it understood the nature of his performance? The idea pleased him. It was something to tell Kainz, if Kainz had been there to speak to.

For he was weary. There is a time when you want the game over. You see you cannot win. The difference between checkmate and stalemate is merely a difference of moral patience. The conqueror sometimes forgets that the victory is not always of his making. Sometimes he wins only because the losing side decides it does not wish to let the winner enjoy his victory any longer. Cowardice saves more lives than bravery ever does, and the stoicism of those who are too wise to fight saves even more.

Why should he bother to explain? As long as his orders were obeyed, he was content. Let others make of his life what they would. He had his own system for dealing with the world now. He left notes for his household staff on his writing-table as he went to his bath. When he returned they were gone. That was as it should be. He did not want to be interrupted by anyone.

Pencils were blunt. They must be sharpened. Teacups

were ugly. They must be replaced. The peerage must be watered by the selling of titles, so it might flow harmlessly away. The valet, to whom he refused to speak, must be taught to tie his tie properly. The man was a booby. The books sent him were unsatisfactory. They must be returned and others procured. He knew that tactic. It was no use their trying to force him out by cutting off supplies. Stalemate should be his, not check theirs. He had only to tire the other side.

He began to have awful nightmares. Through his dreams, if they were dreams and not the sub-conscious reflections cast by sleeplessness, now walked an endless procession of dead lovers. Dead, at least, to him. It began to happen almost every night. The curse of sleeplessness is to show us what the sub-conscious contains, something we should never see, for beneficial to sleep, it is poison to consciousness.

Of all that procession, only Kainz turned to look back at him, so that he could see his face. He saw now when it was too late that the face had been a noble one. He would have spoken, had he had the strength, but sleeplessness drugged his senses utterly. Kainz hurried on.

Then the others came. Paul of Thurn and Taxis, Richard, others of whom he did not even allow himself to remember the names, Varicourt, Mayr, Voelk, Welcker, Hesselschwert, each turning towards him and each without a face, the ugly ghosts of a tyrannical physical necessity.

He had looked so often into the faces of others, in search of the ideal face, that they cancelled each other out and all were featureless. Yet they all had the same face, and that face was his own. He always realized that shortly before dawn. The conclusion was terrible. If he could love only himself, then there was no love that was not circular. From the far end of the procession Kainz's features turned one last time before the figure disappeared. Kainz had had his own face. That love was circular could not be true. There was somewhere another kind of love, which had no name and maybe no identity.

It did not matter where or what, if love was, then it had a nature and an identity. One by one the figures went by, each staring, and each without eyes with which to stare. When he could watch no more he would fall asleep. There must be something more. In his sleep he smiled. It is only in sleep that the sleepless dare to smile. That is the only ease they ever get, and they cannot even see it.

If the ideal did not exist, then at least he could pollute the self. He could debase it. He could show how little it was worth. When we are no longer beautiful, we like best a mirror that reflects us badly. Perhaps in the sudden brief illusory release of sex, with its magnesium light, he could burn the body away and so destroy desire. At least such things made the night shorter.

But there is mercy in the world after all. It came to him as mercy usually does, by accident. Fortunately self-interest is blind. It never realizes that in serving itself it may accidentally be serving others as well. Materialists will never recognize the existence of the spirit. Therefore they can destroy only the body, which is all they can see. In that way sometimes the spirit can get free.

Such was the mercy that liberated him. On Tuesday, 8th June 1886, four physicians sat in a room in Munich and agreed that the King was mad. It was the only way they could remove him from the throne constitutionally, so they did not feel that any examination was necessary. The move came from the Cabinet, not from the Royal family. Dynasties can wait, and are therefore often forebearing, but ambitious men are limited to the term of their office and grow impatient at delay. The King, the Cabinet had heard, wished to sell the crown jewels, and jewels are valuable. Set in crowns, they twinkle down upon ambition, and even a physician knows very well what money is. It is a power which all obey.

Ludwig did well to smile in his sleep, for now there was hope. Now the stalemate was ended. With hope comes dignity, and dignity is the voice of the soul.

Once in his golden cage, and Bajazet was free.

As soon as the medical commission had reached its decision, the news was not long in reaching Neuschwanstein. The King received it calmly and slept well for the first time in many years. His mind had cleared and was at peace. Moonlight invaded the room. It did not wake him. Now he knew what to do, so he slept the refreshed sleep of a man who has work to face in the morning.

XXI

‸

It was his last year, he knew it, and he was glad, for his mind was made up.

With him the direct line ended. The crown would pass to his uncle in time, or to his uncle's sons, but that was not the direct line as he understood it. With him was cut the central scarlet thread. Who can know what it is like to bear in one perishable body the final extinguishable seeds of a race, and to know that once one is dead, that name will never be spoken again of the living, either in affection, in reverence, in amity, or in abuse? He had relatives, cousins, and conjoiners. Some of them would be both wise and efficient. Some would not. But he and Otto were the last in the direct line; and it is great pride and quiet joy to embody and to be the last of any name. It has a quiet uplifted finality. It improves the jaw. One turns to one's ancestors, and one says, now we shall be together. Now we are complete. I shall be with you very soon. I have not disgraced you. Let us sit and talk of what we were.

He was waiting now only on the event, for those who would set sail, even in our day, are still at the command of time and tide.

Landscape, wrote Schelling, should be used as a veil through which one may glimpse a loftier reality. That is true; but sometimes the landscape is shrouded in mist. Ludwig stood at a window and looked across the twilight moonscape of Bavaria.

The wind snapped through Neuschwanstein. It seemed to him that down the unfinished corridors he could hear the slamming of innumerable doors. The arches were full of shadows.

He went and sat in the Romanesque throne room. The Germans are incorrigibly Greek, and looking at the dim murals of Lohengrin, he remembered once more the true legend of the swan. The swan predated Lohengrin and Wagner both. Cygnus was the companion of Phaeton, who mourned his friend so endlessly along the river, that at last Zeus took pity and immortalized the feelings of friendship in the body of the swan. In that sense the swan does not bear love away. The swan itself is love.

His senses were very alert. He peered into the shadows. But there were no shadows there. Even his own ideals no longer stood between him and reality. This was reality, and he sat in the midst of it.

He was almost glad. Before going to bed he watched the mist billowing below him. He was at the still centre at last, and his world became serene. The view was deeply moving, for he was the only one awake to see it. The world was alive again, and from the peaks he seemed to hear a long, contented sigh.

In his blood ran the blood of seven centuries of Dukes, seven Electors, and four Wittelsbach Kings. He would not go down alone. For that reason he would at least pretend to fight, for he was taking a thousand years of history down with him. He would remember that and he was ready. Charles I took his religion to the scaffold with him. Louis XVI took nothing. But at least the walk of both had dignity, for in each of them died not a man, but a society. Theirs was a ritual death. So would be his.

Of the days that followed he remembered only the last, but those clearly. Since what he intended to do would not frighten his enemies until long afterward, first he wanted to frighten them in the only way it was possible to do so.

Early on the morning of June 10th he rose and walked through the hollow castle. It was to say good-bye. He had roused the people he needed, and for a little while they would be loyal. It would be long enough.

He was sad. After all, Neuschwanstein was the Wartberg, too. Around him from the walls looked down the noble prototypes of Hans Sachs, Sigurd, Tannhäuser, Walther van der Vogelweide, and St. Louis. They were painted shadows now, but they had had a meaning once. At the Wartberg Wagner had conceived the *Meistersinger*. Richard had become his friend. And now there were only these paintings left.

In the cold throne room he stood looking out the windows at the mountains riding the mist. At one end of the room twenty semi-circular steps led up to what should have been the throne, but it was not yet installed, nor was it paid for, and it never would be now. He ascended the stairs and gazed out over the room and found it good. It was empty now. It should continue so.

He nodded his head and climbed the stairs to his bedroom. He sat there to wait.

It began to be dawn. The mists began to dissolve, showing more and more the bases of the mountains. At last he could even glimpse the surface of the tarn among the trees. He looked down at it for a long time, for there are a few things in this world which are very good indeed. They make us happy merely to look upon, so they are the things we see first and last. He had spent his childhood near here, at Hohenschwangau. That seemed appropriate.

A servant roused him at five. The party from Munich had arrived and was approaching the castle keep. He followed the servant at once, hastening through the pearl-grey outer courtyard and climbing to the rooms over the keep.

Below him, toiling up the road, he saw Kraft Baron von Crailsheim, the Minister of his Household and of Foreign Affairs; Count Holnstein, whom he had himself raised; Baron von Malsen; and others. Even from this little elevation above them, they looked remarkably futile. He could not see the peasants and the local Fire Brigade he had ordered to guard the gate below him. He heard some sort of parley. The air made the voices clear, but far away. The scene must look rather medieval. He heard the officer of the Brigade announce that he would shoot if the party came any closer.

Baron von Crailsheim broke ranks and ran down the hill. The others swiftly followed. Ludwig grunted. It would be something for them to write about in their memoirs. No doubt they would take refuge at Hohen-schwangau, which was not far away. He found that he felt remarkably well, ordered the Fire Brigade out to arrest them, and sat down to breakfast. The effort was of course futile, but it would at least remind them of the nature of the power they were so eager to destroy, and the lesson would do them no harm.

An hour and a half later the guard returned. The entire party had been arrested. He had no desire to see any of them. He told the guard to lock them up over the keep. One of the men had escaped and was on his way to Munich for reinforcements.

It made little difference. Neuschwanstein was not

equipped for a siege, and he had no desire to withstand one. The pleasure of seeing traitors step forward, he decided, was chiefly that of counting their heads. Inevitably one had omitted a few names, but not many. The omissions were understandable. Traitors, whatever their ages or names, have much in common and therefore look much alike.

He wished to have the matter over. It seemed silly to drag it out, and he had made the only point he wished to make. At least the fools would have a few hours of anxiety in the rooms above the keep. He wandered about the palace. He could see so little from the windows, that he decided to climb the tower. It would be only fitting, this last time, to see the view complete.

Unfortunately, from what motives he could not guess, the key to the tower door had been hidden. On the other hand, the door itself was not strong, and a last breath of clear air would be of immense help.

He made only one mistake. He had not realized that the rescue party from Munich was already in the castle. He went to the base of the tower and began to climb. It was a long climb and it made him breathless. At the top of the stairs was the small locked door to the circular steps leading to the topmost roof. He was concentrating on the view he was about to see.

He reached the landing unprepared. Two men sprang out and thrust his arms into a strait-jacket. He blinked. It was as sudden as that.

He was pleased to see, however, that they still felt enough awe of his person to be scared. They took him downstairs to his own bedroom. He walked in. There were guards posted at the doors and windows. The strait-jacket was highly annoying. It hurt his arms. A little man appeared before him.

"I am Dr. Gudden," it announced. "You may not remember me. I had the honour once to report to you about Prince Otto's condition."

Ludwig merely looked down on him. "On the contrary, I remember you quite well," he said drily. Unbelievably the doctor's black little face reddened into a gratified smile. But then irony was something he would not have expected from a deposed King. The proper use of language can be a defence in depth. The presence of Dr. Gudden did not in the least surprise him. He had known long ago that he would see him again.

"Without examining me, how can you pronounce on the state of my health?"

"An examination is unnecessary," said Gudden blandly. It was clear he believed what he said. He sat down. Inwardly Ludwig frowned, but outwardly he pretended to smile. He needed Gudden in a good mood, but he should pay for the impertinence of sitting down in his presence soon enough. He sat down himself, for it appeared that Dr. Gudden had decided to harangue him. He talked for three hours. Since he was so clearly uncertain of his own abilities, no doubt he wanted to brag about them. From time to time Ludwig smiled. Having an audience seemed to mollify the doctor. After a while the ridiculous strait-jacket was removed.

Ludwig thought that he might be taken to Linderhof, but it appeared that that was out of the question. If he was correct, Dr. Gudden had all the earmarks of a petty sadist. Therefore Ludwig said he wished to go to Linderhof, and waited. Dr. Gudden rose to the bait at once and told him he would be taken to Berg.

Once more Ludwig smiled inwardly. Berg was the place he would have chosen himself. He knew every inch of its grounds, and it would serve his purposes admirably.

He was careful, however, not to appear pleased, for Dr. Gudden was clearly a man who believed in suffering.

He was moved to Berg the next day, in a procession of three carriages, painted blue and silver in the royal colours, and with excellent horses. It was fitting that the peasants should see their King leave them as a King should, with pomp. However his keepers seemed afraid of a demonstration. He was roused early and the party left Neuschwanstein at 4 a.m. Ludwig did not particularly mind. He had made his own plans and would put them into execution soon enough.

It remained only to find the occasion. Whit Sunday, June 13th, seemed as good a day as any. He had spent a troubled night, but as soon as he opened his eyes and saw the sunlight he knew that this Pentecost of 1886 was to be the correct and chosen day. He woke very early. He wanted to get up, but was told not to, so he lay drowsing until six. The dawn was truly lovely. He had forgotten the quality of new-born light. As usual he called for and was given a morning cup of soup.

The cup, he noted with pleasure, was one he had had designed for himself years ago. It was a man's cup, beautifully squat, with a gold repoussée lip, one handle, and gold Chinese figures on a blue ground. It held half a gill. Of course a wide-lipped cup lost its heat rapidly, but since he always drank hot fluids at a gulp, that did not greatly matter. The soup was *consommé* sprinkled with chopped parsley. He found it very good.

It was like the morning of his coronation oath, in a way, except that now there was no terror and no doubt. He looked round the room curiously. There was one answer he would like to have, without the fatigue of asking for it, but perhaps he would find out in time.

It did not seem to be his own room any more. It was

like a room in which he had slept only overnight. That startled him briefly. It had not occurred to him that our possessions, in being extensions of the self, lose identity even before we do, being so to speak the first suburbs to fall.

At one time everything in this room at Berg had meant a great deal to him. He wondered if the familiar rooms downstairs would have become as meaningless.

At eight Dr. Gudden arrived for his morning interview. So, too, Tamburlaine must often have arrived to Bajazet at unexpected hours, to see if the matter had really been brought off, for conquerors are parvenus. They can never be sure that the chair is behind them when they sit down. They have to check. He must not on any account annoy the good doctor now.

The hour chosen for the interview was hardly tactful, but that would be typical of Gudden. Tact, for him, would always be like charm, one of the hallmarks of his betters, a possession to be ignored since he could never have it himself.

Ludwig could hear below him the hammering of carpenters, come to bar the windows of Berg. His cocoon was to be spun around him, it seemed, so that the public might imagine that he had woven it himself. The noise was agonizing.

Gudden was less bumptious than usual. He begged to introduce his assistant, Dr. Grashey, and then left. Ludwig talked to Grashey for half an hour, with considerable surprise. Grashey seemed to have belief in his profession and ability. Therefore he was not ashamed of what he was doing. He was the first man Ludwig had met since Kainz who seemed to have some inkling of self-respect. The spectacle was cheering.

He decided to make a gesture proper to his circumstances, and therefore asked if he might hear Mass. He had no quarrel with God, for they had never met, but politeness did no harm. The request, as he had expected, was refused. That would be Gudden, with his sadism again. Gudden was Protestant. Ludwig smiled. Faith was indeed tidal. It came and went along a thousand shores. But did Dr. Gudden really feel that, even as Protestant, he could control the tides?

At 10 a.m. Gudden sent up a message suggesting that they should go for a walk. Ludwig was only too pleased to agree. He went downstairs, to find as he had imagined that the other rooms had become utterly impersonal. He glanced at them curiously. Once he had been fond of them, but they seemed garish now.

It was raining slightly. The rain was not cold, but warm. He took a large umbrella and an overcoat and stepped outside. In front of them walked the guard, and behind them two keepers. It was somewhat painful to have to listen to Gudden calmly. The man was utterly fatuous. He seemed eager to explain just how he had trapped the King. No doubt Grashey was watching from the windows upstairs. Gudden was confident: he told the keepers to walk farther behind.

To that silly little man, merely to open his mouth was an immortal truth. Gudden seemed to be enjoying himself. It took little prodding to persuade him to take a second walk after dinner. Ludwig was disappointed. Who would play chess against an opponent so incompetent?

Shortly before dinner Grashey was despatched to Munich. Ludwig was relieved. He found he wished the man well. He had no desire to see him disgraced. Competence should be honoured and not disavowed, for it was rare.

He refused to have Gudden dine with him, but fortunately Gudden did not have the impertinence to suggest it. He dined alone, with a keeper instead of a footman, but the wine was excellent, a pale traminer which grew warm in his throat. The night was chilly. Though it was summer, the long twilight got lost among the dark trees along the lake, and the shadows were confused and slippery. It was a quarter to six. He had a demi-tasse with a glass of brandy. Then he rose, called for his umbrella and coat, and had word sent to Dr. Gudden that he was ready for his stroll. It was quite true. He was.

At six-thirty he stood waiting in the vestibule. Dr. Gudden came down the stairs. No doubt he had some nugae of daily wisdom to dispense, and was glad of the royal audience. Ludwig turned to the keeper and had his umbrella refurled, so that it should be slim and dandified and tight. He was helped into his overcoat. The overcoat was shabby, but that did not greatly matter.

It became apparent that Gudden was by no means sure of protocol in the matter of doors. Ludwig smiled and stepped out on to the south garden front.

There was a fountain there. It was not so large as that at Linderhof, being merely a crystal willow tree, but at least it provided the sound of running water. Ludwig looked at it with approval, listening intently. Behind him he heard Gudden tell the keeper that he need not follow them. He stared at the fountain, pleased. It was both kinder and easier that way, and it was as he would have wished. He listened to the small insect noises of the garden, which were very sweet. Then they walked across the lawn to the path which skirted the lake. The evening was agreeable, the stars lustrous. Gudden, however, was clearly not a country man. He seemed to feel that a stroll had a therapeutic merit only. That was a pity. That way he missed so much.

They walked on and entered the wood, the path pushing through it like a tunnel to the other side. There were movements in the wood, the furtive, stealthy, contented sound of growing plants. No doubt to-morrow there would be more flowers in bloom beneath the tree roots than there were to-day. There was something touching about the assurance of small flowers nodding in the security of a tree. They had the frail innocence of children.

All too soon they came out of the wood. Ludwig looked for a while at the shore. The water lapped at consciousness. The lake seemed very large, and Gudden hesitated, looked uncomfortable, and then followed him. He was talking busily. He did not notice what was around him.

Ludwig glanced at the silent, breathlessly waiting wood. Even the insects were still. There was only the lapping of the water. He had always regretted that his body was so large, so clumsy, and so big, but now that had advantages. He grasped Gudden from behind, cutting him off in mid-sentence, and rushed him into the water. It did not take much strength to hold him down. The little man was only an appearance, and had no real vitality. Ludwig straightened up. He knew now who was the executioner who always seemed to wait for him. The executioner was himself.

He left Gudden in the water and went back to the bank. He still had his umbrella crooked over his arm and it was still properly furled. He laid it on the grass, with his hat, his jacket, and his overcoat. Acceptance is final. Rejection alone may be revoked, but this he had accepted. A cool breeze stirred. He turned and walked slowly into the water. For some, their whole life grows towards one opening, and this at last was his. The body longs for survival, but the self longs to be free. It is the self that

268

wins. There was no time for words, but he seemed to feel a presence around him, and the presence was familiar.

It was that part of him that had never been corrupted, and was like a star wandering about with him and flaming up from the depths. It was that part of him no bigger than a thumb that was one with Eternity and sat in the ordinary self, mute, dumb, observant, irrefragable, beyond the other selves he knew. It was that part of him that was capable of salvation, because incapable of sin.

He knew now how great houses die. They die only when the shrine they protect is empty. They die when they must, when faith is dead, for they are the embodiment of the faith that dies and lives again, in that otherwhere where nothing but faith is. He had lost nothing. He was ready for the voyage.

It was quiet on the shores of the lake. In the dimness the mountains bowed and danced, making their eternal prayers against the sky. And through the meshes of the star net wriggled and swam the little souls of time, like boring worms, squirming away from the impenetrable soul of God. Out there in all directions they swarmed towards destiny, spermatozoa, of whom but few would penetrate the world egg. The trees were dusty and fragrant. The birds sounded sleepy, and sang like clockwork birds. Ludwig turned to glance at the limp bloated body of Dr. Gudden, absurdly deferential face down in the water, bobbling close to shore. But he had done with Dr. Gudden. He had done with everything. He was astonished to find that he felt happy, and he had not been happy for a long time. It must be because everything was over.

He stood up to his thighs in the lake. The water eddied gently against the cloth of his trousers, which in turn nibbled against his flesh like fishes. He stared across the waters. Behind him the glow of the lights of Berg rose above the trees, but he saw another glow, the Alpenglow. Then, almost soundlessly, he slipped into the water and lay face down, watching the strange patterns of consciousness below him, like a tourist in a glass-bottomed boat, over a coral garden. And he was glad the night was cool. He had the feeling that he was going home. He felt young again. Slowly the water bubbled around him. It was time.

For death, too, has its fashions. The Romans of the early Empire had the consolation of a civic act, performed with decorum. The Christian Church dangled before us the skyhook of salvation. Science, which can also be merciful, assures us that in the process of natural death the threshold of consciousness is so lowered that the nervous system becomes anaesthetized, so that we cannot fully realize the terms of our extinction.

But suicide by drowning is another matter; deliberate suicide by drowning in a few feet of water when one swims well is not so swift. Subjective time lengthens endlessly. The long corridors stretch interminably, suddenly the sewers of Constantinople, or that underground water temple in which the Egyptians re-enacted the progress of the soul boat. Nor do we, like the heroes of Greece, bound into the heavens of the sky family and twinkle in the stars. For us the stars are farther off than that. Consciousness is wilier than that and more complex.

Slowly the strands of living break under the strain of our final moral act. The great lake is shrouded in a low, coiling mist, that hovers above the waters. The waters themselves are grey. And slowly, as the wooden dugout pushes forward on the outward journey, it breaks the weeds, it clears a passage, as the green strands break their roots. Slower and slower goes the boat through the reeds;

the dead filaments of consciousness eddy in the pewter water.

And there is time, as the immense weights of exhaustion close in like sliding walls, for one last question: what is love?

And far off, at the very end of being, the Self, cold, salt, alone, but again part of the One, far beyond the reaches of speech, has still one last muted power of thought.

Love is stoicism.

Love is dignity.

And love is death.

EPILOGUE

Epilogue

I stood on the bridge above the Iser. The swan was dying. I had never seen a swan die before. I did not want to see it now. And yet I had to do so, for the self is something we sit in, a borrowed chair nailed to the floor, from which we are compelled to watch. It seemed to me, too, that I also was being watched, as the little wild brain of the fox watches from the hedge, afraid to be seen, yet impatient to see how much we know of him.

The swan was dead. I furled my umbrella and I walked away, through the ruins of Munich, in the soft October rain. In the echoes of the rain I caught the whisper of a strangely friendly voice, and the presence of something infinitely gentle all around me, and it said:

Do not mourn uselessly. Remember me.

München-Saddlebag,
October 1953—*February* 1956.